D0207714

Death
À L'Orange

Nancy Fairbanks

BERKLEY PRIME CRIME, NEW YORK

DEATH À L'ORANGE

A Berkley Prime Crime Book / published by arrangement with the author

PRINTING HISTORY
Berkley Prime Crime mass-market edition / June 2002

Visit our website at
www.penguinputnam.com

ISBN: 0-425-18524-9

Berkley Prime Crime books are published
by The Berkley Publishing Group,
a division of Penguin Putnam Inc.,
375 Hudson Street, New York, New York 10014.
The name BERKLEY PRIME CRIME and
the BERKLEY PRIME CRIME design
are trademarks belonging to Penguin Putnam Inc.

PRINTED IN THE UNITED STATES OF AMERICA

10 9 8 7 6 5 4 3 2 1

Acknowledgments

Special thanks to my husband, travel planner, companion on the road, and provider of scientific input; to my son Bill, whose computer expertise makes my website possible; to Mary Sarber, who presented me with the fascinating book *Bouquet de France* by Samuel Chamberlain, which she brought home from her own travels; and to my longtime friend Joan Coleman, for her encouragement and her editorial talents.

I found many books useful in the research and writing of this novel, among them: the abovementioned *Bouquet de France*, *Frommer's Touring Guide to Paris*, the *Michelin Guides to Normandy and Chateaux of the Loire*, *The Traveller's History of France* by Robert Cole, and particularly the delightful *Food Chronology* by James Trager, not to mention all the tourist books packed with pictures and history of the various towns and châteaux we visited.

N.F.

For my son Matthew,
who knows all about traveling with academics

Prologue

Carolyn

Shortly after my husband and I returned from a frightening but lucrative trip to New York City, we received a phone call offering what seemed to be a wonderful opportunity, a tour of Normandy and the Loire Valley at a cost that no one in his right mind would refuse. Being in our right minds, and enthusiastic travelers as well, we accepted. Who wouldn't? It sounded perfect.

The group would comprise faculty and family from our former university; the tour coincided not only with Jason's spring break but also with our son Chris's (although he'd have to leave France several days early); and our younger child, Gwen, had other plans for her Easter vacation. However, she did say that she expected to go on our next trip abroad while her brother stayed home. Ah, children! You'd think they were grade-schoolers instead of eighteen and twenty, respectively.

And then it was France. Especially Northern France. I was a medieval history major as an undergraduate, and Norman history is as fascinating to me as toxins are to Jason, my chemistry professor husband. I could revisit Paris, see the cathedral in Rouen, visit the abbeys founded by William the Conqueror and his queen, Mathilda, and examine the Bayeux tapestry. The very itinerary of the tour sent shivers of delight up my spine.

And the food! Where better to write about food than France? (I am a culinary writer with a book on New Orleans cuisine in progress and a contract to write food columns for newspapers.) Not to mention the fact that we Blues all love good food.

And when better to travel to France than in the spring, when the weather would be cool and pleasant, perhaps even rainy? Rather than hot and hotter, as can be expected in El Paso in April. Our new location pretty much moves from wimpy winter to blazing summer with a month of dust storms in between.

The only drawback that I could see was the promise I made to look out for the sixteen-year-old daughter of Judith Atwater, the woman whose husband had just undergone unexpected bypass surgery and whose tour reservations we would be assuming. But how much trouble could the girl be? I'd already raised one of my own.

I was ecstatic! And how mistaken my expectations were!

The tour began with an accident and ended with a murder. I can still see those two hands clutching the gun, aiming, as our small group gazed, entranced, at a beautiful cathedral shining with golden light in the darkness of a French town. I hear my own voice crying, "No!" and the shocking crack of gunshots. I see the blood and the bodies. And I feel the guilt. Because I might have stopped it.

1
The Dangers of Luggage Carousels

Carolyn

Paris, **Giverny, Rouen,** Mont-Saint-Michel, Caen, Saint-Malo, the Loire Valley—a veritable feast for a culinary writer and history enthusiast. So why was I not full of delight and anticipation after landing in Paris at the Charles de Gaulle Airport? Instead, I moped forlornly by the baggage carousel envisioning the horror of days, maybe weeks, without clean clothes, which I consider of paramount concern for happy traveling. It's a preference I picked up from my mother, who was a stickler for clean clothes.

So what was I to do now? I had neither clean clothes nor any faith in my ability to use a foreign Laundromat if I'd had clothes to wash in one. And our luggage still hadn't appeared. In fact, very few bags were left unclaimed, but those that still trundled by looked as deserted as I felt.

My husband had gone off to do battle with Air France over our lost luggage. My son Chris had been sent to find a representative of our tour company and was undoubtedly using his assignment to check out the young ladies of France, all anorexic, black-clad creatures of mystery—at least to young American males. I remained at my station by the moving belt, looking at each piece that came by in the hope that some clever French baggage handler had managed to unearth our suitcases from the bowels of the plane on which we had flown from London. No such luck. For all I knew, the baggage handlers of the Charles de Gaulle Airport had gone on strike in the middle of unloading our plane, as French workers are wont to do. There were a few other woebegone persons staring at the nearly empty carousel with the same expression of waning hope and dire foreboding that was reflected, I am sure, on my face.

I'd not only have no clean clothes, but also no cosmetics, no jewelry, no umbrella, and no washcloth. The French do not provide washcloths in their hotels! How can one wash one's face without a washcloth? Or one's ears? Ears cannot be washed by sticking them under the shower. They fill with water and no longer function properly. They probably develop infections or fungi. Mother was always adamant that I dry my ears carefully after washing. Funny how you remember every word your mother said, even though she died when you were twelve.

Were we supposed to spend our precious allotment of time in Paris shopping for clothes in strange department stores, where the clerks would speak French and pretend not to understand one's attempts at communicating in their language? Not that I can pronounce French, but still . . . And no doubt, French department stores don't even stock washcloths.

My gloomy musings were interrupted when lights flashed, unintelligible announcements burbled over the loudspeaker system, a new horde of passengers came rushing up to surround me, and a whole new avalanche of suitcases thundered into view. Was there even the remotest possibility that ours would be among them?

"Excuse me, sir," I said to a respectable-looking gentleman who had just stopped beside me. He was wearing a suit, rather than the casual clothes in which Americans usually travel. "Do you speak English?"

"Certainly, madam," he replied. "And several other lan-

guages as well. Do you require someone to translate from
the French for you?" He was actually a fine-looking man,
probably ten years or so my senior, average height, stocky
but not fat, and possessed of a full and somewhat wavy
head of gray hair. And he was an American. The accent
was unmistakably American, possibly even Midwestern,
like mine.

"No, thank you," I replied. "I just wanted to ask if you
came in on Air France from London."

"From London, yes, but ours was a charter from
Chicago O'Hare. We passengers are a conglomeration of
different tour groups, all setting out from Paris to different
parts of France. Not that I am an advocate of tours, but as
it happened, the university at which I teach was sponsor-
ing a tour of Northern France at a price that I simply could
not pass up, being, as I am, a professor specializing in the
history of medieval France. Is something the matter,
madam? You look befuddled."

"You're not Professor Jean-Claude Childeric, are you?"
Then I felt so silly. That was like saying, "Oh, you're from
Chicago. Do you know my husband's mother, Gwenivere
Blue?"

However, the gentleman's face lit up, and he said, "I
perceive that my renown precedes me. Are you, by any
chance, a fellow medievalist, dear lady?"

Now I really was embarrassed. "I am fond of medieval
history," I admitted, "although certainly no expert. A
friend, whose tickets on the Northern France tour my husband and I are using, because her husband just had bypass
surgery, mentioned your—"

"The delightful Mrs. Atwater!" he exclaimed. "And you
must be Mrs. Blue."

"Yes." I was astounded. "Evidently we're going on the
same tour."

"Ah, but that is the least of the amazing coincidences
inherent in this chance meeting, for your friend, Mrs. At-

water, has prevailed upon me to share a room with your son."

"I didn't know that," I said weakly. I had known that Chris was to share a room with someone but had imagined that it would be some other professor's son, maybe even someone Chris had known at our former university. My husband Jason moved us to El Paso, Texas, last year in his pursuit of ever more interesting problems in environmental toxicology.

"I do hope that your offspring is not given to playing loud rock music or staying glued to the television," said the professor jovially, although I detected a hint of serious concern behind this inquiry.

"I'm sure he'll do his best to prove an acceptable roommate," I murmured. Oh dear. Even on so slight an acquaintance, I did not anticipate that Chris would be much taken with Professor Childeric, especially since my son's preferred destination for his spring break had been Padre Island, where half-naked coeds from all over the country would be romping on the beach.

"Dr. Thomas-Smith will be happy to know that you have joined the group," said Dr. Childeric.

"I don't believe I know him."

"Her. She is a professor of nutrition, a spinster."

"And her name is Thomas? How unusual."

"No, dear lady, Thomas-Smith, a hyphenated family name. Be that as it may, Dr. Thomas-Smith's given name is Anna, not Thomas, and she was prevailed upon by Mrs. Atwater to room with the Atwater girl. I'm told that Dr. Thomas-Smith is not happy with the situation, although they have yet to spend a night in the same room. But at least now that you are here, she can relinquish chaperone duties. The girl disappeared at O'Hare, in search of an airport T-shirt, I believe, and caused great consternation."

"Young people do like T-shirts," I replied, hoping that she would not take to disappearing during this tour. Now I began to question my readiness to keep an eye on young Edie in return for a discount on the tour tickets. Judith Atwater hadn't wanted her daughter to miss the educational experience offered by a visit to France.

Surely, I comforted myself, a girl with an interest in French history would soon lose interest in T-shirts and the like when more fascinating experiences were on offer. Our Gwen has always been an inquisitive and cooperative traveler. And even if Edie was a handful, she might become smitten with Chris, my handsome son, who is blond, tanned, and terribly intelligent, although I'm not sure that intelligence is high on the list of desirable male characteristics among high school girls. Still, if she liked him, she might tag around after him. Chris wouldn't be pleased, but I'd always know where she was.

"Why are so many of the bags wrapped in plastic?" I asked. As we talked, I had been keeping an eye on the luggage, but so many suitcases were completely covered with what looked like Saran Wrap that I feared being unable to identify ours if they turned up.

"It is some service offered by the English," Professor Childeric replied. "Perhaps to keep luggage handlers from stealing one's belongings. That does happen, you know. Crime is rampant, even in the most civilized of countries. My wife had her handbag stolen on the Paris Metro as the train approached the Cluny station. I was shocked to think that visitors journeying to one of the world's finest medieval museums have to run such risks."

"It is a wonderful place, isn't it?" I exclaimed enthusiastically. "What a thrill to be able to turn the pages of the Duc du Berry's gorgeous Book of Hours."

Professor Childeric beamed at me and clasped my elbow in delight. "My dear lady," he cried happily, "you are familiar with—" But he was unable to finish because he went sprawling onto the luggage carousel, his head slamming into a large, gray, hard-sided, American Touris-

ter two-suiter. Since his hand was on my elbow, I might
well have followed him into danger had not my son appeared at my side and saved me from a nasty and undigni-
fied spill.

2

Meeting a Gendarme

Carolyn

"Mom, are you okay?" Chris asked as he pulled me to
safety. "What happened?"

"Yes to your first question, and I have no idea to your
second. We'd better rescue the professor." We pushed our
way through the crowd, none of whom thought to do anything but stare at the dazed and groaning traveler being
carried away among the suitcases.

"Help!" he cried. His legs were kicking frantically, one
foot over the lower edge of the carousel, while he clasped
his head with both hands. I could see the blood seeping between his fingers.

"He's hemmed in by the bags, Chris," I said. "You're
going to have to grab his feet."

As my son tried, an even bigger bag toppled over onto
the professor's shoulder. He moaned and tried to move
away. Chris said, "Shit," and reached out again to capture
a foot.

"Watch your language," I gasped, breathless because
we were both chasing after the victim as he circled the
carousel. Chris jumped onto the moving belt himself,
heaved off two bags that were pinning the professor, then

grasped him under the arms and half shoved, half lifted him free. Jean-Claude Childeric staggered and fell to his knees, continuing to moan. I helped him up and kept him from falling over once he was on his feet. The poor man was not only shaken, but his forehead was bleeding copiously.

By the time Chris had jumped off and come back to prop Professor Childeric up on the other side, we had been joined by a French policeman, heavily armed and very stern looking, who proceeded to lecture my brave son and the unfortunate medievalist.

"This man is bleeding!" I broke in.

"Now, Mother," murmured Chris. "Don't make a scene." For no known reason, offspring become embarrassed when their mothers exercise proper indignation in public places.

The policeman had turned to me. "Madame, is not permitted for travelers to ride on baggage facilities. A fine of many francs can be assessed onto such—"

"For goodness' sake, Officer, he fell! Look at his forehead. And my son got up there to rescue him. Where were you when all this was happening?"

Blood was running between the professor's eyebrows and down his nose like red wine from a *bota*. (This is a Spanish wine carrier with a long spout used in a bizarre ritual that involves pouring wine onto one's forehead in such a way that it will eventually run into one's mouth—or perhaps that's a Basque custom rather than Spanish.) In Dr. Childeric's case, it was running off his chin and onto his clothing. I quickly searched my purse for Kleenex and Band-Aids. "It's bad enough that Air France lost my luggage," I said to the officer, "but for the French authorities to harass visitors to the country, one of whom has just been injured in a completely unintended fall—"

"I was pushed!" interrupted Jean-Claude Childeric. Then he translated that remark for the policeman while

Chris and I exchanged surprised looks as I tried to clean the blood away with Kleenex. Why would someone push a traveler onto the baggage carousel? I was now wondering how much wine the professor had imbibed aboard the plane and how appropriate a roommate he would make for my son.

Then I got a good look at the cut on his forehead. It was deep and still bleeding. He must have hit a sharp edge on that suitcase with great force. In which case maybe he *had* been pushed. A frightening thought!

I broke into the discussion between our countryman and the French police officer to say, "This man needs a doctor. He needs stitches. *Dottore. Comprende?*"

"That's Italian, dear lady, not French," said the professor. "Perhaps Spanish, as well. I'm afraid I'm feeling too ill to distinguish."

"Exactly," I agreed. "You need medical attention. Monsieur Gendarme, please summon a doctor immediately."

The policeman produced a cell phone, on which he made a call. No doubt, he said unpleasant things about Americans, but evidently he did summon medical assistance.

"Well, I suppose one can't expect much of the Paris police," I murmured consolingly to the professor as I blotted up more blood from his face with a Kleenex and tried to close the wound and stem the bleeding with two Band-Aids. "They were, after all, founded for the sole purpose of protecting people on their way to and from dinner parties, which seems a somewhat frivolous mission." I used my ministrations as an opportunity to sniff my patient's breath. He didn't *smell* of alcohol. The policeman evidently heard and took amiss my bit of historical information on the Paris police, for he muttered under his breath in French while aiming resentful glances in my direction.

"Frivolous perhaps, but very French, don't you think?" Professor Childeric replied, seemingly cheered by this bit of French history. He then thanked Chris for rescuing him. "I fear that I was quite stunned by my collision with that suitcase. In fact, I may have sustained a second injury. My shoulder is aching abominably. Had you not come to my aid, young man, I might well have been whisked off to some baggage room and arrested as a presumptive terrorist trying to tamper with airplane luggage." He chuckled weakly at his own wit.

"Professor, this is my son Christopher Blue. Chris, Professor Childeric will be your roommate for the duration of the trip." I slipped the first aid kit back into my handbag and turned to greet my husband, who had just arrived on the scene.

"As of now," said Jason, "they don't know what happened to our bags."

"What will we do?" I cried, aghast.

"They've provided us with emergency lost-luggage packets." Jason had three under his arm. "Air France T-shirt and toiletries, I believe."

"What good will a T-shirt do me?" I muttered miserably.

"I'll take it if you don't want it," said a young girl who had joined our group, uninvited. "Hi, Professor Childeric. What happened to your head? You're all bloody. Did you insult that policeman? Did he hit you with his nightstick?"

"Ah, Edie, I see that you have managed to escape once more from Professor Thomas-Smith," said the medievalist. He was sounding weaker. "Mrs. Blue, this is your charge, Edie Atwater."

But the T-shirt-loving Edie was paying no attention to me. She had spotted my son and sidled up to him, eyelashes fluttering. "Hello there. Are you on our tour, too?"

She was a pretty girl, and Chris, from whom I had expected disinterest in high school girls, smiled at her.

Oh dear. Maybe I had a more onerous burden to look forward to with this young lady than trying to keep her

from disappearing into T-shirt shops or harboring a secret
admiration for Chris. I foresaw having to defend my son's
virtue, or hers. This was not a promising introduction to
our tour.

Two men in white rolled up a stretcher, and the policeman insisted that a protesting Professor Childeric allow
himself to be put on the gurney and wheeled away. I felt
very sorry for him, but he did need medical attention. By
way of consolation, I called after him that we'd tell the
tour director what had happened to him so that he would
be well represented in his dealing with French medical
personnel and the police. He raised a hand forlornly as he
disappeared into the crowd.

"Carolyn," said my husband, "you've got blood on your
jacket."

Oh dear, I thought. *No change of clothes, and I picked
this particular afternoon to minister to the wounded. I
don't even have my spot removers; they're in the lost luggage.*

Travel Journal
Day One, Paris, afternoon at the hotel

  Can't believe I did that!
  *But then I couldn't believe it when I discovered that Jean-
Claude Childeric was joining the tour group. A man I've
hated for years. A man I'd almost got over obsessing about.
Not that I've forgiven the S.O.B., but at least I haven't been
thinking about him much.*
  *That's why I signed up for this trip. A first step toward a
less dreary life. Now he's going to ruin it just like he's ruined
everything else.*
  *Even so, I don't go around shoving people. Not since I was
a kid. Must have been his self-congratulatory manner. Or his*

offensive flirtation with that blonde woman by the luggage belt.

Suddenly I felt this bolt of Childeric-loathing, and I gave him a good, hard push.

No plan, no hesitation. Just whomp, and over he went.

No one in the department would believe I had it in me.

And it was so satisfying!

To see him sprawling among the scuffed-up luggage of strangers. His cherished dignity in tatters. Blood all over his head.

I would have laughed out loud if I hadn't been disappearing as fast as I could into the crowd.

That's the really strange thing. I pushed a well-dressed man onto a luggage carrier, and no one noticed.

No one shouted, "Assault" or whatever the French word is.

No one denounced me to the police. I just drifted away in the other direction and picked up my bag about ten feet closer to the carousel entrance. Then turned to watch the hubbub— the blood dripping down his nose. He once described it to me as classic. (I ask you: Who refers to his own nose as classic?)

Some young man jumped up on the belt and hauled him off. That must have hurt. Getting dragged along, hoisted up, and dumped off. He certainly did a lot of groaning. I enjoyed that, too.

Then the blonde woman came at him with Kleenex and Band-Aids.

Professor Hoping-to-Be-the-Next-Dean must have been thoroughly humiliated.

Good!

Best day I've had in a long time.

If he's badly enough hurt, he'll have to go home.

3
A First Taste of Paris

On a recent trip to France one of the things I looked forward to eating was *pâté de foie gras*. It is not, believe me, anything like American chicken liver pâté. The French version is mild, rich, and creamy; it melts on your tongue in a burst of gentle but compelling flavor—a flavor so delightful one almost forgets that some profit-minded farmer force-fed a goose to produce the swollen liver that makes French pâté.

Given the cost (it's expensive) and the anticipation engendered by good French pâté, it is something one hopes to share with loved ones. Accordingly, I could hardly believe that my husband and son slipped out on our first day in Paris while I was napping, ordered pâté without me, and devoured it all. They didn't even bring a crackerful back to the room for the family culinary researcher. And worse, they told me, in vivid detail, how good it had been.

Because the name is so marvelously French, one would think that *pâté de foie gras* originated in France. Where else? But it didn't. Around 400 B.C. a king of Sparta received as a gift from Egypt some plump geese whose purpose was to provide what we now know as *pâté de foie gras*. The question is, did King Agesilaus appreciate the pâté? Or did he consider it an effeminate repast, fit only for nonwarrior types? These enlarged goose livers were popular with the Roman nobility as well as the ancient Egyptians, and only in the eighteenth century did a young French chef, Jean-

Joseph Clausse, whip up pâté for his ducal patron, then governor of Strasbourg in Alsace. It contained black Perigord truffles and became popular all over Europe.

Carolyn Blue, "Have Fork, Will Travel,"
Madison University Banner

Jason

As she always does when struck down by jet lag, Carolyn collapsed into heavy sleep in the hotel room once she had attended to her most urgent concerns. First, she scrubbed the blood of a clumsy medievalist from her jacket. Second, she took a shower. Then, complaining all the while about the indignity of having no clean clothes to wear for goodness knows how long, she hung the various pieces of her only outfit on separate hangers to air on the balcony. I had to point out that other guests of the hotel used the balcony to get to their rooms.

Our hotel was a very peculiar one. From the public rooms, we had to cross a courtyard, take an elevator to the second story of a second building, cross over a second courtyard by way of a crosswalk, then take a second elevator to the third floor of a third building, where we walked along the balcony in question to find our room.

Fearing that passersby might steal her only outfit, Carolyn agreed to suspend it inside an open window. I pointed out that the room was hot, and if we opened the windows, we couldn't very well use the air conditioning promised in the brochure. I needn't have worried. I never did find an air conditioner.

Then Carolyn fretted because *my clothes* could only be aired after I went to bed for the night. Have you ever noticed how obsessive women are about clean clothes and frequent changes, while we men are perfectly happy to wear the same trousers all week as long as we haven't left samples of our dinners on them? It would be interesting to see a statistical analysis of the matter to find out whether this clean-clothes fetish was always part of the female psyche or resulted from the advent of the automatic washing machine.

While I was making a second search for the promised air conditioner, Carolyn burst from the bathroom, wrapped in a towel and coughing violently. She had used the spray deodorant provided in the Air France lost-luggage package. As soon as she opened the bathroom door, the deodorant fumes wafted into the room, and I began to cough as well. God knows what toxic gas lurked in the aerosol. I couldn't identify the chemical because it was disguised by perfume, but I would have liked to know its composition.

I felt rather inconsiderate about leaving her in a room scented with possibly dangerous fumes, but she urged me to go, pointing out that Chris would be anxious to have lunch and begin an exploration of Paris and that he was undoubtedly waiting for me in the lobby. I only hoped that his roommate, Dr. Childeric, with whom I had served on academic committees in the past, would not be with him. Despite the heat and the fumes, Carolyn had dropped into deep sleep before I slipped from the room.

"Listen, Dad," said Chris as we walked next door to a sidewalk café for lunch, "is there any chance I could change rooms with someone? This guy I'm sharing with just spent fifteen minutes telling me how lucky I am because my education will be 'incalculably enhanced' is how he put it, by being around him because he knows everything there is to know about French history, especially medieval French history. Like if I really wanted to know anything about it I couldn't ask Mom."

I had been studying the menu during my son's lament. I did, of course, sympathize with him, and I, too, would rather get my historical tidbits from Carolyn, who wasn't given to droning on and on, but I doubted that there was anyone for Chris to change with and said so. "We're supposed to have a welcome banquet tonight," I remarked. "Shall we eat light now?"

"Light?" Chris looked as if I had suggested that we eat bugs. "I'm hungry."

"I was thinking maybe bread, wine, pâté, cheese—"

"You're kidding, right?"

My son, who has more culinary sophistication than most young men his age, loves pâté and good French cheeses, and he is developing a palate for wine—at home. Carolyn is adamant that he not disobey the law by ordering alcohol in public places until he's twenty-one. However, in France he could have a glass of wine without putting either of us at legal risk.

"Can we afford pâté?" he asked.

"I think, considering what I just made during my week consulting in New York, that we can have an order of pâté."

He grinned with delight. "I'm game if you are. You sure Mom won't flip about the wine?"

"We've already discussed it, and since it's legal in France, we settled on a glass at meals if you want it."

"All *right*!" Chris beamed at me and then added, "If we can afford pâté, how about some caviar, too?"

"On the flight over, your mother told me that the Spanish conquistadors discovered the Indians in South America eating, among other interesting things, the roe of water bugs, which they said tasted like caviar."

"Gross," said my son. "Where does she find stuff like that? If I didn't know better, I'd say she made it up." Then he eyed me suspiciously. "Is that a roundabout way of telling me, no caviar?"

"Just a point of information. But you're right. No caviar."

I ordered our lunch, and Chris returned to his discussion of Professor Childeric. "And he's not only a bore; he's a nut. He said—and I'm not kidding about this—that a 'strapping young fellow like me' could make myself useful by keeping an eye out for his enemies. Enemies? Give me a break! He thinks someone pushed him onto the baggage thingamabob at the airport. Well, he did fall onto it, but why would anyone push him? Probably just embarrassed that I had to haul him off before he disappeared through the leather curtains. I wish I'd let him."

Chris spread newly delivered pâté on a piece of crusty French bread, devoured it, followed with a gulp of white wine, and said, "Oh man, if my fraternity brothers could see me now! They think it's a big night when the cook puts meatballs in the spaghetti at the house."

"Jason Blue?" I glanced toward the new voice and recognized a tall, thin, dark-haired man with an angular face and vague eyes sitting at a table near us—Hugh Fauree, a parasitologist at my former university. I had often chatted with him about things scientific before committee meetings. If I remembered correctly, he was a widower with several relatively young children, whom he had probably brought along.

"Hugh, good to see you. This is my son Chris."

On being invited, Hugh joined us, bringing along a glass of beer and a vegetable salad. "I couldn't help overhearing you about Childeric," he said to Chris. "Consider yourself lucky that he doesn't suspect *you* of pushing him at the airport. He accused me just now in the lobby, and I didn't even see the incident."

"Well, at least you're not rooming with him," said Chris gloomily. Then he brightened. "Say, do you have a roommate?"

"No, I have a room to myself, but it's very small," said

Fauree, "and I'm looking forward to enjoying my nights in single, if cramped, solitude."

Chris looked disappointed. As I had feared, he must have been planning to suggest himself to fill a spot in Fauree's room. "Look, Dad," he said, turning to me, "couldn't you and Mom have a cot put in your room for me?"

"We don't have space for a chair, much less a cot," I replied. "Be glad you got to come along at all."

Looking somewhat sulky, Chris helped himself to bread and Camembert and muttered something about the missed joys of Padre Island, where no one would have wanted to force-feed him medieval French history and the sands were littered with pretty girls his own age.

I asked Fauree why Childeric would think him capable of an airport assault and discovered that the two were nominees for the position as dean of arts and sciences. "They decided to appoint someone from the faculty, and I'm the science candidate," said Fauree. "Childeric and Laura de Sorentino, chair of modern languages, are the arts candidates." He took a long swallow of his beer and added wryly, "For no discernible reason, Childeric seems to think he has the edge, although Laura and I are chairs, and he's never held an administrative post."

"Congratulations," I said.

"Thanks. I figured if I could stand dealing with the biologists, I might as well take on the rest of the college. The selection committee will want another scientist, don't you think?"

"You're a brave man," I replied evasively. "Many a happy scholar has been turned into an unhappy bureaucrat by accepting a deanship."

"Yeah, but isn't one qualification to be a dean stuffiness?" asked Chris, grinning and devouring chunks of pâté. "I'll bet Professor Childeric's got you beat there, Dr. Fauree. He's the most boring man I ever met, and I've been an academic kid all my life."

Fauree started to laugh. "Maybe if you pointed that out to him, Chris, he'd stop suspecting me of skullduggery in the name of ambition."

"Jason Blue!" I found myself grasped by the face, turned, and given a smacking kiss on the mouth. Oh God, I thought, recognizing my assailant, Dr. Roberta Hecht—a friend of Carolyn's, a world-renowned expert on the art of Joan Miró, and a self-proclaimed serial monogamist. She claims to have grown up in the Church of the Latter-Day Saints and given it up for her own version of Mormonism, one more favorable to women. An attractive woman of Amazonian proportions, she does have a certain Mormon aura of robust health and clean living, but there any resemblance ends. Her post-Mormon period includes four husbands that I know of.

"Robbie," I murmured, thinking, where was one's wife when one needed her for protection against casually affectionate women? Since my defense was in my own hands, I hastily directed Robbie's attention elsewhere before she could progress to the French cheek-kissing ritual, for which she was puckering up. "You remember Chris?"

She glanced over my shoulder, spotted Chris, smiled enthusiastically, and transferred the cheek kissing to him. Chris flushed but rose to the occasion and returned the kisses. "You dear, handsome boy! But then you're not a boy anymore, are you?"

Christ! Surely, she wouldn't go after my twenty-year-old son. That would be distressingly inappropriate.

"And who is this handsome fellow?" she asked, releasing Chris and zooming in on Hugh. I introduced them. Roberta couldn't believe she'd never met such a fascinating man, and at her own university. She kissed Hugh, who didn't kiss her back but did look bemused.

"Well, who are you married to this year, Robbie?" I asked heartily in a none-too-subtle attempt to forewarn my colleague.

"No one at all." She dragged a chair over from another table, earning a disapproving look from a French couple, and slid in beside Hugh. "I have snipped my latest matrimonial ribbons with the golden shears of divorce and am as carefree as a Miró bird, but more mobile."

Carefree and on the prowl for number five, I thought.

"Hi, Dr. Blue," said a sugar-sweet young voice. "I'm looking for your wife."

"Carolyn's trying to sleep off jet lag this afternoon, Edie," I said to Judith Atwater's daughter. "Isn't Dr. Thomas-Smith in your room to—"

"Oh, she's gone off to get tickets for some dreary classical concert tomorrow night at a place called Saint Chapel. Hi, Chris. Can I join you? O-o-o, you're drinking wine. That's *so* cool."

I could see that my son not only agreed with her but also was happy to have his sophistication affirmed by a pretty girl. He purloined the last available chair from the table of the French couple. They responded by glaring at him, after which they slapped down some francs and stalked off with their miniature poodle, which had been yapping annoyingly under the table.

"Can I have a glass of wine, Dr. Blue?" Edie gave me a melting glance.

"You're only sixteen," I replied. "I'm not sure what French law is on the subject, but I'd certainly need written permission from your mother."

Edie looked sulky. Roberta Hecht was telling Hugh that he simply had to see some Miró prints she was carrying because they had little squiggles that were surely parasites. "Think of what a paper we could write together, identifying the actual parasites painted by Joan Miró. Interdisciplinary research is very chic. We might even get an article accepted to *Nature*—Miró prints, parasite photos."

"Did Miró know anything about parasites?" Hugh asked, as any practical man of science would. Still, I could tell that he was already falling under the spell of Robbie's maniacally romantic personality. He'd probably never run into anything like it.

"So, Edie," I said, turning to the teenager, who was now clinging to my son's arm and telling him how "cool" it was that he was a real fraternity man. "The concert you mentioned. Could the venue have been Sainte-Chapelle?"

"Maybe," said Edie cautiously.

"Do you remember anything about the program?"

"Oh yeah. *The Four Seasons.* Boy, does that sound—"

"Mom would love it," said Chris. "Vivaldi at Sainte-Chapelle. I wouldn't mind seeing the place myself."

"Me too!" said Edie. "Wow, Vivalti!"

"Let's pick up some tickets and surprise your mother," I suggested to Chris, and we were soon on our way.

Roberta claimed to love Vivaldi as well, and insisted that Hugh accompany her to the concert—as her guest. When he looked reluctant, she exclaimed, "How could a man with a name like Fauree pass up Vivaldi?" Then she punched him playfully on the shoulder. Hugh blinked. Roberta looked at the shoulder with interest and exclaimed, "Great muscle tone! You could be a kayaker."

"I am a kayaker."

"Me too," said Roberta.

Suddenly Hugh Fauree looked much more interested in attending a Vivaldi concert, and I thought with foreboding that my friend might well be paddling in romantic rapids the likes of which he had never encountered.

"Oh, I want to go too," exclaimed Edie.

"Isn't Anna getting you a ticket?" I asked.

"She said I wouldn't like it. She's going with Professor Petar, who's a real cut-off-their-balls feminist." She looked very pleased with this daring choice of words, then amended hastily, "Well, that's what my dad says, anyway."

4
French Lasagna

I recently found myself in Paris—the font of fine food, the Mecca of Haute Cuisine—anticipating the gala welcome banquet that was to launch an exciting tour of Northern France. Was I subsequently titillated by tasty hors d'oeuvres? Entranced by elegant entrées? Delighted by delicious desserts? I was not. A fish mousse of world-class insipidity greeted us at the table, and we were sent on our way with a boring custard pie. In between these disappointments was lasagna. Not even good lasagna. Wine was *not* included. To add insult to injury, we paid $15.65 American for a half-carafe of the house red, a mediocre vintage of no pretensions whatever.

My husband is still indignant over that fifteen plus dollars. He mentions it every time he opens a bottle of wine at home. "This particular Australian Shiraz cost only $10.98," he says, pouring a small portion for tasting. "It's a full bottle, you'll notice, not a half-carafe." He sniffs, then sips appreciatively. "And it's excellent!" My husband likes to get his money's worth when it comes to wine. And I, it would seem, do not like French lasagna. In fact, why would a welcome-to-Paris dinner feature lasagna?

Carolyn Blue, "Have Fork, Will Travel,"
Grand Rapids Post-Meridian

Carolyn

At six-thirty Paris time our group met in a room adjacent to the hotel lobby. Standing among and sitting on bamboo chairs and settees with lavishly flowered, if lumpy, cushions, we introduced ourselves to strangers, renewed friendships with people we had known in the past, and then listened to our guide, Denis. He had a lovely French accent, a dubious grasp of French history, a lively imagination, an extensive wardrobe of black turtlenecks and jeans, and one black sports jacket. Most of this I found out as the tour progressed, but his penchant for lively and fictitious historical discourse was immediately evident.

For instance, he told us that Saint Denis, after whom he was named, had been a native of the Paris region.

"He most certainly was not," muttered Professor Childeric, who had attached himself to me early in the social hour. "He was an Italian sent to Gaul by Pope . . ."

I couldn't help noticing that the medievalist had four stitches holding the wound on his forehead together, that they were sewed with black thread, and that the surrounding area had been painted with a red-orange disinfectant. He looked almost raffish.

"Would you like me to provide you with a gauze pad and clear tape for your forehead?" I whispered.

"You're very thoughtful," he whispered in return. "Unfortunately, the doctor told me to leave the injury uncovered to promote healing and under no circumstances to scrub off the disinfectant. I fear that I must resign myself to looking like some disreputable pugilist until the stitches can be removed."

"The patron saint of our country," Denis was saying, "converted his heathen brethren by introducing them to the use of herbs in their cuisine, thus establishing the French tradition of fine food, which we are about to sample."

Professor Childeric positively growled with indignation

and informed me that nothing whatever was known of the saint's preferences in food, except that he was given to fasting.

In my opinion, I whispered back, the advent of haute cuisine in France was the doing of Catherine de Medici, Italian wife of one of the Kings Henri. She brought her own chefs to the marriage.

"Exactly," said Childeric.

"Sadly, the Bishop of Paris was beheaded by jealous pagans who couldn't tell rosemary from hemlock, after which he delighted his followers and converted his enemies by picking up his head and walking off with it," Denis reported in conclusion.

What a delightful story! I thought.

"Balderdash!" shouted Childeric. "There is absolutely no documentation for that fairy tale."

"It is a tradition that is cherished and attested to by all loyal Frenchmen," retorted Denis cheerfully, making a small but graceful bow in the direction of his critic. "The veneration of Saint Denis was a favorite cause of our own Saint Louis, the tenth King Louis of France."

"Ninth," I murmured discreetly.

"Idiot!" cried Childeric, throwing his hands in the air.

My head whipped around in surprise. Was he talking about me?

"The king who particularly favored the cult of Denis was Louis the Pious, not Saint Louis."

Ah, he was still correcting our guide. How embarrassed I would have been had I named the wrong Louis.

Denis the Guide smiled beatifically at the professor and said, "As you Americans say, 'Whatever.' Now, shall we abandon French history for French cuisine?"

Unhappily, the dinner provided at the tour company's chosen restaurant was neither very good nor very French. In fact, our main course was a lasagna distinguished by leathery pasta, a cheese that no Italian would have allowed in the kitchen, bland tomato sauce, and stringy meat. I would be hard put to write a column in praise of French cuisine on the basis of that meal.

Dinner table conversation was as bizarre as the food was dull. Professor Childeric asked me in a whisper over the fish mousse whether I had observed Dr. Hugh Fauree pushing him onto the baggage carousel at the airport. Surprised, I replied that I hadn't seen Dr. Fauree at all until we met for the predinner lecture. Professor Childeric—he preferred *professor* to *doctor* because Europeans hold professors in such "high esteem"—assured me that Dr. Fauree had indeed pushed him, no doubt hoping to cause a more serious injury than had occurred.

"I'm sure you must be mistaken about Dr. Fauree. He is a very mild-mannered person, not at all the type to cause injury to another."

"Ah, but my dear lady, you are obviously unaware that Dr. Fauree has good cause to wish me ill. We are both candidates for the position of dean of the college of arts and sciences, we and a Professor Laura de Sorentino, an excellent French teacher but hardly a serious candidate. I, on the other hand, am, if I may presume to say so, the favored choice of the administration and the selection committee. No doubt Dr. Fauree is resentful, although I hardly think he should be surprised. I am, after all, a preeminent scholar of the Middle Ages in France."

"But pushing you onto a luggage carousel wouldn't advance his candidacy," I pointed out.

"Any public embarrassment is to be avoided by a candidate for high administrative office at a respected university. I have no doubt that he has already telephoned his supporters with scathing descriptions of my humiliation."

"Dr. Fauree spent the afternoon having lunch with my husband and securing tickets to a Vivaldi concert tomorrow evening at Sainte-Chapelle," I replied soothingly.

"Does that sound like the sort of person who would push a colleague onto a luggage carousel?"

"Vivaldi? Sainte-Chapelle? Is the tour providing—no, obviously not. I must look into a ticket for myself. How unfortunate that my dear wife, who also loves the music of the Baroque, was unable to accompany me. She is playing in a national bridge tournament. A very competitive player, my wife. You say your husband is friendly with Dr. Fauree? Still, Mrs. Blue—may I beg the honor of calling you by your given name? Still, I hope that you will think well enough of me to keep a wary eye out on my behalf, lest another unfortunate *accident* befall me."

"Of course you may call me Carolyn," I replied without promising to act as his bodyguard. Good grief, the man might be a fountain of medieval information, but the impression he made was of a Victorian gentleman suffering from untreated paranoia. "But I'm sure you're wrong about Dr. Fauree," I added. "Jason thinks very highly of him."

"Then how would you explain my fall, dear lady? I have no other enemies that I know of, and I am not a clumsy person."

"You know, I have given what happened some thought, and it occurred to me that you might be the victim of air rage. One reads frequently in the newspapers about passengers and airline personnel being attacked by people driven beyond the bounds of civility by the terrible service, bad weather, and problems caused by an antiquated air traffic control system."

"That is a delightfully imaginative hypothesis, my dear Carolyn, but I fear that I have been the victim of promotion rage rather than air rage, as you so quaintly put it."

Ah well, I could see that I wasn't going to change his mind. Perhaps time and a good night's sleep would put him in a more reasonable frame of mind. I smiled cordially and turned to Jason, who sat on my left. He was poking suspiciously at the just-served lasagna and glad to be distracted.

5
Assorted Tourists

Carolyn

And what of the other tour participants? I found among us an old friend, Robbie Hecht, Miró scholar and romantic adventurer. While we were waiting to be seated at the restaurant, she entertained me with the tale of her latest divorce, during which she and her fourth husband agreed on every detail in the division of property except who got Buster, the offspring of a favorite Irish setter (now deceased) owned by Robbie. In fact, she and the latest husband met and fell in love when he came to buy the puppy. Robbie was claiming right of prior ownership. That controversy was in the courts still, although the divorce was final and Robbie was quite obviously on the lookout for husband number five. She had set her cap with customary enthusiasm for Jason's friend, Hugh Fauree.

I warned her that Hugh had two children, a teenaged boy and a preteen girl, who might not welcome a second wife so soon after their mother's death. Robbie just laughed and said it was about time that she tried her hand at motherhood and that skipping the pregnancy, childbirth, and diaper stages suited her to a tee. She and Hugh sat together during dinner, Hugh obviously flattered by the attentions of a handsome woman who loved kayaking. Evidently women kayakers are hard to find. Even his late wife had not been willing to accompany him on kayaking weekends. Also Robbie showed a remarkable interest in parasites; he confided this to me the next morning at breakfast.

Although I thought their blossoming infatuation quite sweet, Jason disapproved. I said, "Robbie's just looking for Mr. Right, and I wouldn't be surprised to find that Hugh is it."

"I'd be surprised," Jason grumbled. We agreed to disagree and stay out of it, always the most sensible course when mutual friends are beginning a relationship. Another attraction more problematical was that between our son and Edie Atwater, underage enchantress. Chris didn't sit with us because Professor Childeric did, and Edie sat with Chris and flirted blatantly.

Denis announced during dinner that all those who wished to participate in the tour of Paris the next morning should sign up in the lobby of the hotel tonight and meet there at eight-thirty tomorrow to catch the bus. Jean-Claude Childeric snorted and announced that he planned to visit the Cluny. Chris immediately opted for the tour, and Edie followed suit. Disheartened, I realized that perhaps it was my duty to go as well. Professor Childeric assumed aloud that I would want to accompany him to the museum, but Jason replied for me that we were going to the Rodin.

I squeezed Jason's hand appreciatively. And after all, what could Chris and Edie get up to while on a bus full of middle-aged professors and their spouses? However, Anna Thomas-Smith sent me a reproving glance and, looking much put upon, said that she supposed she'd have to go on the tour as well, since Edie needed looking after. I assuaged a guilty conscience by reasoning that, as a professor of home economics with a specialty in nutrition, she probably didn't want to go off on her own to a museum anyway.

I was evidently wrong about that because Dr. Janice

Petar broke away from a conversation, bits of which I overheard after dinner, with Professors Nedda (English drama) and Macauley (creative writing) Drummond about postmodern novels.

"His wife must be the only person in the world who thinks well of that unintelligible stuff Macauley writes," she muttered as she walked up to me. "I'm Janice Petar. I don't think we met when you and your husband were at the university."

"No," I agreed. "Carolyn Blue." I shook her hand. "Did I understand you to say that Dr. Drummond is a published novelist, or does he critique postmodernism?"

"*Mr.* Drummond. He hasn't got a doctorate, and his dreary little novels are published by small presses and are absolute drivel exclaimed over by critics who wouldn't know a good read if it bit them on the ass."

"Really?" What could I say to that? Since she hadn't kept her voice down, Mr. Drummond and his wife were scowling at her.

"I hope you don't plan to saddle poor Anna with the responsibility for that young twit during the whole tour. She'd never have agreed to room with Edie if she hadn't thought you would be doing the chaperoning. Which reminds me—your name, Blue. That's unusual. You're not, by any chance, related to Professor Gwenivere Blue, are you?"

"My mother-in-law," I replied, suppressing a sigh. This lady reminded me of her, except that Janice Petar was younger.

"Good lord!" exclaimed Dr. Petar. "You have my sympathy. Although she is a powerful voice in my field, the chance of getting a mother-in-law like Gwenivere Blue is enough to keep any woman from marrying."

"Fortunately, I was wise enough to woo Carolyn before I let her meet my mother," said Jason. He had just joined us after escaping a conversation with Manfred Unsell, an economics professor who evidently viewed the tour as an opportunity to observe, while disguised as a tourist, the everyday impact of the European Common Market and the Euro.

His wife Grace, in her quiet way, made it clear that she'd just as soon have been at home, where her daughter was soon to give birth to the Unsells' first grandchild. While in France, Grace Unsell was never without a knitting bag, from which she pulled either some half-finished baby item or a cell phone, on which she solicited information on the pregnancy, the obstetrician's latest advice, the intrauterine kicking and somersaulting habits of the fetus, and so forth. I can't say that I blame Grace. I'd have found expectant grandmotherhood more interesting than the impact of the Euro on citizens and tourists in France. Jason wasn't interested in either.

"In fact, we were engaged before you introduced me to your mother," I said to Jason. "This is Dr. Janice Petar, who knows your mother professionally and who thinks we were remiss in letting Anna Thomas-Smith replace us as chaperones on the tour tomorrow."

"Janice, nice to see you again, and believe me, I never volunteered to be a chaperone," said Jason.

"Just like a man," retorted the feminist. "Leave the children to the women. You'll be sorry if your son gets her pregnant. How do you know that the girl is careful about contraception?"

"How do you know she's even sexually active?" Jason replied. Women like his mother get his back up.

Dr. Petar snorted. "Does she act like a shy virgin?"

"Rest easy, Dr. Petar. Our son does know about contraception, and he doesn't seduce underage girls," said Jason.

Another snort. "I doubt that he'll have to. Edie seems bent on seducing him."

I glanced over at the two young people in question and shuddered. Chris was talking to Denis, and Edie was gazing soulfully up at my son with a proprietary hand on his arm. Before we went up to our room, I took Dr. Thomas-Smith aside and told her how much I appreciated her sense of responsibility for young Edie. Then I listened sympathetically to her tale of the horrors of trying to find the girl in O'Hare Airport. Finally, I assured her that I'd be keeping an eye on Edie myself as I had promised her mother.

"I'm delighted to hear it. You and Professor Childeric seem to be good friends," she remarked.

"Actually, I only met the man this afternoon when he fell onto the baggage carousel at the airport," I replied. "My son rescued him."

"Really? I hope the professor wasn't hurt. I did notice the stitching on his forehead."

"Mostly his pride, I imagine," I replied, smiling. "Fortunately, he didn't sustain a concussion."

"But you did sit together at dinner."

"Yes, we have a mutual interest in medieval history, but mostly he thought he'd been pushed at the airport by—ah—someone on the tour. He wanted to know if I'd seen anything."

"My goodness. Had you?"

"Heavens no. Why would anyone who knows him push a medieval history professor in an airport? It was obviously a case of air rage."

"Yes. I read about a man who actually defecated on a meal tray because he didn't like airline food. A highly unsanitary method of protest." The nutritionist then engaged me in a rather technical discussion of teenagers' eating habits.

One does accumulate a lot of information when associating with academics. Had I been touring with any other group, I might never have learned the name of the pope who sent Saint Denis to France or the postmenopausal effect on a woman's bones of twenty-four ounces of milk a day during her teen years.

Travel Journal
Day One, after dinner in Paris

   Now that shameless libertine is going after a married woman. Impressing her with all sorts of medieval foolishness. Maybe I should warn her that he's not to be trusted.
   Or maybe I should just give him another shove.
   Must put thoughts like that aside and concentrate on ignoring him.
   Dinner a disappointment. I wonder if the sauce on that lasagna contained horsemeat? It was very lean and tough.
   Thank God Childeric is going to the Cluny tomorrow. Now I know the place to avoid.
   If he continues to accuse Fauree of pushing him, that should cause some resentment.
   Maybe C. will ruin his own chances of becoming dean.
   I hope so.

6

Aphrodisiac Art

Jason

On our first night in Paris, Carolyn complained about having to wear an Air France T-shirt to bed. Personally, I thought she looked quite fetching, and pointed out that our daughter liked to sleep in T-shirts. My wife replied that teenagers, being hormonally impaired, would wear anything favored by their contemporaries.

More worrisome to Carolyn was the continuing nonappearance of our luggage. "I am not going anywhere in

three-day-old clothes," she declared. "You and Chris will
have to buy me something."

"But we're going to the Rodin tomorrow," I protested.

"Not in dirty clothes."

"Carolyn, the French don't even wear deodorant," I ar-
gued. "They won't notice."

"The women don't shave their legs and underarms either, but that doesn't mean I'd go out in public covered
with hair," she retorted. Needless to say, without the
promised air conditioning, the room was very hot, and neither of us slept well. Carolyn awoke the next morning with
a tension headache. While she was describing it in terms of
a medieval torture that involved tightening a band on the
prisoner's head until he or she fainted or died, the desk
called to say that our bags were sitting outside our door.

"They'll have been stolen by now," Carolyn exclaimed
when she heard. Fortunately, they hadn't been, and she
made a miraculous recovery as she pulled out her washcloth and her cosmetics bag with its nontoxic deodorant.
My wife has a thing about washcloths. I had to shower second because she was so anxious to use hers.

Our first breakfast in Paris consisted of the traditional
croissants and coffee, over which we all discussed our
plans for the day. Childeric was going to the Cluny to wal-
low in medieval artifacts, and no one offered to accompany him, although he made another try at talking Carolyn
into it. He even invited me along, but only as a ploy to solicit her reconsideration. I had to wonder whether he was
infatuated with my wife. He wouldn't be the first, not that
Carolyn encourages or even notices that sort of thing.

Those opting for the tour with the guide, aside from my
son and his groupie, were a sedate group: the Unsells, accompanied by her knitting and his long-winded warnings
about the dangers of investing in European stocks when
the new currency was so shaky; Anna Thomas-Smith, who
had little to say for herself but called young Edie *Edwina*

whenever her behavior seemed unacceptable (on the third such occasion the girl muttered, "You're not my mother," and Dr. Thomas-Smith replied, "No, but I certainly wish she were here"); Ivan and Estrella Markarov (Markarov is a computer science professor and his wife, a professor of preschool education who was shocked to hear that we'd be looking at naked statues); and Carl and Ingrid Jensen, respectively, an ag professor with an interest in cows and a county home economist who, when she heard that Carolyn wrote about food, gave her a casserole recipe whose basic ingredient was canned cream of mushroom soup.

I had envisioned Carolyn and I wandering through the gardens at the museum, which had been the sculptor's mansion, a formal, two-story stone building with ranks of tall, many-paned windows. These mildly romantic plans for a private day didn't work out. As soon as Carolyn mentioned where we were going, Roberta Hecht invited herself along, which is not surprising since she's an art historian and Miró did odd sculptures as well as curious paintings. That Roberta talked Hugh Fauree into accompanying us was a surprise. I've never known him to express an interest in sculpture. However, he let himself be persuaded—poor fellow! I'm sure he had no idea what she had in mind. I did because I heard her say to Carolyn that she hoped all those naked statues, suggestively entwined, would give Hugh ideas.

In addition to Hugh and Roberta, two other couples joined us. Jeremy and Hester Foxcroft are art professors and New Englanders. He specializes in traditional landscapes and she, in wildly modern art glass, of which the postmodernist Drummonds approved, although they didn't approve of Rodin. They invited Hester to accompany them on a trip to the Jeu de Paume, which had some "very avant garde exhibits." Her husband Jeremy talked her out of avant garde and was called a "reactionary" by Macauley Drummond.

The second couple was named de Sorentino. He is a plastic surgeon and she, the chair of modern languages, a strikingly beautiful woman with the gentle face of a young Madonna and the silver-streaked black hair of an older woman. This lady was the third dean candidate, the one not yet accused of anything by Childeric.

We had a very pleasant day. The others were new to the Rodin, and all were pleased with it. How could they not be? The museum attendants were not on strike, and the house is a beautiful venue for Auguste Rodin's powerful sculpture, which was displayed not only inside, but also outside in a lovely garden. Even the weather cooperated. It was warm, but a light breeze floated through the windows and cooled us outside as well. Much more comfortable than our room at the hotel.

Roberta may have been a bit too obvious in her enthusiasm for the erotic statues, but Hugh responded favorably to her art-as-aphrodisiac ploy as well as her art-critic-at-large explanations. The Foxcrofts both sketched busily, she some of the less representational works inside, he various scenes in the garden, myself included, unfortunately. There is nothing more embarrassing than being asked to sit for an artist.

Dr. de Sorentino, whose name is Lorenzo, compared his wife's face to that of every female statue and found Rodin lacking. The man acted as if he had personally created his wife. Laura de Sorentino seemed enchanted by the sculptor and carried on conversations in fluent French with natives, who were obviously charmed with whatever she had to say, or possibly with how she looked and how well she spoke their language.

She and Carolyn seemed to form an immediate bond and sat together for some time talking and laughing in the garden, after which we all went out to lunch at a small, family-owned café that served only chicken dishes. The special of the day was Poulet Marengo, a dish prepared for

Napoleon after he defeated the Austrians at the battle of Marengo. Carolyn told us that, since the Emperor had been hungry and the supply wagons had not yet caught up with the army, the chef was forced to make do with what he could find in the area: a bottle of cognac, a scrawny chicken, six crayfish, olive oil, garlic, and tomatoes. She ordered the dish for herself, sharing the contents of an earthenware pot with the Foxcrofts and me. Lorenzo de Sorentino insisted on some sort of Italian chicken and became very irritable when his wife didn't like it and said they should have let Carolyn choose for them, too.

With Laura's help, Carolyn managed to prevail on the proprietress for the recipe and ask why her version contained mushrooms instead of crayfish, white wine instead of cognac, tomato paste instead of tomatoes, and deep-fried eggs. The lady, red-faced from her morning in a hot kitchen, replied that she was a woman of the Lyonnais and made Chicken Marengo in the traditional way, as had her mother and grandmother, who knew more about good food than any army cook, even if the man had served Napoleon Bonaparte, who, after all, hadn't been a real Frenchman. Carolyn and Laura dissolved into giggles as soon as the proprietress had returned to her kitchen.

With our several chicken dishes we had loaves of crusty French bread and carafes of cold white wine. It was an excellent midday meal, much better than dinner last night.

"Well," Carolyn said later as we took the Metro back to the hotel, "finally some food to write about."

7
The Prozac Dean

Carolyn

I had the most amazing conversation with Laura de Sorentino before we all went off to lunch. We were sitting together in the museum garden while my reluctant husband posed for a sketch by a landscape artist named Foxcroft, who had one of those slow, nasal, Down-East accents. If he hadn't been so completely involved in his sketch and in a verbal color analysis of fall in New England, I'd have taken him for a farmer from New Hampshire or Vermont. The conversation loosened up my embarrassed-to-be-sketched husband, who chimed in with information on the toxins in various oil paints. I'm sure Professor Foxcroft was amazed to learn how dangerous certain paints would be if he chose to eat, sniff, or paint himself with them. Still, he took the information in good part. Not everyone does.

At any rate, Laura introduced our remarkable chat by telling me how strange it was that all three finalists for the dean position should wind up on the same tour. "I realize that you know Childeric and Fauree personally, but you probably didn't know about me. I hope it doesn't make you uneasy seeing that Hugh is your husband's friend."

"Not at all," I replied. "I like to see women advancing into administrative positions. Not that I wasn't a stay-at-home mom for years, but even I'm trying to establish a career. I guess I'd be called the late-blooming, empty-nest entrée to the world of working women," I added wryly.

"The Empty-Nest Writer? I like that." She laughed and added, "If I get the dean's position, I suppose I'll be called the Prozac Dean."

I have to admit that her statement took me by surprise.

"I am a good chair."

"I'm sure you are."

"But I wouldn't have been ten years ago. Oh, I was a good teacher. Isn't that odd? I was horribly shy in any place but the classroom and very unsure of myself socially, for which I can thank Lorenzo. Being married to a plastic surgeon is not, believe me, a bed of roses."

"But I heard him say Rodin never sculpted a female who could compare to you."

"What he meant was Rodin couldn't compare to him— my husband. Every time I got comfortable with my face or figure, Lorenzo proposed some small improvement he could and did make. He considers me his creation."

I'm afraid I just stared at her in shock.

"I got so depressed that I started going to a psychiatrist. I was considering leaving Lorenzo and quitting teaching. Instead my therapist prescribed Prozac, and it made all the difference. The last time Lorenzo suggested a bit of surgery to improve me, I told him to bugger off." She chuckled happily. "Not a very ladylike thing to say. Lorenzo was terribly offended."

"I can imagine," I replied, grinning.

"Anyway, Prozac was a godsend. Suddenly—well, gradually—I was able to talk to people, and then I started heading off disputes in the department. Pretty soon I was being appointed to contentious committees with the idea that I'd make peace so something could get done. And it was so much fun! And people were so appreciative! The department got together, decided that they wanted me as chair, and petitioned the dean. The old chair left in a huff for another university, and everyone stopped squabbling; infighting had been the hallmark of our department. I used to cringe when we had departmental meetings and people started shouting at each other. Now I just speak up and talk them into something they can agree on."

She seemed so amazed and delighted with this new talent that I had to feel happy for her. It occurred to me that she'd probably make a much better dean than Jean-Claude Childeric, who thought he had the position sewed up. As interesting a fund of medieval information as he had, people in other disciplines would probably prefer someone who was interested in them and their problems.

"Of course, I doubt that I'll get the appointment, and that's fine. I'm happy where I am. In fact, just being nominated gives me new confidence. Lorenzo's latest campaign is to get me to dye my hair. Imagine! I don't have time for things like that."

"It's beautiful just the way it is," I said. "What's wrong with your husband? Any normal man would be delighted to be married to a woman as beautiful and intelligent as you," I added indignantly. Then, of course, it occurred to me that I wasn't being very diplomatic about her husband.

However, she was already saying, with remarkable good cheer, "Oh, Lorenzo's just shallow. That's another thing that depressed me in the old days, but now"—she shrugged expressively—"who cares?"

"I never realized that Prozac was so effective."

"It's a miracle drug," she said enthusiastically. "If I become dean, I'm going to organize Prozac Day and invite all students suffering from depression."

I suppose I looked dubious at that idea. "Just kidding," she said. "Our president would be horrified, mostly because he'd be afraid the university would have to provide the pills. They *are* expensive. On the other hand, it takes a whole box of chocolates to accomplish what one little pill will do without making you fat. Maybe I'll just have a sampler embroidered for my office. *Prozac at work here.*"

We were both laughing helplessly when Jason escaped from Professor Foxcroft and told us that we should consider getting some lunch.

The Prozac Dean? She'd probably be terrific!

Chicken Marengo

I obtained the following recipe from the owner and chef at a small restaurant in Paris. Although she took offense when I questioned the historical accuracy of the ingredients, her version of Chicken Marengo is very tasty. It may not have been what was served to Napoleon after his victory against the Austrians, but I have no doubt that he would have preferred it had he been given the choice.

• Cut a *small roasting chicken (around 3 pounds)* into pieces.

• Heat *3 tbs. olive oil* and *2 tbs. butter* in an earthen casserole or heavy Dutch oven, and sauté the chicken until golden brown on all sides.

• Add *1 tsp. chopped shallots, salt, pepper, 1 tsp. dried tarragon, 1 clove finely chopped garlic, 1 cup dry white wine,* and cook until wine is reduced by half.

• Add *2 tbs. tomato paste* and *1 cup chicken bouillon* or *1 cup liquid from cooking ½ lb. mushrooms in salted water,* reserving mushrooms to add later.

• When chicken is tender, place pieces on a heated platter. Reduce sauce and stir in *1 tbs. flour* blended with *1 tbs. butter.* Put mushrooms on the chicken, strain sauce over it, garnish with *parsley,* and serve hot.

• To satisfy Napoleonic tradition, garnish with *crayfish (cooked, presumably)*. To satisfy the lady from Lyon, surround the chicken with *deep-fried eggs*.

Carolyn Blue, "Have Fork, Will Travel,"
San Mateo Messenger

8
Killer Beef

Carolyn

"I'll have beef tartare," I said to the waiter. Since the tour wasn't providing dinner, a number of us met before the concert at a sidewalk café in the neighborhood.

"Is Madame aware that the *boeuf* is—how to say?—not cook-ed?" asked the waiter.

"If it were cook-ed," I replied sweetly, "it wouldn't be beef tartare, would it?"

"Oh, gross," said Edie Atwater. "Raw meat?"

"It's awesome," Chris assured her. "I'll have it, too, and a glass of the house red."

"I'll have what he's having," Edie chimed in, evidently overcome by infatuation to the extent of no longer finding raw beef "gross."

"Without the wine," added Jason.

Edie pouted. Chris grinned. I thought that I'd have to watch those two. She was practically sitting in his lap at the crowded table, and Estrella Markarov, the bilingual preschool education professor, was eyeing them with disapproval. That afternoon Anna Thomas-Smith had hinted vaguely at improper conduct during the tour of Paris.

Anna and I did have an interesting conversation about fat in the human diet. Anna says that Paleolithic man was taller than later Bronze Age man and had no heart disease, unlike modern man, because he had a perfect diet: game meat, occasional fish or shell fish, lots of fruits, nuts, and veggies, but most important, no dairy products and little or no grain. Their diet didn't sound very gourmet to me and certainly not very French.

Anna then gave me a recipe that substituted nonfat evaporated milk for butter and whole milk in béchamel sauce. Since she'd mentioned the sauce, I told her that a seventeenth-century French financier of that name, a man with large investments in the Newfoundland fisheries, had created the sauce himself to make dried codfish palatable to his countrymen, who hated it. If I were still cooking, I might try her version of Béchamel's recipe myself, but would I like it? I comforted myself for having such unhealthy thoughts and tastes by remembering that the French, despite a diet appallingly rich in fat and cholesterol, have a long life expectancy. But I digress.

Carl Jensen, the bovine expert, said in his slow, flat Midwestern accent, "Take my advice, Mrs. Blue. Don't eat any beef at all. They've got mad cow disease in France."

"Indeed," said Manfred Unsell, interrupting an argument with his wife Grace over his desire to order a whole bottle of wine when she planned to drink only one glass.

Unsell was a tall, portly man with a hawk nose and a very red face that contrasted sharply with his black hair.

Maybe the red face and nose were an indication that he felt a need for four glasses of wine with dinner.

"The national fear of mad cow disease is having an ominous impact on the cattle industry here," Unsell remarked. "Farmers are facing bankruptcy. In fact, the whole European Union is at risk. Austria has banned imported German beef; the German chancellor had to reassure his constituency of the safety of German sausage—"

"Bo-vine spongi-form en-ce-phal-o-pathy," interrupted Jensen, separating the three words into their component syllables. "A terrible fate for an innocent cow. I've seen the poor creatures in England. Staggering, falling down. A pitiful sight. No future but a sure and painful death. It can be passed on to humans, Mrs. Blue."

Jason murmured, "Creutzfeldt-Jacob disease."

I sighed. It was going to be hard to write columns about French cuisine if all these knowledgeable men kept providing unwelcome input.

"Mercy, Carl," said Ingrid Jensen, who was as tall, sturdy, and blond as her husband, "let the poor woman enjoy her beef. As long as it's well done—that's what I always tell my county extension classes," said Ingrid. "Cook it enough, and you don't have to worry about parasites and such."

"Madam," said Jean-Claude Childeric, who had once again attached himself to me, "*boeuf tartare* would not be the famous dish that it is if it were cooked. It must be raw! The beef, as well as the egg yokes that bind it."

"Raw!" Ingrid Jensen looked horrified. She had evidently missed my initial conversation with the waiter. "Why, I'd never let my students use *eggs* that are raw, or even half-cooked. 'Cook 'em hard,' I say. 'Don't take chances.'"

"We don't have that egg disease in the Southwest," I said, then nodded to the waiter and murmured stubbornly, "I will have the beef tartare."

"If you'd seen a cow die, its poor brain turned to mush—" Jensen began.

"I'm not a cow," I replied, "and only three human cases have been reported in France according to the *New York Times*."

"Market conditions are often influenced more by public hysteria than actual statistics," Unsell remarked. "Of course, it all started here on the continent with the export of English bone-meal animal feeds."

"The animals are eating each other?" gasped Estrella Markarov.

"Only in a manner of speaking," said Unsell. "Animal parts that were unusable in any ordinary way were found to make good additions to feed. A very profitable business for the English until the unfortunate advent of mad cow disease. As I understand it, no one is even sure that the feed causes the disease in other animals."

"Oh, I think there's no question that it does," said Jason. "BSE seems to be an offshoot of sheep scrapies. Sheep parts ground up and fed to cows caused BSE, which in turn causes nv—that's new variant— Creutzfeldt-Jacob in humans—all related to one another through autopsy results."

My beef tartare arrived, and I eyed it warily. Even if only three human cases had turned up in France—and the entrée did look delicious—I didn't want to die of some dreadful degenerative brain disease. On the other hand, one little taste—I took it—ah, so yummy. The capers, the onions, the spices, the beef tenderloin—ground and—

"What *is* in question is the mechanism," Jason added. "A lively debate in scientific circles. Some say prions are the infective agent—meaning protein only."

Jason went on to discuss proteins and nucleic acids, but I hadn't the faintest idea what he was talking about. I did wish that he and especially Dr. Jensen would discuss it somewhere else. Markarov's wife Estrella and Grace Unsell had both turned a bit green as the descriptions of mad cow disease were enlarged. They probably weren't used to unpleasant scientific discussions in inappropriate settings. Unfortunately, I am.

Professor Childeric, sitting beside me and eating something in sauce, obviously hated being left out of any discussion. "These plagues and problems in the food chain have affected European civilization for centuries," he informed us.

"Oh, are you an expert on the science of food?" asked Janice Petar.

She had joined our party, although without her friend Anna Thomas-Smith, who had a terrible headache as a result of spending the day chasing after Edie, or so Janice said. An interesting-looking woman, I thought, glancing at her as she zoomed in on Childeric. She was small and rather muscular with weathered, brown skin and short-cropped hair.

When she mentioned Anna's headache to me before dinner, she had cast me an accusing look. However, it was nothing compared to the malice of the look she shot at Jean-Claude Childeric. It suddenly occurred to me that if Professor Childeric really had been pushed at the airport and the culprit hadn't been an air-rage attacker, Janice Petar might be the person who did it. Not that I had noticed her there, but then we hadn't yet been introduced. I'd have to keep my eye on Dr. Petar.

"Or do you rely on others to provide you expertise in scientific matters?" Janice asked.

Childeric looked quite taken aback at her tone and stammered that he certainly *was* a bit of an expert on French food, especially the cuisine of the Middle Ages. "Take Saint Anthony's fire," he began.

"That *is* an interesting example," Jason agreed. "Fungus on the rye crop that got into the bread, causing erysipelas."

Oh dear, they were off again, and I knew for a fact that Saint Anthony's fire was an unpleasant topic.

Our guide, Denis, was passing the table at the time and said with his mischievous grin, "*Oui.* It was called Saint Anthony's fire because the good saint wished it on those who did not properly honor him."

"Nonsense," snapped Childeric. "It was because the intercession of Saint Anthony was thought to cure the disease."

"I believe Saint Anthony suffered from it," said Estrella Markarov. "That is why it was named for him."

"Cellulitis," Fauree called from their table. "Caused by streptococcus bacteria."

I looked up from my delicious entrée to see Childeric sending a furious glance at his rival in the dean's race. Hugh chuckled and turned away while Ivan Markarov, who had a longish beard and dishwater blond hair, was shoveling in a mouthful of beef tartare and beaming at me. "Is good. No?" he asked. "I think I have Tartar in genes."

I couldn't help adding, "Marco Polo saw Tartars eating various chopped raw meats seasoned with garlic when he visited the Yunan province. Maybe that's where the name of the dish came from."

"Enjoy good food while food is on table," said Markarov.

Was that an old Tartar folk saying? Had the Tartars had tables? I'd always thought they spent all their time in the saddle and slept in the open or, at best, in tents.

"Is interesting problem," he continued, turning dark eyes with a slight oriental slant on my husband. "Genes in cow, maybe in people, make prion infectious. No?"

"I believe so," Jason agreed. "Although I am not a biologist. For instance, I had no idea that Saint Anthony's fire also referred to a bacterial infection."

"Saint Anthony's fire has nothing to do with strep throat," said Childeric. "Fauree has his facts wrong. The scientific name for Saint Anthony's fire is epi—epi something."

"Perhaps everyone is thinking of ergotism," I intervened. "Thousands of people in Europe went crazy and died from that, and nobody knew until the late sixteenth century that it was caused by something on rye wheat."

"Is true," said Markarov. "Russian Tsar, Peter, was going to attack Turks, but whole army gets sick from rye bread." Then he turned to Jason. "I, as computer science person, sometimes work with chemists. You are chemist, no? Who does research on environmental toxins, no? Before I leave Russia, I am noticing many bad air and water. Is serious problem."

His previously thoughtful wife gave him a smile of melting devotion. Then she told us she had just realized that mad cow disease was God's answer to the sins of man. "When our Lord created the creatures of the fields and forests, he made cows and sheep herbivores. *Our greed* has turned them into cannibals, and now we are paying the price. The plague has entered our own houses."

"My little sugar beet is being very holy woman, no?" said Markarov, patting his wife affectionately before he returned to his next bite of beef tartare. "She is making this former atheist into worshipper." He didn't seem worried that his wife's God might strike him down for the sins of man. Personally, I was glad I had managed to finish my entrée before I learned that I might be bringing a holy curse down on my head. The threat of Whatsis-Jacob disease was bad enough.

"Could be God. Who knows?" said Carl Jensen

gloomily. "But I can tell you, I worry about our herds in the U.S. of A. If folks abroad don't get a handle on this, we could all end up eating chicken."

But not yet, I thought. I could safely publish a recipe for beef tartare in my column since the American cow wasn't yet infected.

"Did I read recently that chickens may carry the disease as well?" Jason asked.

"We're going to be late for the concert if we don't hurry," I said. No use considering dessert when someone at the table was sure to find a dire consequence of eating whatever I chose. Perhaps I'd write a column on how to ruin someone's dinner.

Do-It-Yourself Beef Tartare Americaine

Beef tartare (also called steak tartare or beef steak tartare) probably originated among invading tribesmen descended from the hordes of Genghis Khan. Some legends say Tartars were in the habit of shredding raw red meat with their knives and eating it. Others claim that they put raw beef under their saddles, where the pounding it underwent during long rides and the sweat of the horses tenderized it. We have more palatable recipes for beef tartare these days. No restaurant chef would consider marinating it in horse sweat.

However, with mad cow disease sweeping Europe, perhaps we Americans should keep the tradition alive while it is still safe to do so. Our cattle do not yet have mad cow disease, and believe me, beef tartare is scrumptious. If you live in a section of the United States where eggs are not infected with bad things, here is my own recipe, which I call Beef Tartare Americaine. If you do have the egg problem, skip the raw yolks, mix the ingredients yourself to your own taste, and serve the dish.

• Cut the fat from *2 lbs. raw, top-quality beef tender-loin or fillet*. Grind in a blender or food processor until the meat is finely chopped. Divide into 4 balls and chill in refrigerator until ready to serve.

• Finely chop *½ cup onion* and *3 tbs. parsley*.

• Serve the beef on cold plates by shaping each ball into a mound and indenting the top to receive a *raw egg yolk*. Arrange *capers*, chopped onion, and chopped parsley around the sides.

• Allow guests to mix their own tartare and flavor it to taste with *Tabasco, Worcestershire sauce, Dijon mustard, salt, pepper, cut lemon*, and a good *bourbon whiskey*, all arranged on a lazy Susan in the middle of the table. (For European tastes, you can provide *cognac* or even *port* as a substitute for bourbon.)

• To be accompanied by *thin slices of dark bread or buttered toast*.

• If you don't want to use raw eggs, you can mix the tartare to your own taste from among the above ingredients, form small balls with the meat mixture, roll the balls in the *chopped parsley*, chill, and serve on a toothpick as finger food.

Carolyn Blue, "Have Fork, Will Travel,"
Reno Mountain Times

9
Vivaldi Adventures

Europeans first came across chocolate when Cortés saw Montezuma drinking a thick, bitter beverage the Aztecs believed was a cure for dysentery and also a purveyor of aphrodisiac effects, which made it the drink of choice at wedding celebrations. Cortés himself wrote to Carlos I that it combated fatigue and might even taste good if sweetened. The Maya used it for religious rituals, and in Nicaragua, cacao beans served as money; ten cacao beans bought the favors of many a willing woman.

Hot chocolate soon became a favorite drink in Spain and Portugal, but the French were not so easily swayed. Two different foreign queens introduced it to the French court, Anne of Austria in 1615 and Marie-Terese of Spain in 1660, but even after the drink became popular and was endorsed by the medical establishment in Paris, shocking rumors circulated that chocolate was an aphrodisiac. Then in 1670 a noblewoman, who had overindulged in hot chocolate during pregnancy, was said to have given birth to a black baby. After the French Revolution, chocolate was considered too aristocratic and Catholic (Jesuits having been accused of trying to monopolize the trade in cocoa) for hardworking, Protestant citizens.

However, at that time the French had never tasted a chocolate truffle. It fell to a Dutch cocoa merchant in 1815 to produce the first edible (as opposed to liquid) chocolate, for which Conrad J. van Houten deserves

our thanks. There's nothing more delicious (or addic-
tive) than a chocolate truffle flavored with a tasty
liqueur.

Carolyn Blue, "Have Fork, Will Travel,"
Oakland Weekly Shopper

Carolyn

Sainte-Chapelle is to churches what a chocolate-raspberry
truffle is to candy—an absolutely delicious, beautiful, inspirational confection of a building. Saint Louis ordered its
construction to house the Crown of Thorns, which he purchased at great cost during the thirteenth century from
John III, the impecunious Emperor in Constantinople. This
building-as-reliquary, completed in only three years, was
constructed almost entirely of stained glass, with lovely,
narrow windows soaring between pillars to Gothic points
in a burst of color that takes the breath away.

What a glorious place to hear the music of Vivaldi, even
considering that I had seated myself between Chris and
Edie to head off any possible amorous conduct. She sulked
throughout *The Four Seasons,* while behind us Grace Unsell's cell phone rang in the middle of "Spring." Grace had
to put down the almost completed baby bootie on her knitting needles to carry on a whispered conversation about
her daughter's experiences with false labor. Frenchmen
glared. Frenchwomen who understood English eaves-
dropped and whispered advice. Manfred Unsell tried to
take the phone away from his wife, at which she told him
that she hadn't wanted to come to France anyway and
would be perfectly happy to leave for home this very
minute. Then an usher made them both leave before the

beginning of "Summer." It was all very embarrassing and detracted from the inspirational nature of the experience.

As did the events that preceded and followed the concert. We were, in fact, late leaving the restaurant because the waiter refused to provide separate checks. Before we left, Roberta, who was seated at another table with Hugh, the de Sorentinos, and the Drummonds, stood up and said to Lorenzo de Sorentino, "Fuck off." Then she gave him a push, almost knocking him from his chair, and strode out of the restaurant. Poor Hugh was caught between his obvious desire to follow her and the need to pay the bill first. I myself don't like the "f" word, although I know that Robbie uses it in moments of great stress, but Estrella Markarov gasped and looked as if she might faint.

As we were all scrambling by Metro and on foot to get to the concert in time, Robbie told me that Lorenzo, the plastic surgeon, had had the gall to suggest that she consider breast reduction in the near future before hers began to sag or cause her back problems. "He actually said that in front of Hugh," she whispered, changing hands on her Metro strap. "I was so embarrassed. You may not have noticed, but Laura didn't take it very well either. She said, 'When will you ever learn, Lorenzo?' and knocked a glass of red wine in his lap. Angry that he was ogling other women's breasts, I suppose." Then Robbie laughed exuberantly. "I don't think they'll be going to the concert."

I felt rather sorry for Laura. She seemed the sort to love Sainte-Chapelle and Vivaldi. Professor Childeric, who had been staying close to me, heard this story and said, "Hardly proper conduct for a dean candidate. Pouring red wine on a spouse in public."

"I'm sure it was an accident," I murmured.

"And where is your spouse, Dr. Childeric?" asked Janice Petar. She was clinging to a Metro strap beside him. "For that matter, why are you, *the* expert on France, going on this very ordinary tour? Perhaps you're hoping to hit on some naïve lady in the absence of your wife. That would hardly be proper conduct for a—"

"Hit on?" Childeric interrupted. "I do not *hit on*—"

"Oh, save it," she snapped and left the car ahead of us when the doors opened at our stop.

"That woman hates me," he murmured, obviously amazed. "And for no reason that I'm aware of. Except—" He nodded sagely at an insight that had evidently just come to him. "Perhaps she's an adherent of one of the other candidates and plans a campaign to slander my good name, to create a last-minute scandal when it would be too late for me to defend myself. Very clever of Fauree."

"I don't think he even knows Janice," I replied. "Science and women's studies are not two fields that—"

"Of course. Exactly! A feminist would be a supporter of the female candidate. Laura de Sorentino put her up to this. She probably had someone push me at the airport, too. Or did it herself. It's a plot to humiliate me at every turn."

He had grasped my arm and was by then propelling me up the stairs at a rate much faster than I cared to climb. Where was Jason when I needed him? Gasping for breath, I glanced around and spotted my husband on the landing with Markarov and Hugh, engaged in what had all the earmarks of intense scientific conversation. Good grief, were they planning to mount a multidisciplinary assault on some arcane problem?

"Professor, you'll have to slow down. I'm going to fall on my face if I don't get a chance to catch my breath."

Childeric was all solicitous apologies.

"And I do think you're imagining plots. These are perfectly respectable, well-meaning academicians like yourself, hardly the sort of people to endanger your physical well-being or your good name." Although after that race upstairs and his wild imaginings, I was tempted to give him a shove myself. When finally we reached Louis IX's lovely chapel, I was pathetically glad to sit down.

Then there was the return to the hotel. Robbie and Hugh did not accompany us. Perhaps she had heard Childeric's accusations and repeated them to Hugh. Having been expelled, the Unsells were no longer with us. Chris and Edie persisted in lagging behind, forcing me to crane my neck in order to keep them under surveillance, and my husband and Markarov continued their avid conversation, leaving me with Estrella, who talked my ear off both riding and walking.

The gist of her conversation was as follows: She was a de la Garza. No doubt I had heard of her family, which was very prominent in New Mexico, an ancient and aristocratic Spanish bloodline, but that didn't keep her from espousing the cause of poor Hispanic children who needed both preschool education, which their parents couldn't afford, and bilingual education, because their parents didn't speak English at home. In fact, she had studied the program at our university and found it most impressive, didn't I?

As I have no preschool children, I'd never heard of it. Then she told me about her first husband, the eminent Professor Arthur Conway, a good Catholic and an internationally renowned expert on communication with autistic children. And I wasn't to believe the jealous critics who claimed that those who assisted autistic children to communicate on typewriters were either stupid, misled, or charlatans. Arthur himself had trained many of the best facilitators in the field, researchers who, by guiding little fingers on the keyboard, discovered loving children and brilliant minds inside those mute babies.

Whatever her first husband had been doing, it sounded suspiciously like something Jason read to me from the *Skeptical Inquirer*, Ouiji board science he had called it. I politely refrained from mentioning that article to Estrella.

Unfortunately, she continued, God had taken Arthur to his bosom. Her dear first spouse had been struck down on a golf course by the crazed parent of an autistic child under

treatment, struck down and killed with a nine iron. The attacker was now in a hospital for the criminally insane, and
Arthur was undoubtedly in heaven as a result of his own
virtue and Estrella's prayers for him. Then Estrella informed me that, after going through a period of grief when
she thought of joining a convent, she had decided that
God's plan for her was to remarry and have children of her
own, something she and Arthur had been unable to accomplish.

"You may think me too old," she said to me.

"Not at all," I replied politely.

"But I'm only forty-five and have the perfect hips and
bosom for motherhood."

She did have wide hips and a generous bosom. "Perfect," I agreed.

"How could God ignore my prayers when I have
brought my dear Ivan into the arms of the true church, not
to mention other converts among my students?"

"How indeed?" I responded, spotting the hotel and
wishing I were safe in my bed. Tonight I'd sleep well because I knew that tomorrow I'd have clean clothes to wear.
Oh lord, Chris and Edie were holding hands. "Excuse me,"
I said to the future mother of Russian-Hispanic, bilingual,
preschooled, Roman Catholic children, and I hastened
back to my son and my duties as chaperone.

10
It's Raining Flowerpots

Carolyn

"Did you enjoy the concert?" I asked Chris as I snatched his hand from Edie's.

"It was too hot in there," Edie responded for him. "Seems to me they could put in air conditioning even if that is an old building."

"Not easily," I murmured. "I was really asking if you enjoyed the music."

Edie shrugged. "It was okay. But when Mrs. U.'s phone rang and the French guy kicked them out—now, that was cool. Did you see Dr. Unsell? I'll bet he's never been kicked out of anywhere. Chris and I just about died laughing. Say, Mrs. Blue, would you mind if Chris walked me to my room? Those courtyards at the hotel are creepy at night."

"Indeed they are," I agreed. "And because your mother is such a dear friend and placed your safety in my hands, I'll walk you to your room myself."

"But—"

"Hey, Denis," Chris called as we entered the hotel.

"While you're talking to Denis, Chris, ask him what we'll be doing tomorrow."

"I can tell you that. We're going to see some artist's flower garden," said Edie. "I'll just tag along and talk to Denis, too."

"Nonsense. Jason," I called to my husband, "you and I need to escort Edie to her room. Those creepy courtyards, you know." Jason didn't even hear me.

However, Dr. Childeric came to my rescue by saying gallantly, "I shall be delighted to escort you lovely ladies to your rooms." He linked his arms through ours and led us off toward the dreaded courtyards. Oh well, it was kind of him to offer. The first courtyard was indeed dark and overgrown with shrubbery.

"My room's on the second floor of the next building," said the pouting Edie. "I can get up there on my own. Dr. Thomas-Smith will be waiting for me. She thinks sex-crazed French guys are sneaking around everywhere, looking to jump American girls."

We didn't get to hear the rest of Anna Thomas-Smith's warnings about lascivious Frenchmen because a round object trailing shrubbery plummeted in front of us, caromed off Professor Childeric's shoulder, and burst on the courtyard stones. Edie shrieked. I leapt backward, my stockingless shins stinging, and Professor Childeric staggered. Somehow, a flowerpot had fallen almost on top of us from the balcony above. Had we entered that courtyard just a step or two earlier, one of us might have been dead. I was so frightened that I felt dizzy.

Having heard the crash and the shrieking, hotel employees raced out to rescue us. Edie was found to be unhurt but giggling rather hysterically. I had shard cuts on my legs and even one on my cheek, along with a fine spray of dirt from the pot explosion. Dr. Childeric clutched his shoulder and rocked, moaning. Had the pot been *meant* to hit him? I wondered uneasily.

When Denis arrived and offered to escort Edie to her room, she asked pitifully, "Where's Chris?"

"Gone to bed," said Denis.

Relieved to hear that, I turned Edie over to Denis and let the desk clerk help me to a stone bench.

Professor Childeric joined me there. "Fauree," the medievalist gasped. "He tried to kill me."

"We just saw him in the lobby. He couldn't have got upstairs in time to push a pot over." Could he?

"I didn't see him," the professor objected suspiciously, as if I were part of the imagined plot. "My God, I think something's broken. The pain is—excruciating." He continued to rock. "Or Laura de Sorentino. *She* wasn't in the lobby."

"Laura's too slender to have moved a pot filled with dirt and vines," I objected.

"Then her husband. Or that Petar woman. She looks too muscular to even *be* a woman. I don't remember seeing her after the concert. Or at the concert, for that matter. She probably slipped away to lie in wait for me."

Even in the shadowy courtyard, I could see the sweat on his forehead and the paleness of his skin. "Really, Dr. Childeric," I said as soothingly as I could, "the pot probably fell off on its own." I turned to the two clerks who now hovered anxiously beside us. To one, I said, "This man needs a doctor. Don't you, Professor Childeric?"

"Yes," he groaned.

The first clerk rushed off.

To the second, I said, "You should take care that your pots aren't positioned in such a way that they can teeter and fall off on unsuspecting guests."

The clerk protested that the hotel's pots did not *teeter.* Childeric insisted that the pot had been aimed at him.

"Oui," said the clerk. "I weel call the gendarmes."

"And the doctor?"

"Soon, madame. He eez being sent for."

"Good." A terrible weariness flooded over me. "I think I'll go to bed." I stood up, somewhat unsteadily.

"Excellent, madame. Pierre weel escort you."

"Don't leave me, Carolyn," begged Jean-Claude Childeric, sounding frightened.

"I stay weeth you, Professor, until the doctor, he come. Pierre, he take ze lady away. I theenk she is for faint."

Pierre took my arm, and I was soon in my own room, showering off the shrubbery dirt and perspiration in blessedly cool water, placing Band-Aids on my cuts, which were, fortunately, more painful than serious, donning my full-length nightgown—so much more comfy than a T-shirt. At last I climbed into bed to consider what had happened. I was sorry to have deserted Professor Childeric, especially after he had been so kind as to offer himself as an escort, but I *had* been feeling faint. Also on the verge of tears. The incident had frightened me badly.

Could someone be targeting him? And if so, why? This was his second accident in as many days, and whereas one might, in the midst of a crowd, trip and fall onto a luggage carousel, or be pushed by some impatient and furious passenger, surely being almost pulverized by a pot was not as likely to be an accident. On the other hand, who would *do* such a thing?

I wondered where Janice Petar's room was. She seemed to have a deep-seated dislike of the man. As for an opposing dean candidate, that was silly. When Jason came in, full of enthusiasm for a problem he and Markarov had been discussing, I voiced my fears and speculations to him.

Jason cuddled me sympathetically and listened. Then he kissed my Band-Aid-dressed forehead injury, and said, "Don't let Childeric's paranoia infect you, love. Academics do not try to kill each other with heavy clay pots. But pots have been known to fall off balconies. It happens."

"Umm," I replied, willing to be comforted. "I think there's another cut on my ankle that needs attention."

"My pleasure." Jason tossed off the duvet.

"And on my shin," I suggested. To think Chris had wanted to share our room. What luck it was so small.

11
Monet's Revenge

Jason

After her fright the night before, Carolyn had calmed down and now looked forward to the group's visit to Monet's gardens at Giverny. She even listened to Denis's talk on the bus until he made the mistake of embroidering on the truth. Evidently Monet did not personally plant every flower and tree or nearly drown in a lily pond while carrying on a romantic liaison with a female gardening enthusiast, not his wife. Carolyn snorted at these fabrications and fell asleep, leaving me to chat with Markarov, behind me, and Hugh, who sat across the aisle dividing his attention between me and Roberta.

We three scientists amused ourselves with plans for the investigation of mad cow disease—Hugh to do the biology, Ivan to provide computer programs, and I to design necessary chemical experiments. The challenge lay in the fact that none of us was really an expert on his given segment of the project. However, it passed the time enjoyably and foiled Roberta's attempts to divert all Hugh's attention to herself.

I'm sorry to admit that we continued to chat when we reached the gardens, which are, admittedly, delightful—a riot of colorful flower clumps, exotic trees, bridges, wandering paths, and of course, the lily ponds that figure endlessly in Monet's paintings. Either the man became obsessed with water lilies, or he ran out of inspiration. Carolyn would know.

At any rate, while Hugh, Ivan, and I strolled along the paths immersed in scientific discussion, Carolyn got stuck with Jean-Claude Childeric, whose arm was now in a sling. It seems that the falling pot had dislocated his shoulder. The man was having a serious run of ill luck on this tour.

While he told Carolyn about the excruciating pain he had experienced in the hospital, Carolyn nodded, murmured sympathetically, and took pictures of the garden with such abandon that I considered the financial benefits of buying her a digital camera to save on film and developing. All the while Childeric continued to talk. After he had bemoaned his injury, he regaled her with the name and medicinal or cosmetic function of every herb ever used in the Middle Ages. She did seem interested.

Behind us Roberta Hecht was less good-natured, for not only had I purloined her latest romantic target, but she was being deluged with the names of saints to whom a woman could pray for the blessing of conception, not the least of whom was the Virgin Mary herself. Evidently Ivan's wife wanted to have a child, an unlikely event in my estimation, although I was just guessing at her age and consequent infertility.

Ivan seemed happy enough at the prospect of parenthood. He said, blowing a kiss over his shoulder toward his wife, "My pretty little samovar is hoping we be parents soon. Is not a fine thing for famous American scholar wish to make me a papa?"

Even as he interrupted our discussion with this remark, Carolyn spotted a vista in whose foreground she wanted me. Although she turned away from Childeric to tell me where to pose, he continued to talk. Rosemary was his topic at that moment, and the man has a very penetrating voice. While Ivan and Hugh stood out of range and Carolyn maneuvered to focus me in her camera sights with an arched bridge in the background, Childeric cited references to rosemary in the plays of Shakespeare, evidently to illustrate that medieval interest in herbs continued into the Renaissance and beyond.

Completely self-absorbed, jacket draped jauntily over his shoulders to accommodate his disabled arm, he ambled along beside a bamboo grove saying, "Of course, you will remember, my dear Carolyn, Ophelia's reference to rosemary: 'There's rosemary. That's for remembrance.' A very touching scene. And in *Winter's Tale* there is a reference to rosemary and rue, which keep all winter long, a very desirable trait since castles must have become quite odoriferous in—Agh-g-gh." Childeric had interrupted himself with an electrifying bellow of anguish.

Crouched in an awkward position to get her picture, Carolyn fell over in astonishment and fear. While Ivan stayed to help her up, Hugh and I sprinted along the path toward Childeric, who was bent over, keening, one hand covering his eyes.

"What's wrong, man?" asked Hugh.

"You!" screamed the medievalist. "I recognize your voice. How dare you spray me with some noxious gas and then ask what's wrong?"

Hugh and I exchanged puzzled glances.

"I'm blinded," roared Childeric. "You've blinded me."

Since his eyes were covered, I couldn't fathom how he'd know that he couldn't see. Still, something had obviously happened. I could smell the pungent, lingering odor of some gas or mist. "Insecticide?" I guessed, not at all sure of this hypothesis.

"We are in a garden," Hugh agreed.

Childeric moaned as we led him to a bench and other tourists crowded around. "My God," he said, "not only am I blind, but I'll probably die of cancer. My skin is burning, my eyes are burning, I'm—"

He was on the edge of hysteria, and people surrounding us were saying, "What have they done to him?"

"Water," said Hugh. "We'd better rinse him down. That's bound to help." He spotted a gardener with hose in hand and grabbed it.

"Wait," I cautioned. "Ivan! Find an official and ask what insecticide they use. Do you speak French?"

"Oui, monsieur," Ivan replied and loped off.

Roberta came to join us, took the hose from Hugh, said to Childeric, "Stop whining. I'm going to wash all that stuff off you," and proceeded to do so before I could warn her that she might be turning a chemical to acid by mixing it with water.

Although Childeric leapt up when hit by the stream of cold water and tried to fend her off with his free hand, the dousing seemed to do him no harm. His moaning turned to indignation, and he even admitted that he could see, after all. That being the case, Hugh and I restrained him while Roberta continued to give him a very thorough wash-down, ignoring his repeated complaints about the plot to destroy his suit and his dignity.

"Better a dose of embarrassment than having your skin peel off or your cells mutate," she responded with cheerful pragmatism. "I heard you say something about cancer, and Hugh was talking earlier about cell mutation."

"I knew you were behind this," Childeric snarled at Hugh. "You and your hulking girlfriend."

"Hulking?" Robbie turned the hose on his face, in response to which he yelped and tried to shield himself. "Stop that, you nincompoop," she ordered. "You want to leave it in your eyes?"

At that point a French official arrived, accompanied by Ivan and Estrella, who was explaining the situation in Spanish. Either the official did not understand Spanish, even spoken slowly and with many accompanying gestures by a woman determined to communicate, or he chose not to respond. Ivan murmured to me that the official had stopped understanding Russian-accented French as soon as he heard that a visitor had been attacked, presumably by a gardener.

The official then admonished us for attacking a visitor with the garden's hose. We were to know that all implements for the maintenance of the Giverny gardens were the property of the Claude-Monet Foundation and not to be used by visitors, who would be ejected forthwith if found—

He got no further, for the lovely Laura de Sorentino arrived with her husband. Lorenzo saw Roberta, wielding the hose, and retreated hastily. A smiling Laura introduced herself to the official, who actually kissed her hand. Then she asked us what the problem was and listened attentively to the story. To Childeric she said, "You poor man. Just let me try to sort this out for you. Are you in pain? Do you need a physician? Lorenzo!"

Her husband, now lurking nervously on the edge of the crowd and, incidentally, talking with suspicious intimacy to my wife, refused to offer any medical attention to someone suffering from insecticide poisoning, about which he knew nothing and for which he did not care to put his reputation and insurance coverage at risk. His wife tossed him a glance of contempt, but de Sorentino didn't seem to notice.

Childeric, rather ungraciously I thought, said that her efforts were not needed here, especially since she was probably a party to the attack. She looked at Childeric with great sympathy and patted his good shoulder, as if his terrible experience had scattered his wits. I was beginning to find the whole scene amusing and glanced at Carolyn to see if she, too, was entertained. She was, but evidently by Lorenzo.

Then Laura turned back to the official, who had never taken his eyes from her. The poor fellow seemed mesmerized by the beauty of her face or, perhaps, by her impeccable command of his language. In my experience Frenchmen can be very picky about the spoken French of male foreigners and inordinately tolerant of a foreign woman's attempt to speak their language, especially if the woman is pretty. Laura had his full attention as she explained that someone had lurked in the bamboo grove and attacked this world-renowned expert on the Middle Ages in France and, indeed, on all things French, with a deadly insecticide spray.

Childeric forgot for a moment that he considered her an enemy and preened, while the official bowed respectfully in his direction. Had these quick-thinking and knowledgeable men of science not intervened with the Giverny hose, Laura continued, no doubt Professor Jean-Claude Childeric would now be dead. Since Fauree was chuckling and translating for me, I found myself highly flattered to be described as knowledgeable and quick-thinking, although it was Robbie who had actually taken charge.

Childeric, on the other hand, turned pale when the probability of his own death was mentioned, and the official breathed *"Mon Dieu,"* no doubt at the prospect of the foundation being held responsible for the death of an eminent scholar. He protested that no gardener in the employ of Giverny would do such a thing.

I then called upon the aforementioned quick thinking to ask what insecticide the garden employed, information that was necessary to the further and successful treatment of Professor Childeric. A gardener was sent for and arrived looking both nervous and stubborn in his Giverny coverall.

Much discussion and translation ensued, Ivan, Laura, the official, and the gardener running on in French and occasionally translating for the rest of us. Carolyn had edged away from Lorenzo and into the group. Childeric was now too busy contemplating the destruction of his clothing and dignity to join in.

It gradually became evident that the fellow who supplied the insecticide believed in organic gardening and had made the compound himself according to a secret recipe inherited from his father (who had worked for Monet) and improved on by himself for the benefit of the foundation and the garden. He refused to reveal ingredients or their amounts in the secret mixture but burst into a flood of indignant French when it was suggested that his spray might injure the eminent scholar. He replied that the spray would not make the professor grow, but that it would keep bugs off him. Furthermore, the ingredients were perfectly safe to ingest or to rub on one's arthritic knees.

"Capsaicin," I surmised. No wonder Childeric's skin and eyes burned. Still, having been rapidly doused with water, thus diluting the chili pepper derivative, he should be safe enough, although it was obvious that he did not feel at all grateful for our intervention and Roberta's decisive action with the hose.

"Shouldn't someone be looking for the miscreant who sprayed Professor Childeric?" Carolyn asked. Laura translated.

"It was Fauree," said Childeric.

"Ah ha!" cried the foundation official. "One of your own countrymen, then?"

"Hugh was with me," I protested.

"You probably helped him." Childeric gave me a furious look. "I see now that the whole science contingent is banding together to destroy me."

"They were behind you on the path, Professor Childeric," my wife explained.

"How would you know, Carolyn? I was talking to you at the time. In fact, how did you escape the deadly spray yourself?" He was now eyeing my wife suspiciously.

"She was taking my picture, not talking to you," I snapped.

The official threw up his hands and advised us to settle

the matter among ourselves, unless we wished for a gendarme to take us all in for questioning, which would probably involve incarceration and the confiscation of our
passports.

"You're going to arrest us and let the real criminal escape?" Carolyn exclaimed. While Laura translated, the rest
of us peered at the bamboo grove. However, it was obvious that no one was lurking there after all the fuss. Grudg-
ingly, the official sent the gardener to investigate. The man
found nothing but a spray can, half full of his secret potion,
abandoned among the bamboo stalks.

Childeric's accusation had brought to my attention the
possibility that my own wife could have been injured had
she not fallen back to take my picture. Also Childeric *had*
been attacked. That was incontrovertible, just as there was
no possibility that Hugh was the attacker. Unless it was the
gardener or some other employee of Giverny, whoever had
done the spraying couldn't have known that the insecticide
was relatively innocuous. The attack might have had serious, even fatal results. Something dangerous was afoot. I
could no longer pass off as accidents Childeric's fall at
Charles de Gaulle and the plummeting pot in the courtyard
last night. Because in each instance, my own wife could
have, inadvertently, been a victim instead of Childeric, I
vowed to keep her at my side for the rest of the trip and,
more important, to keep her away from Childeric.

The gardener spoke solemnly to the official. The official nodded. Hugh began to laugh. "The man says that
there is no plot, only the ghost of Claude Monet, returning
to protect his garden from rude foreigners, who can never
appreciate the splendor the great painter created here. How
else could a spray used only by himself, the inventor, have
been directed against this stranger? No employee of the
foundation would dare to take up the secret spray. He says
that we should go away."

While Hugh was translating, the official began to speak

angrily in French to the gardener. Laura picked up the translation. "The official says the gardener should shut his mouth and tend to his flowers. It is not his place to drive away visitors to a treasure of France, which is praised and marveled at the world over. The gardener says—"

"What I'd like," Roberta interrupted, "is to find a nice café with a tree-shaded patio, handsome French boys waiting tables, and a good bar."

"Most fine thought," Ivan agreed.

"I think the foundation should provide dry clothes for Professor Childeric, Professor Fauree, and my husband," said Carolyn. "They're all soaking wet, which can't be healthy."

Since the sun was shining brightly on our heads, I rather thought I'd dry out in no time, but Childeric began to complain about his suit, which would shrink in the sunshine. He pointed out bitterly that we scientists had nothing to worry about, being casually dressed, but he had his dignity and his wardrobe to protect. Which is why the three of us, none happy about it, ended the visit to Giverny wearing Claude-Monet Foundation coveralls. Childeric was furious.

12
Young Love Foiled

Carolyn

No wonder Monet's paintings so often featured his own garden. It's gorgeous! I changed film twice because there were so many views and individual flowers I couldn't resist: the lily ponds with willows leaning down to brush the water and cast misty reflections; the dark green bridges, which seem to arch magically from the surrounding trees and shrubs; one particular huge, round, shaggy flower of lavender-pink that I zoomed in on as it perched splendidly among its smaller sisters and large, floppy leaves. I did hope that photo would come out—and a stack of white bells bursting from a stalk, their throats lavender spotted. I'm not much of a gardener, but I loved the place.

It had been a wonderful day, except for the attack on Professor Childeric. I suppose a gardener could have made a mistake and been afraid to own up, what with all the fuss afterward. Childeric seemed none the worse for the spraying, but still I decided to ask Jason how dangerous insecticide could be. I don't use it myself. It smells bad and makes sticky places on the woodwork that attract dirt and become disgusting. I do have a service that sprays outside. That seems to keep down the scorpions, which are the most fearful household bug in El Paso. I screamed and ran out of the room when I saw that first scorpion waving his poisonous tail at me.

As our tour group was making its way to the exit, I glanced down a bypath, half obscured by yellow-green bushes underlaid with purple-hearted yellow pansies. There amid the greenery was my twenty-year-old son kissing sixteen-year-old Edie Atwater. I must admit that she was clutching him like a Venus flytrap devouring a bug. Still, I whirled aside from the main path to confront them, taking my surprised husband with me. He had been sniffing the air and mumbling about what else the gardener could have put in the homemade bug spray. As if anyone cared now that Childeric seemed to have survived the dousing with everything but his suit and self-esteem intact.

I cleared my throat loudly like a stereotypical stage parent, and Chris leapt away from Edie. With some difficulty. She did not seem as embarrassed to be discovered as Chris did. "Jason, perhaps you'd escort Edie back to the group and ask Anna to take charge of her," I suggested.

Jason hurried a scowling Miss Edie down the path toward the disappearing tour group. I turned and said, "Christopher—"

"Oh, oh," he interrupted. "Now, I'm in for it."

"Not funny," I replied. "That girl is only sixteen. And I'm supposed to be chaperoning her. Judith Atwater is not going to be happy if she hears that instead of looking after Edie, I left her to my grown-up son, who has no more sense than to kiss an underage girl."

"Aside from the fact that she came on to me, I can see your point, Mom," said Chris. "I don't suppose you'd accept the argument that I'm just a captive of my hormones?"

"I would not."

"Or that, being male, I'm gender bound to refuse quiche and accept kisses from pretty girls?"

Gender bound? It's hard to give your son a maternal lecture when you're being overcome by a case of the giggles. "Just for that, you don't get to order quiche the whole time we're in France, Mr. Macho. In fact, I think this deterioration in your moral fiber must be a result of the wine you're drinking at dinner."

"Hey, come on, Mom, what was I supposed to do? Give her a push?"

"Only in a gentlemanly way," I answered, turning back toward the main path. "My considered advice is avoid her if you can't fend her off."

Grinning, Chris put his arm around my shoulder. "Makes me sound like a wimp, doesn't it? Can't fend off a sixteen-year-old. Tell you what. I'll hang out with Denis. Maybe if she won't go away, she'll kiss Denis instead."

I sighed. "That won't do either. She'll just have to sit with me. If she wants to flirt, she can practice on your father."

Chris burst out laughing, and I had to join him. Jason is famous for his methods of fending off amorous young things: wedges of wood to keep his door wide open during office hours; serious suggestions that the way to please him is to study hard, these suggestions accompanied by reading lists complete with Library of Congress call numbers and scientific explanations that glaze their eyes. Oh, Jason is a wily one, and I don't suppose I can realistically expect such expertise in my twenty-year-old son, but I could give him advice. "Why don't you try telling her all about chemistry," I suggested.

"Jeez," he replied glumly.

Jason awaited us at the exit from the garden. "Edie's been safely stowed with Anna Thomas-Smith, sulking like a two-year-old and being called Edwina for her trouble." He then glanced inquiringly from me to Chris.

"And I've been duly chastised," Chris answered for both of us. "Mom says you and she will keep Edie under surveillance."

"Wonderful," my husband grumbled. "I'm sure we'll find her conversation very stimulating." He explained that Denis had announced a café break in the village before we reboarded the bus. Chris went off to look for Denis while Jason and I strolled at our leisure and found a charming café with a terrace overlooking the town. The view was lovely; the table, umbrella shaded. A gentle breeze stirred the trees; and best of all, no one sitting on that terrace was from our tour group.

"I'm glad to have a moment alone," Jason said after we had both ordered Kir Royales and been served a little bonus, a bowl of crunchy bits that were garlic infused. I sighed with pleasure, relaxed in my chair, and told Jason that Edie seemed to have been the aggressor in the scene we had stumbled on. My husband nodded, unsurprised. I then said Chris had decided to discourage Edie by hanging out with Denis, which should take care of that problem, although I'd be stuck with Edie.

Finally, I reminded myself that girls Edie's age were not only obsessed with boys but going through that difficult phase of rebelling against their mothers—or in this case, mother figures. I would have to be more sympathetic to her problems. She was, after all, marooned in a foreign country with a group of middle-aged academics. No wonder her interest in Chris was less than ladylike.

"I don't know what to make of the incident with Professor Childeric," I continued. "I don't for a moment believe that Hugh or Laura is plotting against him, but something's going on. Do you think Janice Petar—well, you were behind us. Did you notice her in the area? Or anyone else looking suspicious? Of course, it could have been a mistake, I suppose. Some gardener trying out the spray can or even spraying those stalks—"

"Bamboo," said Jason, who has a penchant for exact designations.

"Yes, thank you." At least, he doesn't know the Latin names of plants and trees. "He might have sprayed Professor Childeric by mistake, after which he was afraid to confess. Didn't you gather that the head gardener felt that only he should use the spray?"

"Carolyn, I have no idea what happened back there, but that's one accident too many for me. Had that been a manufactured insecticide, Childeric could have suffered long-term consequences or even been killed, depending on what was in the stuff and how fast he was treated."

Well, that answered my proposed question, but it certainly didn't ease my mind.

"I'd really appreciate it if you'd avoid Childeric," Jason continued. "I realize the man's full of information that interests you—"

"True, but he can be rather pedantic about imparting it," I added to relieve my husband's mind. "Lectures are nice in their place, and maybe he wouldn't keep giving them if Denis were more knowledgeable and less fanciful, but still, one does like interactive conversation once in a while as opposed to—"

"Good," Jason interrupted with satisfaction. "I was afraid you'd miss his insights. So you will try to avoid Childeric? I don't want you falling victim to some mishap aimed at him. That pot that smashed in the hotel courtyard and even the insecticide could have been lethal."

"Poor man. What can he have done? If everyone ostracizes him, he'll have no one to talk to."

"For God's sake, Carolyn," Jason exclaimed, "surely you don't find that windbag attractive!"

I retorted sharply, "Have you ever known me to chase after other men?"

"Well, I didn't mean—"

"Maybe if you spent less time talking research with Hugh and Ivan—you'd think we were at a scientific meeting instead of on tour—I wouldn't find myself—"

"Would Madame and Monsieur care for another order of drinks?" asked our server.

"Saved by the waiter," said Jason.

"I certainly would," I replied, "and another bowl of those crunchies."

"Madame?"

"I wonder if you could give me the recipe for them," I continued without trying to define the word *crunchies* for him. His eyes bugged out in bewildered consternation. What could be more satisfying than confounding a French waiter? As soon as he had scuttled back into the café, no doubt to seek help from the manager, Jason and I grinned at each other, and our little altercation was forgotten.

13
Conclusions on Sex, Crime, and Revenge

Jason

Although Carolyn had had a talk with Chris, I felt that I, too, should intervene. I took him aside after dinner, not a very memorable one, and said, "About Edie—"

"Come on, Dad, nothing's going to happen between Edie and me. I already promised Mom—"

"It may be harder than you think to keep that promise," I interrupted. "Edie seems to be a very determined young woman, and you're the only person even near her age in this group."

"Are you saying be nice to her, but don't touch?" Chris asked, beginning to look confused. "Or stay the hell away from her? Or what?"

"She's a minor in the eyes of the law, and of her parents, who, unfortunately, aren't here to keep her in line. You understand the term *statutory rape,* don't you? It has nothing to do with consent when it comes to young girls."

"I won't—"

"Be tempted? Of course, you will. She's a pretty girl. And not only infatuated but feeling rebellious and off the leash. At least, she'd like to be. Your mother and Anna are doing what they can. You have to do your part. We'd like to be sure you don't ruin your future, that you don't even put yourself in a position where she could make a false accusation if she takes your rejection amiss."

Chris looked astonished. "I never thought of that." He considered the possibility. "How about this? I won't let Denis out of my sight."

"Good. We'd also like to enjoy this vacation ourselves, so if you have any idea that Denis is getting interested in her—"

"He hasn't really seemed—"

"She hasn't turned her full attention on him."

Chris sighed. "How did I get into this, anyway? I just wanted to enjoy France."

"Didn't we all?" I replied. "It's looking less and less like we're going to."

The Kir Royale

Did you know that before Dom Pierre Perignon discovered that cork was the best substance for keeping the bubbles in sparkling wine, cellarmasters tried bark, rolled grape leaves, and nastiest, a skim of olive oil? Only cork worked, and Louis XIV loved the Benedictine monk's champagne, as did the Sun King's court. Who wouldn't? And a lovely way to drink it is in a Kir Royale cocktail.

Basically the yummy Kir Royale is a flute of *ice cold champagne* with a dash of *crème de cassis* (black currant liqueur). Bartenders differ on whether the *teaspoon of cassis* should be put into the flute before the cold champagne is poured over it or the champagne poured and then topped with the cassis. No one disagrees that the drink should be made flute by flute and served immediately.

There are several nice variations: a *lemon twist* on the rim, a *raspberry or blackberry* floating in the cocktail, or halved *strawberries* sweetened with *sugar* and put in before the champagne and cassis.

My favorite variation is a mixture of cassis and *chambord* (raspberry liqueur) poured in before the champagne. However you fix the Kir Royale, you and your guests will love it; it's delicious and festive.

Carolyn Blue, "Have Fork, Will Travel,"
Oak Ridge Times

Carolyn

Jason was asleep by the time I'd finished writing a newspaper column to send to Paul Fallon, the vice president of the newspaper syndicate in New York. I considered going to the lobby to fax it, but I didn't really want to walk through those "creepy" courtyards alone. That realization forced me to think about the strange incidents that were occurring on our tour. Jason was right. There were too many to ignore, but what was really going on? Obviously, the occurrences were connected to Childeric because he'd been the target two—no, three—times. But did I believe that it was connected to the competition for dean? No. That was ridiculous.

Staring at the lighted screen of my laptop, which displayed the copy of my article, I felt the urge to write down what I could remember of the happenings. Maybe if I did that, I'd see useful connections. In other words, I was again letting curiosity lure me into considering what seemed to be a mystery. Not, thank God, one that involved missing or dead people.

I gave in to the impulse, but in a very sensible and methodical way. I clicked on the Table function at the top of the screen, created a table . . . and found I couldn't get enough words in the little boxes. Computers are so frus-

Clue List

Day	Place	Victim	Injury	Means
1	airport Paris	Childeric	head cut shoulder	shove
2	courtyard	Childeric me	shoulder shins	pot
3	Giverny	Childeric	clothes dignity skin	insecticide

trating. Next, I entered items under headings. It wasn't terribly neat. I couldn't even manage to run the bottom line
all the way across the page. But still, when I was finished,
my information was laid out in front of me.

After studying the chart, two things occurred to me:

First, although Hugh Fauree was Dr. Childeric's prime
suspect, no one had seen Hugh at the first two scenes, and
he could not have sprayed Dr. Childeric with insecticide at
Giverny because he had been behind him on the path, not
hiding in the bamboo grove.

Second, in all three instances I could have been injured
myself: at Charles de Gaulle, if Chris hadn't pulled me
back when I might have fallen with Childeric; in the hotel
courtyard, when I had been injured, although not seriously;
and at Giverny, if I hadn't dropped back to take Jason's

Clue List

Present	Suspect(s)	Motive
Childeric Chris me	Fauree	deanship
strangers	stranger	air rage
Childeric Edie	Fauree	deanship
me	Petar	hates JPC
Childeric	Fauree Robbie Lauria Jason	deanship " " "
Jason me	gardener	accident?

picture. However, the thought that anyone might be after me was silly. I wasn't even a dean candidate.

In other words, I had no idea who might be staging these attacks. If someone was and it was the same person every time, it had to be someone other than Chris, Edie, Jason, and Hugh. Janice Petar seemed to be the only person who really disliked Dr. Childeric, although I had no idea why. Hugh was getting to dislike him, but that was because Childeric was picking on him.

Travel Journal
Day Three, Giverny

Last night I got the S.O.B. with a flowerpot. Arm in a sling. Shoulder evidently dislocated. Must have been painful. Good.

Today he was accusing the other dean candidates of trying to kill him and acting like a wounded warrior in the academic wars. Man's an ass. Wish I'd realized that years ago.

So why did Carolyn Blue walk through Giverny with him? She should have realized by now that his company is dangerous.

It made me very angry. With both of them. Angry enough to stalk them through the garden.

Beautiful place, but I wasn't paying much attention to the flowers. His fault.

I found this sprayer in a bamboo grove, something in the can. I was thinking fertilizer when I caught him alone and gave him two or three squirts from behind a tree. The sprayer had a good range, but the stuff turned out to be some innocuous bug spray. Well, maybe not completely innocuous. His face and hands were still red tonight. Kind of like he'd been scalded. Not bad, but I'd rather that he got soaked with liquid cow manure. Something that really reeked.

At the time, C. thought he'd been blinded. The others thought it was a toxic insecticide. Then the Hecht woman turned the hose on him. That was fun. C. likes to be well dressed. Good clothes, no wrinkles, hair just so. He looked like a drowned rat. And acted like one. The two scientists got soaked too, and the garden authorities made a fuss. Snotty French. My mother hated that word—snotty—never let me use it. C. is French. Maybe they'll all think twice now about having anything to do with him.

And no one saw me. I circled around and came up behind the big scene he made, no one the wiser.

Maybe I'm invisible, and I never realized it till now.

Childeric did that to me.

Only fair that I return the favor.
Still, I suppose I'd better keep a low profile for a while.
Versailles tomorrow. Heard Denis say thunderstorms pre-
dicted. Maybe C. will get hit by lightning.

14
A Feminist Mother of Nine

Carolyn

The plans for day four were a visit to Versailles, a sail at dusk on the Seine, and an evening dinner aboard ship. It sounded charming, but after our first three days, I was wary. Also, it was hard to look forward to the company of Edie. No doubt she would have been thinking the same thing had she known she was to sit with me on the bus and at dinner and enjoy the delights of Louis XIV's palace in my company.

I did try to enlist Anna Thomas-Smith to spend at least part of the day with Edie, explaining with some embarrassment that I had caught the girl kissing my son. Anna's response was a kind but firm no. She sympathized with my problem but pointed out that she was not the person who had promised to take care of Edie. Nor was she getting a tour discount for rooming with the girl. "I do have friends of my own on the tour, Carolyn," she said, "and hope to spend my days, at least, with adults."

Well, she had a point, and I felt guilty for sticking her with Edie yesterday afternoon while I lectured Chris. Anna was quite nice about accepting my apology and responded by advising me to watch out for lecherous Frenchmen, both on my own behalf and Edie's, and to keep an eye on Chris, who seemed a nice boy but was possibly being influenced by the lax morals of the country.

Although I have, of course, read about the amorous and hedonistic French, they've never struck me that way—except in the matter of food and wine. In fact, they seem practical, frugal, and somewhat standoffish, admirable traits when you think about it. I read an article once that advised tourists to refrain from smiling at strangers on the street in France because the French assume that such behavior indicates simplemindedness. Perhaps Charles the Simple, the king who gave away Normandy to the Vikings, had been in the habit of smiling at strangers.

At any rate, Anna and I parted friends, and we all set out on a bus for Versailles. Chris sat up front with Denis and Marguerite, who was to be our special guide in Versailles. Edie sat beside me, refusing my offer of the window seat and suggesting that I might prefer to sit with Dr. Childeric, since I seemed to like *him*. Jason sat beside Ivan, with Hugh across the aisle caught between the intellectual excitement of scientific discussion and the more obvious allure of Robbie.

Edie was blatantly uninterested in anything either Denis or I had to say about Versailles, but very interested in my son's attentions to Marguerite. Then suddenly she announced that, since I didn't want to sit with Dr. Childeric, she would, her idea being that if she had to listen to French history, she might as well get it from the expert. The professor was sitting by himself, when I glanced over. Not only was his arm still in the sling, but his face looked severely sunburned. Was that the result of the homemade bug spray? The red skin had, more or less, erased the antiseptic that had stained his forehead, but his four black stitches now looked loose and even more unsightly. Poor man. Maybe he'd appreciate Edie's company.

While I was debating the matter, Edie hopped across the

aisle and informed the astonished medievalist that she'd just *love* to hear about all the lecherous Louies who had lived at Versailles. What history professor could resist an invitation to impart knowledge to an eager young thing, even if her choice of words left something to be desired? I closed my eyes and had a lovely nap.

For the most part, the day at Versailles was overcast or raining, and the gloomy weather was somewhat depressing after the frightening events of the days before. I'm not particularly fond of eighteenth-century history or palaces, but Versailles is certainly memorable—for its size, its ostentation, and its immense gardens. It started out as a hunting lodge built by Louis XIII so he wouldn't have to sleep out in the cold while galloping about the countryside, looking for animals to kill. On his death, the lodge passed to Louis XIV, who from 1661 on poured money into buildings and interior decorations. After his death in 1715, Louis XV inherited the results.

The tour of all this splendor was punctuated by verbal outbursts from Marguerite, who never hesitated to lambaste Japanese tourists who persisted in taking pictures where none were allowed and to shout angrily at other guides who dared to interrupt her lectures. I personally enjoyed Marguerite's talks enough to resent competing guides, too, even Denis, who occasionally disagreed with her.

When we reached The Queen's Inner Chambers, the fun really began. Louis XV's queen, Marie Leczinska, of whom I had never heard, inhabited these rooms. Because her father, Stanislas I, had to leave Poland and raise her in poverty, she had been thought extremely fortunate to be chosen as a French royal bride, a selection made on the grounds that she was suitably Catholic and unlikely to gain any partisans in court.

However, her forty-three years in France were pretty much downhill from the royal wedding at Fountainebleau in 1725. Before the bridal year had passed, Louis lost interest and began taking a long series of mistresses. Nonetheless, the unhappy Marie of Poland gave birth, in public, to nine royal children in ten years. Denis swore it was thirteen children; Marguerite disagreed in her accustomed aggressive fashion.

Whoever was right, Edie thought having so many children was "gross." Ingrid Jensen voiced dismay at the idea of giving birth in front of an audience of courtiers. Estrella Markarov, no doubt thinking of her own childbearing hopes, said children were a gift from God, no matter what the number or circumstances. Marguerite became peeved at the interruptions and snarled for quiet, after which she went on to tell us that the Polish queen, after the ninth child, announced that henceforth her bedroom door was closed to the king on saints' days.

"That's almost as good as birth control, at least if there's nothing better available," Robbie offered humorously.

"The queen was obeying the church, not practicing birth control," a shocked Estrella retorted. "Roman Catholic women do not use birth control, then or now."

"Church say no sex on saints' days?" asked Ivan, looking worried. "How many saints' days are?"

"The church has changed its position on abstinence," Estrella murmured, blushing.

"Many thanks to Pope for that!" Ivan exclaimed, beaming as he gave his wife a hug. "Sex is like warm stone in cold bed, no? Too much cold nights make mens sad."

"Really, Dr. Markarov!" murmured Anna. "There are young people present."

Her comment went unheard by all but Edie, who sniggered knowingly. The call for propriety had been drowned out by Janice Petar, who said, "That makes the queen an early feminist. I'll have to include her in a lecture. There's nothing more edifying than a woman who turns the rules of the patriarchy against those who thought them up."

"I rather imagine she just got tired of having children," I murmured to Jason, and we all moved on toward our rendevous with the gardens of Versailles, all of us except Grace, who said it was about to rain. Therefore, she would just sit here beside this nice French lady and knit until we returned. She had found one of the ubiquitous national monument attendants, and the two of them sat down amid the satin and gilt and mirrors for a grandmotherly chat.

The rest of us went out to view the long, long vistas of formal paths and lawns, with statues and fountains, trees and hedges adding decoration. I'm happy to say no one suffered any injuries, although I was keeping my eyes open for the perpetrator.

15
Drenched on Royal Grounds

Orange Bliss

Orangeries were popular with French kings and nobles. At Fontainebleau the sixteenth-century orangerie of the Valois kings began with one tree, planted in a tub in Spain by Eleanor of Castile, acquired by the constable of France, confiscated by the Queen Mother, Louise of Savoy, and moved later to Versailles. It finally died 335 years later without having produced one orange. The few fruits borne by these indoor trees were not tasty. When the trees even blossomed, it was cause for celebration.

The welfare of the Versailles orange trees was inquired after by Louis XIV, even during military campaigns. They provided orange blossoms to decorate the palace, particularly the Hall of Mirrors, and the flowers were admired for their sweet fragrance and beauty. One wonders whether the Sun King inquired as solicitously after the well-being of his queen as he did after that of his orange trees. As for the lack of fruit, faux oranges suspended amid the leaves and blossoms like Christmas ornaments remedied that.

Fortunately, the French were able to import real oranges from countries more favorable to their cultivation. Here is a delicious French recipe, simplified for American use.

• Peel, section, and remove seeds and filaments from *4 oranges*. Cut into small pieces and reserve juice.

• Whip *¾ cup heavy cream* and mix in *4 tbs. sugar, 1½ tbs. Grand Marnier, 4 tbs. chopped walnuts, 2½ tbs. orange juice,* and the orange pieces.

• Ladle into 4 dessert goblets. Use *orange leaves,* if available, or *maraschino cherries* to decorate the individual servings. Chill thoroughly in the refrigerator before serving.

Carolyn Blue, "Have Fork, Will Travel,"
Manchester Times

Carolyn

No doubt the various Kings Louis viewed the park and the buildings with satisfaction, but it seemed to me that Versailles could not have been much fun to live at. Yester-

day's sunshine at Giverny had given way to dark clouds. I
heard other tourists talking of storms elsewhere, high
winds, rain, lightning strikes, power outages, and a man
killed when his crane blew over. Thank goodness, I was
carrying an umbrella.

Professor Childeric managed to break away from Edie
and once more attached himself to me for a chat about yesterday's insecticide attack. "It must have been Fauree," he
assured me. "Who but a biologist would think of using bug
spray as a weapon?"

"His field is parasites, not bugs," I replied, noting that
Jason looked quite irritated, although we were now view-
ing a lovely five-tiered fountain in the middle of a pond.
On every tier there were statues and water spurting. Very
nice. Was Jason angry because I hadn't been able to avoid
the disaster-prone Dr. Childeric or because Edie had attached herself to him, having lost or abandoned the attention of the medievalist? She was literally hanging on my
husband's arm, looking up at him with a melting smile. I
heard Jason ask whether her generation was concerned
about global warming and the greenhouse effect.

Before she could answer, if she had any ideas on the
subject, a sudden wind came up and blew fountain water
onto the four of us, not to mention quite a few other un-
wary tourists. Jeremy Foxcroft, sketching the fountain in
pastels, was left with a soggy piece of paper. Edie giggled
like a six-year-old running through a sprinkler on a hot
day. Jason gave himself a wet-collie shake and eyed the
dark clouds rolling in, while Professor Childeric complained bitterly, as if the wind had risen specifically to ruin
his day and his tweed sports jacket with the professorial
leather elbow patches. Rain then fell, and he crowded
under my umbrella, saying that water would spot his silk
tie.

I was remarking that we should all be glad the rain
wasn't as dangerous here as in other parts of France—he

seemed to feel no sympathy for the deceased crane opera-
tor—when the wind turned my umbrella inside out, thun-
der rumbled, and a lightning bolt struck nearby, barely
missing a statue of some Greek god. Without even pausing
to help me, the professor headed for shelter. Edie, whose
wet T-shirt clung and revealed that she was braless, took
off after Professor Childeric. Jason joined me, saying,
"Saved by a timely storm," and helped with my umbrella.

We took refuge in the orangerie and admired the three
thousand orange trees until the lightning abated, then wandered off to look for Edie and view stone dogs spewing
streams of water from opposite sides of a runoff basin, a
number of really excellent statues from Greek mythology,
and finally a huge equestrian sculpture, probably of Louis
XIV, where other members of our group were congregated.
There we did find our missing foster child.

Carl Jensen seemed to be studying the legs and buttocks
of the rearing horse, while his wife remarked that she'd
never seen a horse like that at the state fair. "Shapeless
head, don't you think, Carl?" Lorenzo de Sorentino
seemed more interested in the rider's face, and I liked the
king's shoulder-length hair and silly hat.

"So, Sorentino," said Macauley Drummond, "are you
considering plastic surgery on his majesty? A nose job
maybe? Those French kings were a bit long in the beak."

Lorenzo ignored him, but Drummond persisted. "Take
Nedda, what would you propose for her?"

Overhearing Drummond's question, Nedda abruptly
ended her disquisition on the brilliance of his novels. Janice Petar turned away from Anna, with whom she had been
chatting about how silly Jean-Claude had looked when
drenched by the fountain, and snorted, "Brilliant? Drummond's books? More like an exercise in patriarchal rub-
bish."

"Are you saying you've actually read one of my novels?" Macauley asked. "I'd have thought you stuck pretty much to the drivel put out by the feminist presses, Janice."

"I prefer fiction that says something in an intelligible and literate fashion," she replied.

"Oh really. Whom would *you* recommend?"

"E. Annie Proulx, for one, and so do the critics. If you've won any prizes, I haven't heard about it. Proulx won them all with *The Shipping News*."

"Ugly loser makes it big in the ice and mud of small-town Newfoundland. Fascinating subject." Drummond turned his back on her and continued to prod the plastic surgeon. "Take a look at Nedda here. What would you do for her?"

Finally Lorenzo turned around. "Well, I'd start off by shaving her head."

"Lorenzo," his wife murmured warningly.

Nedda Drummond did have tightly frizzy, singularly colorless hair, but she was perfectly able to defend herself. "You may not like my hair, de Sorentino, but we scholars don't worry about such trivia. I believe my list of publications and honors speaks for itself."

Her husband's laughter boomed out until de Sorentino continued, "And then I'd paste your wife's Brillo hair on top of your bald pate, Drummond. It would make a marvelous topper for those pretentious ear-to-shoulder locks of yours."

The plastic surgeon walked off; rolling her eyes, his wife strolled in the other direction; and I sighed, thinking that if our fellow travelers became any more disagreeable, maybe I could talk Laura into slipping them all some Prozac. Time for perusing the gardens being over, the onset of another bout of rain and wind sent us hurrying back to meet our guides in the central building. There we found that at least one of us had been enjoying herself.

Grace Unsell had gathered a coterie of four women, two of whom spoke English and acted as translators. They

were all offering advice by cell phone to Grace's pregnant
daughter, who was getting no sleep because the baby
kicked her so hard at night that not only her nightgown, but
the covers, bulged with the force of determined little feet.
A very chic matron was singing a French lullaby into the
cell phone when we arrived. It was guaranteed to calm a
child in the womb, we were assured by a Belgian, although
she herself recommended herb tea and a gentle rubbing of
the wife's stomach.

Female bonding could save the world, I thought, if the
men could only be persuaded to let it work.

Well, it hadn't been too bad a day so far. Quarrels, certainly. Wind gusts, drenchings from fountains and rain
clouds, a bit of scary lightning, but no physical damage
done. Until Jean-Claude Childeric managed to fall down in
the aisle of the bus. He claimed that Janice had tripped him
in an assault motivated by feminist solidarity with Laura.
Janice hooted with laughter. Childeric retorted that his
ankle was sprained and he might well sue her.

Sitting across the aisle one seat forward from Janice
was Anna, who had relented in her desire to spend her days
away from teenagers and boxed Edie in by the window.
However, Edie would not stay boxed when she saw a
means of escape. She jumped up, climbed over her roommate, and rushed to Childeric's side, giving my son and
then me a lofty toss of the head. Then she draped
Childeric's good arm over her shoulder and helped him to
the back of the bus, while he complained about his
sprained ankle and his aching shoulder, which had been
jarred by his fall.

Had she decided that she preferred medieval history to
science? Or did she think Chris or I or both of us would be
jealous of her attentions to Childeric? I, for one, was delighted that she'd found someone to occupy her time without inconveniencing Anna, and Chris seemed to be more
interested in Marguerite than the girl he had kissed just

yesterday. Yes, it was proving to be a better day than those that preceded it, and we had a lovely cruise and dinner on the Seine to look forward to.

The cruise was very pretty, but there was no dinner on the Seine. In fact, there was no dinner worth mentioning. I wrote an article on indoor orange groves for Paul Fallon, wondering all the while whether he'd found more papers interested in my columns. Since I had to stay up past my bedtime to write them, it would be nice to make more money doing it.

Then I asked myself, did Childeric's fall on the bus merit addition to my clue list? Probably not. Probably he'd tripped over his own feet, and he hadn't been limping much by the time Edie got him to the back of the bus. He had, however, accused Janice, and he had been beside Janice when he tripped. Who was on the other side? Lorenzo and Laura, Lorenzo on the aisle side. Would he do that to forward his wife's candidacy? I sighed, pulled up my clue list, and added Childeric's ankle to the bottom. Hooray! I managed to get the bottom line all the way across.

So what did my list tell me? If all these happenings weren't accidents, they could all be motivated by the competition for the dean's position, but one had to postulate that candidates, their spouses, their friends, and/or one woman motivated by dislike would be willing to hurt someone to influence the selection. Did I believe that?

Travel Journal
Day Four, Versailles

What do I have to do to isolate C.? Shoot the rest of them? Edie Atwater, of all people, rescued the bastard from having to sit on the bus by himself. Then Carolyn let him under her umbrella.

A lightning bolt almost hit a statue in the park at Versailles but missed C. entirely. Enjoyed watching him fume when a fountain and then a rainstorm soaked him, but that isn't good enough. And it wasn't my doing. Maybe I need to plan ahead instead of acting on impulse.

The best I could do just winging it was trip him. Not very exciting, but it hurt like hell. You could hear him whining about the pain all over the bus.

Then the damn Atwater girl propped him up and spent the ride home fawning on him, telling him what a wonderful scholar he is.

Right! His most successful paper was based on my research, and he never so much as mentioned my name.

My God, but I'd like to get even.

The thing is—how? Nothing works. And here I am, tempted to skip the boat ride and dinner tonight because I can't stand to be in the same room with him.

16
The Dubious Delights of Rouen

Jason

Carolyn had such high hopes for the Seine cruise and dinner, and the *cruise* was spectacular. We drifted sedately by all those handsome riverside buildings under a white sky. Late in the afternoon the horizon streaked with rose, mauve, and blue, while pink-tinted clouds drifted up from perches atop the statues and towers of the city until finally the sun sank down behind the darkening silhouettes. We took pictures. We mourned the end of the display; then we went in search of Denis, for we had seen no preparations aboard to feed us the promised feast.

He shrugged, smiling, and replied, "Didn't I say? These boat dinners, they are . . . *très* inferior. I have picked a fine café ashore." No one was pleased to hear it. No one was pleased with the dinner that followed. Carolyn's final word on that meal was: "It's not worth so much as mention in my notebook." She was very testy by the time we returned to the hotel, more so when Denis informed us that our packed bags should be outside our doors by 11 P.M. for pickup.

"If you have my suitcase, what am I supposed to do with my nightgown and toiletries tomorrow?" she asked. "Carry them under my arm all day in Rouen?"

"Madame, have you never been touring before? Everyone carries a small bag onto the bus," Denis replied.

"Then where do I put my camera, film, notebooks, pens, and travel books if my small bag is filled with a nightgown and toiletries?" Carolyn retorted.

"Surely, Madame's nightgown is not so . . . voluminous?" He treated her to his charming smile. Carolyn did not respond.

"You can have nightie room in my backpack, Mom," said Chris.

"Can I too, Chris?" Edie asked. "My nightie is ever so tiny."

Before Chris could answer, Carolyn grasped Edie by the arm and hustled her off toward the courtyard of the falling flowerpots.

However, Carolyn was more cheerful the next morning. When she awoke, our bags were still on the balcony, so she prevailed upon me to stuff her nightgown into an outside pocket. Then when we were leaving the hotel, she spotted the bags beside the bus and stopped the driver from loading hers until she could dispose of her toiletries. Having triumphed over tour regulations, she said happily, "I can hardly wait to see Rouen. It was a seat of Norman power. William the Conqueror and his queen, Mathilda—"

"Ah, my dear Carolyn," Childeric interrupted, "you must share the ride with me. We can discuss—"

I grasped Carolyn's arm and hustled her away before the hotel marquee could collapse on him and injure her as well. I've never thought of myself as a superstitious person, but this tour was getting on my nerves. Carolyn swept up Edie as we wove through the chatting crowd of academics toward the bus door.

"Well, Dr. Blue," the girl exclaimed coyly, "I do believe you're jealous of Mrs. Blue and Dr. Childeric, but don't you worry. I'll divert his attention." With that, she tossed a glance at Chris, as if to say, *I can have anyone I want. I don't need you*, and she attached herself to Childeric. *Bet-*

ter him than me, I thought, and settled down to enjoy my wife's company.

Carolyn

I **can't believe** I slept all the way to Rouen. No wonder Jason likes to spend his time with Ivan and Hugh. When I woke up, he was sitting at the back talking science. I caught Dr. Jensen, the bovine specialist, casting them envious glances, like a little boy who wants to but despairs of being invited to join the other boys in the tree house. Chris had a tree house when he was eight, in which he and his friends gathered to play space war. By the time he was nine, the tree house was forsaken because his sister had sneaked in while he was away at camp and defiled his hideaway with ruffled curtains and Barbie dolls who enacted melodramatic scenes of Gwen's composing.

I took a sip from my plastic water bottle and climbed off the bus, enthusiastically looking forward to the walking tour. Rouen has been here two thousand years or more. Gauls, Romans, Normans, and Frenchmen have walked these narrow streets that now feature elaborate wood and plaster houses leaning precariously toward one another.

"Watch out, Childeric," Robbie called. "That house is about to tip over on you." Everyone but the professor laughed. He clutched his injured shoulder protectively.

We listened as Denis told us that the Butter Tower was built with the offerings of Normans who couldn't give up butter for Lent. I came to sympathize because Norman butter is special, rich and somehow more delightful in flavor than other butters. We visited a plague cemetery that had a courtyard surrounded by typical wood and plaster architecture. Denis said the poor were buried in pits in the center courtyard while the rich were buried inside, with the second floor reserved for bones.

In later years orphan children were housed at one end.

To allay their fears of ghosts, black cats were enclosed in the walls to frighten away the dead. The cat skeletons there were found more recently during renovations. Estrella Markarov was distressed to think of the poor little children subjected to such fear and hoped that they were comforted by their faith and by visiting or resident priests.

Ingrid said to Denis, "The poor cats were buried alive? That's—that's barbarous." Denis replied that it was their dying cries that frightened away the ghosts.

Childeric growled, "What nonsense."

I myself had no idea whether or not the story was true, but it was interesting, and creepy. The plague, the corpses, the cats, the children, even the gloomy skies overhead gave me a feeling of impending doom, which I had to shake off to admire the soaring beauty of the cathedral that held, according to Denis, the tombs of such romantic figures as Richard the Lionhearted. "Was that the crusader king?" I asked Denis. "Isn't he buried somewhere else?" Childeric tried to answer my question, but Jason whisked me away when the professor approached.

Other tombs belonged to Rollo, the Norse adventurer to whom Charles the Simple gave the dukedom in return for a cessation of Viking raids up the Seine; and to William Longsword, a later Duke of Normandy, so named, according to Denis, for the "length of his male member."

At this, Professor Childeric was so offended, both morally and academically, that he shouted, "Have you no shame, man? He was called Longsword because his legs were so long that his feet dragged when he rode a horse."

To me it seemed more likely that the duke had wielded a particularly long sword in combat, but it was something I could look up at home, without having to contradict the modern combatants. "Who the hell cares?" Jason muttered. "Why can't the man just shut up and stop infuriating everyone? No wonder things keep happening to him."

Since *I* cared about what the nickname of the Norman

duke meant, I failed to agree with my husband's complaint, and he gave me a narrow look. "Don't tell me you feel sorry for that ass?" Such language is not typical of Jason, so I hastened to point out the interesting carvings of biblical stories on the portals as we left. "Hardly anyone could read then, so they had to get their lessons chiseled in the stone. Imagine trying to teach chemistry that way to illiterates."

"We do teach chemistry with pictures," Jason replied, relaxing and smiling at me, "and I've had students who are borderline illiterate. Didn't you hear Nedda Drummond talking last night about refusing to teach Freshman English because she had so many students who didn't read and couldn't write?"

We continued chatting happily, trying to take in all the sights while heeding Denis's exhortations to mind the traffic and not cross against the lights because the tour company reprimanded him if cars ran over his tourists. Finally we came in view of the famous clock on the Rue du Gros-Horlage. Childeric came over to give me some "accurate information" on the clock, and I listened absently and admired its beauty. Placed at the foot of the bell tower, it is huge, its face gold and blue with a sunray design and hands that terminate in animal figures.

I squinted, trying to make out what animal it was. Others were speculating aloud. "Looks like a rat to me," said Macauley Drummond.

"How clever," exclaimed his wife Nedda. "How symbolic in a town that suffered so severely from bubonic plague, which was carried by the fleas on rats. The clock tells us that Time brings death to us all."

"Looks like a sheep to me," said Carl Jensen.

"And how do you interpret that, Carl?" asked Drummond. "Sheep bring mad cow disease to us all?" He snickered and added, "Not very poetic."

"No mad cow disease back then," said Jensen. "France only got that just lately."

"Perhaps our knowledgeable guide would care to enlighten us," said Childeric. Then he made a strange grunting sound and, with one hand against my back, shoved me.

I found myself stumbling into the street and falling in front of a large bicycle ridden by a husky, red-faced man in a cap. I couldn't get out of the way, or do anything but continue my fall. Although the incident must have occurred in seconds, it seemed to drag on in slow motion, accompanied by paralyzing fear. The collision with the bicycle flattened me on the cobblestones, and my body shuddered with the shock of the impact.

If you've ever been run down, you know that it's no laughing matter. It hurts! Especially if you're a relatively small woman, small in comparison to a large man peddling his ancient, heavy bicycle with muscular ferocity. I felt frightened and faint as people crowded around me. On his knees beside me in an instant, Jason told me not to move. The rider shouted angrily in French, no doubt protesting my invasion of his right-of-way. Dr. Jensen knelt beside Jason and began to feel my arms, legs, and ribs, all the while assuring me that he'd diagnosed many a broken cow bone.

Someone, Janice I think, demanded to know why Jean-Claude Childeric had pushed me, and as I began to think more clearly, I wondered myself. It was definitely he who had propelled me into the street, not Jason, not anyone else. I had smelled the distinctive cologne he wore as I sprawled forward. The professor insisted that someone had pushed *him*. *He* was the intended victim, not me!

"Well, my wife is the person who was hurt," snapped Jason. "Why don't you stay away from her?"

"Mom, are you okay?" Chris loomed at my feet, peering at me anxiously.

"I didn't mean her any harm," Childeric protested. "We're both victims here."

"I do believe you're a jinx, Childeric, old man," said Macauley Drummond in what I was coming to recognize as his typically nasty brand of sarcasm. "Maybe we'd all better stay away from *you*."

17
The Medicinal Qualities of Calvados

Carolyn

With Jason on one side and Chris on the other, I hobbled toward the Place du Vieux-Marche and a visit to the stunningly modern church of Sainte Joan of Arc. Outside, a dark, conical roof swept up at a slant from its height-of-a-man overhang to a point that seemed to pierce the overcast sky. Lower sections of the roof swooped away from the cone and sent triangular points almost to the ground. The architecture had an original and dark simplicity, but lovely war-salvaged stained glass lighted the inside.

En route Denis entertained the group with the tale of Rouen's patron saint, Romain, an eighth-century bishop who saved the terrorized city from a monster called Gargoyle. Silly me! I thought a gargoyle was an ugly monster head protruding from a cathedral, a carving that drained water from the roof and frightened off demons. Jason and Chris were discussing the best strategy for protecting me from Childeric accidents. They struck on some plan too complicated for my befuddled mind to take in, and Chris went off to implement it.

As a result, when we had lunch at a sidewalk café near the church, I found myself seated with ladies. Childeric was boxed into a table with the men, who could presumably defend themselves against whatever ill fortune might befall. My companions were Robbie, Janice, Anna, and of course, Edie. Liking them all (well, the jury was out on Edie, but I was trying), I was happy enough and ordered seafood crepes and white wine. I have to tell you that, although the crepe and sauce were very nice, the seafood bits were sandy. There is nothing more disconcerting than finding sand in your food by chewing on some. It's not as if you can separate it out like a bone, a piece of gristle, or an olive pit and remove it from your mouth with ladylike delicacy.

My mother advised patting one's mouth inconspicuously with a napkin, thereby transferring the indigestible item into the napkin. With sand-laced food, you must either spit out the whole mouthful, which is hard to do inconspicuously, or swallow it, which makes one fear for the state of one's digestive tract. And to be confronted with this problem while aches were springing up everywhere in my body was really too much.

Robbie had ordered mussels in Normandy sauce and, because she knew about my writing, offered me a taste. I refused a mussel. If my seafood bits were sandy, think of how much sand a whole mussel might contain! I did try the Normandy sauce, and it was excellent, flavored by the rich cream for which the region is famous. To that were added flavors from the mussels, onion, herbs, and other things. I can't tell you everything I detected because my arm hurt, and I didn't make notes. Also, the conversation had begun to command my attention.

"Can you believe that Hugh's room has only one bed, one *single* bed? It's downright inconvenient, I can tell you that," Robbie complained.

I should have changed the direction of the conversation

right then. After all, Edie was at our table and listening avidly.

"So it occurred to me that we could shift the room arrangements." Robbie's trademark smile flashed around the circle. "Then Hugh and I could room together. He's such a love."

Anna sent her a warning frown, then glanced significantly in Edie's direction.

Edie said, "Oh, don't mind me. I know that if people my age do it, so do people your age. Married, unmarried, whatever. I think it's cool."

Anna gritted her teeth and said, "You are the most irresponsible girl. If I were your mother, I'd keep you locked in your room."

"Well, you're not my mother, thank God," Edie retorted. "Hey, Dr. Hecht, I'd give you my bed if it would do you any good, but—"

"That's a start," said Robbie enthusiastically. "But Hugh and I can't move in with Anna. On the other hand, Anna, you could move in with Janice, and then Hugh and I could move into your room."

"I think not," said Janice. "Two single women, one a feminist? Ingrid Jensen would love that. The woman has a mortal fear of homosexuality. She'd be telling everyone on the tour that we're gay."

"Wow! Are you?" asked Edie.

Janice eyed her with sardonic amusement. "We're not. Are you?"

"Me? Hey, I like guys." Edie's eyes began to dance. "So how about this? Now that it's settled you're not lesbians, Dr. Thomas-Smith moves in with you, Dr. Petar. I mean, she'd probably rather have you for a roommate than me. She can't stand me! And you probably don't like Dr. Hecht because she likes guys and sex. I mean she's been married a bunch of times, and now she's after Dr. Fauree. So, like

she said, she and Dr. Fauree can have my room, and I'll—
I'll move in with Chris!"

"And Dr. Childeric?" asked Janice dryly.

"He can take Dr. Fauree's single room. Not likely anyone would want to move in with him if he's as dangerous
as Dr. Drummond said." She was smiling broadly as she
turned to me. "Gee, Mrs. Blue, you don't want your son
rooming with a professor who's on someone's hit list, do
you?"

"Since I was the one who had an accident today, I think
we can assume that there is no *hit list*," I replied.

Edie shrugged. "Oh well, I think Dr. Drummond was
just being . . . snotty. About the jinx business." She turned
to Anna and added, "I hope you noticed I didn't say he was
being an asshole, although he was."

"You are not moving in with Chris," said Anna. "Carolyn, don't you have anything to say?"

A groan would have expressed what I had to say. My
bones felt as if I'd been kicked and trampled by a column
of Nazis in jackboots, whatever those are. I'm afraid I
didn't acquit myself very well in my surrogate mother role.
The waiter approached, and I ordered an apple tart (Normandy is also famous for its apples) and a Calvados.

"Alcohol will not solve this problem," said Anna.

"You're really hurting, aren't you?" My friend Robbie
was now studying me thoughtfully. From the look on her
face, I gathered that large bruises must have been appear-
ing on mine, not to mention on the clothed parts of my bat-
tered person.

"I really am," I agreed.

"Yeah, you look awful, Mrs. Blue," said Edie.

What a source of joy the girl was. I couldn't wait to return her to her mother.

Robbie pulled a bottle of Tylenol from the backpack
slung over her chair and passed it to me. "You better take
some. They might help."

I snatched the bottle eagerly, fumbled with the lid as the waiter set my Calvados on the table, and washed down four pills with one swallow of the bottled water I carry. Then I picked up the Calvados, which I don't even like, and took a big gulp. I ordered it because one can't write about Normandy without mentioning Calvados, another specialty of the area since it's made of local apples.

"Carolyn, don't do that!" Anna protested. "The combination of alcohol and acetaminophen will destroy your liver."

I don't know about my liver, but the Calvados went straight to my head, perhaps dissolving the synapses, or whatever, that connect pain to the perception of it. "Anna," I said, more relaxed now that I saw a less painful future in the offing, "I really can't worry about my liver right now. It doesn't hurt. The rest of me does." Then I took another swallow, and it burned right down to my tummy. Good stuff!

Anna turned to Edie. "You are not going to room with Chris," she said calmly. "You're staying with me, which does not make me any happier than it makes you, but your only alternative is to go home."

"You can't send me home. I'm too young to travel by myself."

"Yes, you are, although I am sure there are girls your age who could easily and safely make the trip by themselves. You, on the other hand, would miss your plane by running off to a T-shirt shop or never arrive home at all because you saw fit to run off with some drug-addicted biker with a pierced tongue."

"Meany," said Edie and giggled.

She was enjoying the debate. I really should have done something about her sassy way with Anna, but my apple tart arrived—*tarte aux pommes*—and it looked very tasty. There probably wasn't a grain of sand in it. I took an appreciative bite and followed it with a slug of healthful Calvados. I must tell you that the two make a lovely combination. Lovely.

Anna was watching me and shaking her head, feeling very sorry for me and worrying about my liver, no doubt. Nice lady. I took another bite of tart and finished my Calvados.

Robbie said, "You're looking better already. Can I have a bite of your tart?"

"Order your own tart." I waved to the waiter.

"Hey, I'm the one who provided the painkillers."

"Maybe," I agreed, "but I think the Calvados is what's doing the job. I'll have another," I said to the waiter. He didn't blink an eye.

Anna had risen and moved across the café to speak to Jason. Was she ratting on me, telling him I was getting drunk and raucous? Well, I wasn't. I was just feeling a bit better.

"So about switching the room assignments around." Robbie was nothing if not persistent.

"Did you ever consider," Janice asked, "that this open sexual liaison may hurt Hugh's chances to be appointed dean?"

"Now, there's an old-fashioned thought," said Robbie gaily. "No, Janice, that never occurred to me. Anyway, it's the selection committee that counts, and how are they going to know? Are you going to call them up and snitch?"

"Maybe they sent along a spy since all three candidates are on the tour."

Edie giggled, and Robbie joined her. Then Robbie's tart and my second Calvados arrived. Maybe I'd write a column on the gourmet and analgesic properties of Calvados and *tarte aux pommes*. At the time, that seemed like an inspired idea.

18
How to Come Up
Smelling Like a Horse

Jason

"Dr. Blue?"

I looked up from dessert to find Anna standing beside me, looking worried.

"Ah, my dear Anna," said Childeric heartily, "joining the male table, are you? Had enough of ladies' chatter?"

She ignored him and murmured, "Dr. Blue, I'm afraid your wife is experiencing a good deal of pain from that bicycle accident."

"I'm so sorry to hear it," said Childeric. "How can we be of service to the charming—"

"She's talking to me, Childeric," I said impatiently. "Stop butting in, will you?"

"I certainly didn't mean to interfere." Childeric was now offended. "However, as a friend of your wife's—"

"Pushing her in front of a bicycle is not an act of friendship," I retorted.

"As I was saying," said Anna. "Carolyn is drinking Calvados while taking acetaminophen, not a safe combination and one that I'm sure she wouldn't risk if she weren't in pain. Perhaps she'd be better off resting in her hotel room."

I rose immediately, followed Anna to the ladies' table, and knelt beside my wife. "Anna says you're hurting, sweetheart."

"Well." Carolyn thought about it, then sampled what looked like a tart and sipped the Calvados, which she doesn't even care for. "This is a lovely combination," she informed me. "Actually, I'm feeling better, but I'm afraid I'm getting a bit tipsy."

"How much have you had?"

"One tart and two liqueurs. Works wonders. I may recommend it to my readers."

"How would you feel about skipping the afternoon tour and going back to the hotel for a nap?" I suggested. When Carolyn looked dubious, I added, "You know you like an afternoon nap when you have the time."

"True." She smiled at me and sipped a bit more Calvados. "But I'd miss the res' of the tour. Who knows? We might get something decent for dinner. Something I could write about. Is it a tour dinner? If i's more lasagna, I jus' might go for the nap."

"Carolyn, you poor thing, you're sloshed," said Robbie. "Go home and sleep it off. Maybe the acetaminophen will have worked on the bruises by then."

"Cool," said Edie. "Now if you threaten to call my mom, I'll tell her you got drunk at lunch, Mrs. Blue."

"Isn' she a horrid girl?" said Carolyn cheerfully. "The leas' Judith could do was warn me about her."

"So let's go back to the hotel, Caro," I persisted. "A nice nap—"

"Proceeded by a good soak in a hot tub," suggested Anna.

"Ummm," Carolyn agreed. "That does soun' lovely. But there'll be wonderful things to see, and I won't get to—"

"I'll go back to take pictures if you want," I promised. "I'd even offer to take notes, but it's doubtful Denis will say anything you'd want to pass on to your readers, and I'm not to listening to Childeric any more than I have to."

"He probably didn' mean to push me in front of the bus," said my wife magnanimously.

"Bicycle, not bus," said Edie.

"You didn' get hit. It felt like a bus."

At that point I did manage to fend off Carolyn's idea that another Calvados might be good for her, and having left money on the table to pay her bill, I escorted her back to the hotel before she could change her mind.

Carolyn

The hot soak in the bathtub helped, and the nap was even better. I woke up at the end of the afternoon hurting, but not unbearably. The knock that had awakened me sounded again, and I fumbled for my robe, found Jason's instead, and pulled it on over my nightie. Then rubbing my eyes, I limped to the door, thinking I wasn't that much better after all. Even my hand hurt as I unlocked the door. Had the bicycle run over my hand?

"My dear Carolyn, I just had to stop by to assure myself you were not seriously injured. I'd rather have thrown myself under that bicycle than see any harm come to you at the hands of my enemies."

"Professor Childeric?" What was he doing at my door?

"Jean-Claude. Please call me Jean-Claude." He then stepped around me into the room. "Given the bond between us, surely we need not stand on ceremony, although of course in public your husband might be appeased if you—"

"What are you talking about?" I stammered. I had turned to face him, and he reached beyond me and closed the door.

"Your husband. I fear he suspects our feelings for each other. He's seems quite set on keeping us apart."

Childeric still had his hand on the knob of the closed door, thus boxing me in. Finally he pulled the hand back but used it to take mine. He had a warm, damp palm.

"Dr. Blue's feeling insecure, no doubt. It must be hard to realize that your wife has more in common with another man, not to mention a tender regard for—"

I yanked my hand away and edged sideways.

"Ah, my dear, there's no need to be frightened of discovery. He's still with the tour. I must say that it was very insensitive of him to leave you alone, but scientists are not known for gallantry, are they? I'm here now to comfort you."

Then the man actually put his good arm around me. "Let go this instant," I demanded and tried wiggle away. He hung on. The arm in the sling was pressing against my breasts, while his good arm had trapped one of mine to my side as he reached around and clutched my elbow. I don't know when I've been more shocked and embarrassed.

He, in the meantime, was smiling at me fatuously and saying, "Don't be shy, my love. With a rapport like ours—"

"Are you out of your mind? The only rapport we have is a mutual interest in—" Since the lower part of my arm was free, I used it to push at his chest, much good that did.

"Ah, such passion!" he exclaimed.

"A mutual interest in medieval history," I gasped, "does not give you the right to—to—"

"Make a declaration of affection that you have been hoping to hear?" he finished for me. "I knew from the moment we gazed into each other's eyes and you stroked the blood from my forehead so sweetly, that we were destined—"

With a wrench I managed to drag my elbow free, after which I punched him in the shoulder. He howled in pain and staggered back.

"You, sir," I panted, "are a—are a horse's—patootie! Get out of my room!"

The professor's eyes, which had filled with tears in reaction to the pain of his injured shoulder, then rounded with astonishment. "Carolyn—"

"Out!" Having backed toward the bed, I snatched a silly-looking, ruffled lamp from the bedside table and brandished it at him. Jean-Claude Childeric backed up and fumbled for the doorknob, his mouth still agape with astonishment and his face redder than it had been after exposure to the capsaicin spray. Jason had told me about capsaicin. In concentrated form, it raises blisters on the skin. Childeric bolted out the door. With a shaking hand, I followed to turn the lock, then replaced the little lamp on its table, dropped abruptly onto the bed, and burst into tears.

I was just having a good cry and blowing my nose with Kleenex taken from the travel pack in my handbag, when I heard him tapping at my door again. Indignant, I grabbed up the lamp, rushed forward, and swung the door open, crying, "If you don't go away, I'm going to call the police."

Anna stood in the hallway. "Carolyn?"

I gulped. "Anna?" I didn't know what to say. I'm sure she hadn't expected to be greeted by a tearstained woman wielding a ruffled lamp.

"Was that Jean-Claude Childeric I saw scurrying away from your door?" she asked, an expression of concern on her face.

I'm afraid I burst into tears again, and under her sympathetic questioning, the whole humiliating story poured out. "I don't think I did anything to encourage him," I sniffled. "Discussing medieval history isn't—can't be interpreted as—as flirtatious. Can it?" We were both sitting on the bed, Anna patting my hand consolingly.

"I've never even been alone with him until he forced his way into my room."

"Some men, for all their seeming gentility and charm," she said, "have no real respect for women."

"I don't think he's charming," I responded bitterly. "He's a horrid, arrogant—"

"I quite agree. I think you should—"

"And I called him a horse's—a horse's patootie."

"Did you?" Anna looked—well, impressed, or perhaps amused. "I hope he took it to heart," she said. "Now, I think the thing to do is tell your husband about this—"

"Tell Jason? He'd be furious."

"With you?"

"No, with Childeric."

"And rightly so. In fact, perhaps we should warn some of the other women, just in case he looks elsewhere for female victims."

"Good heavens. Surely, you don't think he makes a habit of this?"

"I've heard rumors," said Anna.

I was beginning to calm down and consider the whole embarrassing event. If this story got around the tour group, I'd feel like a fool. "Let me think about it, Anna." I ran distracted fingers into my hair, inadvertently probed one of my bruises, and groaned.

"The bicycle accident?" she asked.

"The bicycle accident," I agreed. "Robbie's Tylenol is wearing off, and struggling with Professor Childeric didn't help."

"The man should pay for what he's done," she said. "You shouldn't let him get away with this." She glanced down at a tube she held in her hand. "Still, it's your decision, of course." She placed the tube, which was about eight inches long, in my hand. "Dr. Jensen left the tour to find this for you," she said. "He promises, if you rub it into your bruises or anywhere you hurt, you'll feel a lot better."

"What is it?" I asked, unable to translate the French lettering on the plastic.

"Liniment would be my guess," Anna replied.

"I guess that means I've now been treated twice by a vet. If he is a vet."

"I think he's just a cow specialist, but I don't doubt the ointment is safe to use. Lots of country people use liniment on their horses and themselves to ease pain. It can't hurt to try."

"I suppose not. And thank you. Both of you. Well, I'll thank Dr. Jensen myself, but if you see him . . . I'm dithering, aren't I?"

"You're upset," she said kindly. "And undoubtedly in

pain. Rub some of that cream on and go back to bed. Maybe by tomorrow you'll be fit enough to dodge the next bicycle." Then her face tightened. "Or the next amorous professor."

"Bite your tongue," I replied, trying to look more cheerful. "I guess you got stuck with Edie again. I'm so sorry. Did she—"

"She had a perfectly boring afternoon, mostly in my company," Anna replied. "Which serves her right. She's an ill-mannered girl." With that, Anna went back to her room and, probably, the company of that ill-mannered girl. I didn't envy her.

The liver-destroying alcohol and Tylenol having worn off completely after my three-hour nap and subsequent visitors, I looked thoughtfully at the large tube in my hand. Then I unscrewed the cap and sniffed. Well, it wasn't French perfume, but my aches and pains were making themselves known. I slipped off Jason's robe and rubbed an experimental dab on an arm that was turning red and purple. Dear Dr. Jensen. Thoughtful Anna. That one spot felt better. Soon I was applying dollops freely—on road-collision areas, on bicycle-collision areas, and on places where my bones simply ached.

Whoever was responsible for my injuries—Professor Childeric or some enemy of his or just some crazy person; after my most recent shock, I blamed Childeric—I wished an equally painful accident on them. With the scent of horse medicine soaking into my skin and wafting through the room, I imagined Jason's expression when he returned. And when would that be? And lord, was I going to tell him about Childeric? I could hardly believe what had happened myself.

Perhaps Jason had decided to join the tour dinner, after all. If so, I'd have more time to decide what and what not to tell my husband. For a wonder, I wasn't even hungry.

19
Suspicions and Quiche

Carolyn

While I waited to see if Jason would return, I thought about Jean-Claude Childeric and all the accidents we'd shared or nearly shared—the airport, the falling pot, the insecticide. Had being endangered together made him think there was a romantic connection between us? Or had he somehow arranged the accidents in order to—what? Scare me to death so that I'd be vulnerable to his advances? He'd certainly had the worst of the first three. So maybe his idea had been to make me feel sorry for him. But this last. I could have been killed. What good would that do him?

And why was he making passes at a married woman? As much as he wanted to be dean, that was hardly the way to go about it. I could have made a terrible fuss and ruined his reputation. I still could, but I'd be too abysmally embarrassed to do it. No wonder men get away with sexual harassment.

At that point in my confused musings, Jason arrived with a bag containing mussels browned in the shell, quiche, salad, and apple tarts. No Calvados, but Carl Jensen's liniment had helped, so I felt able to do without Calvados. And Jason had brought a half-bottle of wine.

"I thought you might rather eat in," he explained as he laid the dinner out on the lamp table. "Are you feeling better?"

"Much better," I assured him. "I've followed everyone's advice, even to rubbing on Carl Jensen's horse liniment. Do I still smell funny?" I held out an arm for Jason to sniff. "Well, I didn't listen to Anna when she told me not to mix alcohol and Tylenol. Do you think my liver is shriveling even as we speak?"

"More likely swelling up," Jason replied. "Pretty soon you'll turn yellow."

"Thanks a lot." I tried the mussels and, surprisingly, they were tasty, but I think it was the stuff on top that made them so palatable. I had two and even looked for a recipe when I got back to the States since I didn't feel up to pursuing one that night at whatever establishment Jason had visited to get our dinner. Jason had the other six. "Is Chris joining us?" I asked.

"No, he's braving the tour dinner."

"Teenaged boys will eat anything."

"He's twenty, but given the food at his fraternity house, you're right." Jason poured me some wine, and I sampled the quiche. Mushroom. Very nice. We sat on the bed eating and discussing what could be going on with the tour. Any topic would do as long as I didn't have to mention Jean-Claude Childeric's visit to my room.

"That bicycle accident frightened me," I admitted.

"Me too," Jason replied. "It *was* Childeric who pushed you."

"Well, bumped into me, but he did say he was pushed." Why was I still defending him? "Obviously, someone is doing these things," I added hurriedly, "but who could it be? Edie? She's peeved with me for keeping her away from Chris."

"Well, if she pushed Childeric to get to you, she didn't accomplish much. Anna made her toe the line this afternoon. Didn't you say Janice dislikes him?"

"No question." The salad had a nice light dressing on very fresh greens. "But I can't remember seeing her near any of the . . . accidents. Can you think of anyone else who seems to have a grudge?"

"Drummond?" Jason suggested. "As far as I can tell, he doesn't like anyone. And de Sorentino. He's a rather unpleasant fellow."

"Could it be a Munchausen's syndrome sort of thing? I saw that . . . where? . . . a TV hospital series, I suppose. He hurts someone and then looks like a hero when he steps in to cure them."

"Two problems with that hypothesis. He's a plastic surgeon, and the only medical interest he's shown in any of us is cosmetic."

I had to giggle because I'd had a silly thought. "It's Carl Jensen. He got me knocked into the street so that he could go out searching for horse liniment to cure me. Or Dr. Unsell. He wants to see how the Common Market and the Euro have affected hospital services in France, so he's trying to send us all to the hospital."

"Seriously, Carolyn."

"All right. I had a scary thought while I was soaking in the tub. There's Ivan. He seems nice enough, but he is Russian, and it was a Russian Mafia type who—"

"Take my word for it, Carolyn, Ivan Markarov is not a member of the Russian Mafia," said Jason.

"Oh, you'd think that because he's scientific. You're as bad as Childeric thinking all the scientists are plotting against him because he has a better chance at being dean than Hugh."

"Who says he has a better chance of being anything but an asshole?" my husband demanded sharply.

"Jason Blue. Is that any way to talk in mixed company? I may just have to eat both tarts myself."

Moules Gratinées

Butter was introduced to Western Europe in the fifth century by the Vandals. I wonder if the villagers considered wholesale barbarian rape and pillage a fair trade-off for the delights of butter? And did they realize that, by using it instead of olive oil, they were endangering their health? Those Vandals! After all the damage they left behind, they added heart disease to the toll.

Still, butter is lovely, especially butter made in Normandy. I've come to the conclusion that Norman butter can make anything good, even things you don't usually like— mussels, for instance. Here is a Norman recipe for a first course that combines butter and mussels to advantage.

• Vigorously scrub the sand from *2 qts. of mussels.*

• Steam in *½ cup white wine* with *pepper to taste* and *several slices of carrots and onions.*

• Save the broth and shells after removing the mussels from the shells.

• Cream some butter with *chopped and crushed garlic, finely chopped parsley, pepper, and salt (unless the butter is salted).*

• Place each mussel in a half-shell, sprinkle with the leftover broth, add to each shell a layer of the butter, and brown briefly in a hot oven.

Carolyn Blue, "Have Fork, Will Travel,"
Bisbee Arizona News

As soon as I had finished writing a column, I tried to pull up my list of clues, to which I certainly needed to add my own injury. The file was gone! I'll never understand how computers manage to devour whole files. I had to start all over again.

Clue List

Day	Place	Victim	Injury	Means
1	airport Paris	Childeric	head cut	shove
2	courtyard	Childeric me	shoulder shins	pot
3	Giverny	Childeric	clothes dignity skin	insecticide
4	Versailles	Childeric	ankle (probably an accident)	trip
5	Rouen	me	bruises	pushed into bicycle

After looking over my list, my thought that the first three attacks could have been aimed at me was reinforced; I had even sustained minor injuries from the falling pot. The third, Childeric tripping on the bus, was probably a real accident, and I had been the one hurt in Rouen. Although Edie might dislike me, she couldn't have pushed the pot because she was with me in the courtyard, and I

Clue List

Present	Suspect(s)	Motive
Childeric Chris me	Fauree	deanship
Childeric Edie me	Fauree Petar	deanship hates JCC
Childeric Jason me Fauree	Fauree Robbie Laura Jason gardener	deanship " " " accident
everyone	Janice Lorenzo?	hates JCC deanship
everyone 	 Ivan Edie enemies of Childeric	Childeric felt I snubbed him? lust? Mafia hates me?

wasn't sure that a girl that slim could have shoved a man of Dr. Childeric's girth hard enough to push me in front of a bicycle.

No one else on the tour seemed to dislike me or would have any reason that I knew of to wish me ill. The idea that Childeric might have set up the attacks under some delusion of unrequited love seemed ludicrous, so I discarded it, while vowing to stay away from the medievalist. Without knowing all the reasons, Jason would be relieved.

That left Ivan. Had he been recruited by Russian gangsters to frighten me or worse? Maybe they had threatened relatives of his in the old country unless he cooperated, and he was cozying up to Jason in order to get close to me and to divert attention from himself. Where had he been during the other attacks? Perhaps tomorrow I could ask a few discreet questions and find out. I saved my clue list, turned off my computer, and slipped into bed to snuggle up beside Jason, terrified at the idea that someone might be stalking me.

Travel Journal
Day Five, Rouen

Pity about Carolyn. I meant to get C., that pompous bastard. What a pleasure it would have been to see him flattened by an irate Frenchman on a rickety bicycle.

Still Carolyn's not likely to get anywhere near C. after this. On the other hand, that brainless Edie Atwater reacted this afternoon to Chris Blue hanging out with the guide by trying to attach herself to C. again.

And Hecht. She's ruining Fauree's chances at the deanship. Not that I care who gets it as long as it's not C. But she's dead wrong to think all this public sex isn't getting back to the committee. As soon as they heard that C. had picked up someone's ticket cheap, the way the Blues did, the committee would have got themselves a spy to watch the three candidates, see how they interacted. Wonder who the spy is.

Damn administration. Spies everywhere. Probably why I never made full professor after C. got through with me.

He'll pay.

20
Honfleur, Tourist's Delight

French mayonnaise and French fried potatoes—delicious both separately and together. I sampled the combination in Honfleur on the Normandy coast.

Mayonnaise was reputedly invented by the Duc de Richelieu. He named it after Mahon, a British fort on the Balearic Island of Minorca and the scene of his great victory during the Seven-Years' War. When not fighting wars, Richelieu was quite the man about town and is said to have invited guests to dine under his roof in the nude. Perhaps all that creamy female skin inspired the recipe for mayonnaise.

And war has inspired other landmarks in culinary history. Napoleon, for instance, offered a prize for an invention that would preserve rations for an army on the move. Vacuum-packed food was the result in 1808. Napoleon III wanted a synthetic butter for his army, and a scientist produced it from suet, chopped cows' udders, and warm milk in 1867. Sounds disgusting, doesn't it?

As for French fries, potatoes had a checkered history in France once they were brought over from the New World. In 1540 they were considered an ornamental plant to be exhibited as an exotic in royal gardens but not eaten. By 1618 the Duke of Burgundy banned the planting of potatoes because they were reputed to cause leprosy. Only in the late eighteenth century did potatoes overcome suspicion and become a popular food. Louis XVI accomplished this by various ruses and publicity stunts invented by Antoine-Auguste Parmetier. First, they planted land outside Paris with potatoes and set soldiers to guard the fields day and night. Then they gave the soldiers a night off, and local farmers, overcome with curiosity, stole the plants to put in their own fields. Finally, the king gave an all-potato dinner party at which Marie Antoinette wore potato flowers in her hair. (I didn't even know potatoes produced flowers.) Benjamin Franklin attended the royal potato feast. Soon potatoes were considered fashionable both by the court and by the general populace, and Parmetier published a book on how to grow and cook potatoes.

Viva les pommes frites!

Carolyn Blue, "Have Fork, Will Travel,"
Cheyenne Gazette

Carolyn

Honfleur is a lovely town; its harbor is crowded with yachts and sailing vessels whose masts reflect in the water like a leafless forest. Here, too, are reflected, seemingly a phantom city beneath the sea, the multistoried stone houses that wall in the harbor with their slate roofs sprouting chimneys and dormer windows. How lovely it would be to sit in one such window, I thought at the time, and stare out at the bustle of the Quai Sainte-Catherine or at the salt houses of the Quai Saint-Étienne, from which fishermen sailed to the rich and dangerous waters of the Newfoundland Banks. Or I could curl in a window seat and imagine the adventurers who sailed from Honfleur centuries ago to found Quebec, to reach Brazil, and to reconnoiter the Saint Lawrence Seaway.

On the other hand, those houses are narrow. They probably have no elevators. Would I have wanted to climb six, seven, eight stories to inhabit that dormered room of my imagination? Certainly not that day. I ached still, not unbearably, but I foresaw that the rest of this trip would involve continued personal discomfort accompanied by unease bordering on fear.

Still, I fell in love with Honfleur. Who could not after seeing Saint Catherine's Church, which was thrown up by sixteenth-century shipwrights in the form of a ship's hull? In this charming church, the builders, who were the bedrock of the town's economy, gathered to worship for many centuries.

And Honfleur has also been known for over a century and a half as an inspiration to artists. It still has many fine galleries, in one of which I saw an oil that I coveted, a portrait of a ghostly Mardi Gras girl in flowered hat and ribbon streamers, yet very young, pale, and sad. The saleswoman certainly thought I should buy it and offered a price reduction, free shipping, even financing. Ivan and Estrella were with us, I keeping a wary eye on that possible gangster disguised as an academic. He thought we should buy the portrait because the painter was Russian and because Ivan could not buy it himself, being a man looking forward to fatherhood and its many long-term expenses.

Estrella nodded approvingly. Wild expenditures were not for those who hoped to be parents, and the girl in the picture was too pasty-faced for her taste. Jason pointed out that he, too, was a father, one with two offspring in college, and extravagant expenditures were not to his taste at this time, although he did like the picture. Ah, well. I was feeling melancholy and didn't argue. The Frenchwoman did. She followed us out into the rain, elaborating on the growing fame of the artist and the probable increase in value of the painting in ten years' time.

Art as investment. That consideration hadn't occurred to me. If it had, I might have suggested to Jason that he was less than twenty years from retirement and needed to be on the lookout for such fine investments. Undoubtedly, Jason would have replied, "Who plans to retire? Not me. They'll have to carry me out of the lab in a pine box."

Mortuary salesmen tend to start calling one after the age of forty, our age, not theirs, with offers of elaborate prepaid funerals, early casket selection before inflation drives the prices beyond our means, and so forth. Ghoulish telemarketers! We've formulated a marvelously discouraging reply: Whoever answers the telephone responds, "We'd be interested in a price quote on your least expensive pine box. Is there a discount for two? We could keep them in the garage. Oh, and do you actually have to convert to Judaism to be eligible for the day-after-death, unembalmed-corpse burial?" Even the children have taken part in this form of family entertainment.

After we fled the gallery with the saleswoman at our heels, Jason and Ivan walked ahead, so I was paired with Estrella, who gave me a perfect opening for a bit of sleuthing. She asked how I was feeling after my accident yesterday, and I replied that I was still in pain. Then I asked if she had seen it, and she replied that she had indeed. She had been one person away from Professor Childeric and seen him lurch forward into me.

My heart rate increased as I realized that had Ivan been standing with her, he might well have shoved Childeric into me, hoping to frighten or kill me while Childeric took the blame. My next question was critical. "Was Ivan with you? I wonder if either of you noticed who was behind Professor Childeric."

Estrella looked thoughtful. "Ivan must have been with Hugh or Jason. He *will* become involved in those scientific conversations." She smiled indulgently. "And I didn't notice anyone else. I assumed at the time that Professor

Childeric tripped. He must be quite a clumsy person. Didn't I hear that he tripped at the airport, too?"

"Yes, Chris and I rescued him. You didn't see that one, I take it?"

"No, Ivan was getting the luggage while I looked for the tour representative."

"Did he see anyone push Professor Childeric?"

"I think he'd have mentioned it if he had, Carolyn. Isn't it strange that he insists on being called Professor? The rest of us are on a first-name basis by now, but he . . ." While I remembered, with a shudder, the professor imploring me to call him Jean-Claude, Estrella chatted on, saying that she preferred to be called Dr. or Mrs. I decided that I'd have to ask Jason and Hugh if Ivan had been with them when I was shoved in front of the bicycle. I soon found out that Jason hadn't been with either of them. I'd talk to Hugh next, although, of course, Childeric would say that it was Hugh who had pushed him.

We caught up with Hugh and Robbie several streets over. Ivan and Estrella had wandered off, so I could ask more questions without revealing that I was thinking of Ivan as the culprit in my injury. Since Hugh immediately fell into conversation with Jason, I asked Robbie first. She told me that Hugh had been with her when I was hurt, that she hadn't seen anyone push Childeric, and that she doubted anyone *had* pushed him. Then she added that, considering the things Childeric had said to her when she was trying to save him from pesticide poisoning at Giverny, she'd have been happy to give the man a push herself. However, she'd have made sure no one was in front of him, unless it was a horse doing its business, in which case she'd have pushed Childeric into the horse dung.

"There weren't any horses," I remarked. "Was Ivan with you and Hugh?"

"No."

"Was he near Childeric?"

"Actually, from where I stood, I couldn't see Childeric. And I didn't see Ivan either. Surely you're not thinking Ivan—"

"Oh, I'm just trying to find someone who might have seen Childeric pushed."

"Mark my words," said Robbie. "That man is a mean person. He probably pushed you because you were dodging him yesterday. You were, weren't you?"

"Well, I did promise Jason—"

"Good. Stay away from him. We'll all stay away from him. Serve him right." Then she spotted a jewelry shop and dragged Hugh in.

Could Robbie be right? I wondered. Would Childeric have given me a push in a fit of pique because I'd stopped providing him with an attentive audience? Was his visit to my room a last desperate attempt to prove to himself that I was, in fact, infatuated? If so, how could I explain the other attacks? Before Chris and I rescued him at the luggage carousel, he'd just met me. And he certainly couldn't have pushed the pot over on me because he'd been beside me. And whom could he have talked into doing it for him?

Back to Ivan. I still hadn't accounted for his whereabouts when I met with grief yesterday. More questions were needed.

21
Honfleur, Sailor's Delight

Carolyn

There were also delightful boutiques in Honfleur, which I had reason to visit that morning under less pleasant circumstances. We made the mistake of heading back toward the harbor to admire the boats. "Are you two still plotting an attack on mad cow disease?" I called ahead to Jason and Hugh. Jason replied that they were discussing which team had the best chance to win the NBA championship.

Hugh added, "I say the Lakers, but Jason—"

"Hugh's absolutely right," said Robbie and hustled ahead to take my husband's arm. I heard her suggesting a little bet as Hugh fell back to walk with me.

Time to see what I could find out about the attack on me. Not that I was interested in clearing the detestable Professor Childeric, but I did want to know who was responsible. First, I asked what Hugh had seen when the bicycle hit me, and he replied that he'd seen Childeric push me. "Gave you quite a whack with his good hand."

"You didn't see anyone push him?"

"I did not," said Hugh.

"Could you see behind him?"

"I didn't need to. I don't believe that nonsense about someone pushing him, any more than you should believe it when he says I pushed him. The man's paranoid, but that's no reason to take it out on you just because you and Jason are my friends."

There was a new motive. I suppressed a sigh and tried one more time. "Did you by any chance see Ivan when it happened?"

"Christ! Is he saying Ivan pushed him because Ivan's a friend of mine?"

"No, no, Hugh. I'm just trying to figure where people were when it happened, in case someone really did push him. If Ivan was closer, he might have seen something."

"So ask Ivan."

Hugh was getting irritated, so I changed the subject by inquiring after his children. He told me that his teenaged son didn't seem to be recovering from the death of his mother, that in fact, Sam's grades had dropped, and he was having a problem with what the school counselor called "anger management." "I guess that means he's pissed off all the time at school. He sure is at home." Looking woebegone, Hugh added, "God, I wish June were alive. She'd know what to do with him. But then if she were alive, he probably wouldn't be acting the way he is. He even seems to resent his sister and me, like we're getting over Bebe's death too fast."

"Maybe he needs grief therapy, Hugh," I suggested. Jason and Robbie had disappeared into a crowd at the wharf, where a boat was pulling in with much shouting of sailors, a scruffy-looking lot, in my opinion. All of them needed a shave. Or maybe they were espousing the popular unshaven look. Thank goodness Chris hasn't been tempted to go around looking mangy, and Jason's beard is always neatly clipped and, in my opinion, very attractive.

"What's grief therapy?" Hugh asked. "I'm ready to try anything."

"Well, you could send him to a therapist, or even get him into a group of young people who've lost loved ones. They meet with a therapist and—"

A shriek, a splash, and louder shouting interrupted my impromptu counseling session. According to people at the very edge of the crowd, Robbie had just fallen into the harbor. Neither Hugh nor I was close enough when she went in to see for ourselves. I could only hope Jason had been there. Hugh was muttering, "That damn Childeric," as he pushed his way forward with me following at his heels until I could see the water but not my friend.

The rain falling on my umbrella was cold (some of it had seeped down my neck during our walk to the wharf), and I'm sure the harbor water was even colder. It seemed to take forever for Robbie to surface, and I was terrified, remembering the horror of just such an event in my own recent past. Then she emerged between the two boats and, swimming powerfully, headed away from the quai, much to everyone's shock. We thought she must be disoriented and shouted for her to turn around, while Denis wrung his hands over yet another incident on his watch. As people milled about debating rescue options, Jason grabbed a life preserver and called to her. Since she didn't turn, he couldn't fling it out. Sailors on fishing boats to either side flourished life jackets and preservers and shouted advice in French, but still Robbie continued to swim, passing the end of the boat on her right.

More quick-witted and boat-oriented, Hugh saw what she was doing and ran down the wharf, from which he jumped off into a rowboat beside the fishing vessel that Robbie had circled. While he cut the dory loose from its mother boat and took up the oars, the sailors' shouts increased in volume. I presume they thought he was stealing their rowboat. Police arrived, and the tumult increased, added to by townsfolk and other tourists crowding in to witness the excitement. Gathering my wits, reasoning that Robbie wouldn't have jumped, I tried to memorize the names of those in the immediate area: the Macauleys, the

Foxcrofts, and the Markarovs. They were the people nearest Jason.

Meanwhile Robbie swam past the end of a second boat, heading for the bow, or whatever, of the next. Hugh shouted to her. Him, she heard, for she turned her head at the last moment, reversed directions, and began to swim toward him as he rowed toward her. In less than a minute she was scrambling into the rowboat, her soaked clothes clinging fetchingly to her generous curves. Ingrid Jensen called out that someone should throw a blanket over Robbie. I'm not sure whether Ingrid was offended by the wet-clothing-on-voluptuous-woman display or afraid that Robbie would catch cold.

Robbie took up oars, and the two of them rowed back toward the wharf. The sailors, who had previously excoriated Hugh for stealing their dory, were now whistling and grinning and staring at Robbie as they lowered a rope ladder. They cheered her lustily as she climbed aboard, followed by Hugh, whom they pretty much ignored.

Within moments our friends had jumped ashore from the fishing boat. The mishap ended safely, thank God, but still someone had again been pushed into danger, the perpetrator unknown. Robbie verified that such was the case, although she denied being in danger. She and Hugh hadn't enough words of praise for each other, he for her "great crawl" and rowing, she for his quick-witted rescue, not that she needed it; there was a ladder up to the wharf several boats down, and she had been heading for that.

Ingrid may have called for a blanket, but Grace Unsell was the person who actually, with the help of Laura de Sorentino translating, borrowed one from a French woman in the crowd.

"Now I'll have to go out and buy a new outfit from the skin out and the toes up," said Robbie gaily. "I can't run around all day in wet clothes, or even this nice French lady's blanket. *Merci, madame,*" she said, smiling, to the

French grandmother, who had been chatting with Grace after fetching the blanket. "Anyone seen a good boutique?"

"Oh, I saw a terrific place two streets over," said Hester, a person who peered into every window, no doubt looking for objects that would inspire a scary glass sculpture. Ultimately, there were four of us who visited the boutique: Robbie, Hester, myself, and the French grandmother, who wanted her blanket back.

22
Revelations in a Dressing Room

Carolyn

The proprietress of the boutique looked quite distressed when Robbie, dripping on the carpet, led our little group in. However, when my friend announced that she needed a whole new outfit, the lady placed her on a chair and offered various selections. Then they disappeared into a dressing room, the proprietress carrying an armload of Robbie's choices and a pressed linen towel so that my friend could dry off before trying on clothes. Finally the lady returned the soggy blanket to the French grandmother with ten dollars in francs for its rehabilitation and Robbie's thanks.

I, in the meantime, browsed the store's offerings and chose for myself a beautiful art deco hair clip, copied, according to the owner, from a Lalique brooch. It was so pretty that Jason didn't even ask the price. Having made my purchase and realized that Robbie hadn't reappeared after ten minutes or more, I became worried and hunted her down in a dressing room. There I found her sitting on a stool shivering.

"Oh, Robbie, you've caught cold. Let me help you out of those wet clothes," I offered.

"I caught a fright," she replied in a trembling voice. "Whoever pushed me wanted to make damn sure I didn't manage to keep my balance and stay dry."

I sat down on the carpet in front of her and took both her hands in mine. "And here I thought you were enjoying the whole thing. That was quite an act you put on out there."

She nodded. "Give me a minute, and I'll get back into the part."

"This tour is becoming a lot too scary for my taste," I said.

"Yeah, tell me about it. Can't believe what happened to you yesterday. And what the hell could anyone have against the two of us? You think it's Childeric?"

"I don't know, but I won't be so quick to defend him from now on. He came to my room yesterday afternoon before Jason got back and made a pass at me."

"You're kidding!" My friend stopped looking shaken and said, "Tell all."

After I had described the scene, she exclaimed, "That lecherous old bastard! Man, I wish I hadn't saved his hide at Giverny. If I'd left that stuff on him, maybe his skin would have peeled off." Her eyes were narrowed angrily. "What shall we do to him?"

"For now, you should get out of those clothes, dry off, and find something to buy."

"Right. And then we'll get even." She jumped off the stool, stripped down with my help—wet clothes aren't easy to remove—dried off with the linen towel, and in less than five minutes had chosen tight moss green pants with matching boots and a high-collared blouse whose first button was fastened right in the middle of her cleavage. "Don't tell Hugh I was such a weenie," she murmured as we left the dressing room.

I suppose fellow kayakers want to be thought of as fearless. "I won't tell Hugh if you don't tell Jason about Childeric."

"Deal. We'll take care of the old fart ourselves."

I shuddered to think of what she might have in mind.

Hugh was bowled over by the newly outfitted Robbie, but by then she could have left the store wearing a burlap monk's robe, and he'd have been impressed. Hester bought a black dress that clung to her from ears to ankles. It had a slit on one side to the hip and crisscrossed ribbons in back to hold the bodice in place. She skipped out into the street where the men were drinking cassis with the Drummonds under a café umbrella and modeled it for Jeremy, who stammered, "Won't you catch cold?"

"I never catch cold as long as my neck is warm," she replied solemnly.

That was a theory I'd never heard. With her whole back and one leg exposed, she certainly wasn't following the keep-your-head-covered-and-the-trunk-of-your-body-layered-on-cold-days school of thought.

"And think how much my mother will hate it," Hester added. Jeremy nodded, evidently seeing benefit in that proposed poke to the maternal eye. Hester turned to me and explained, "My mother thinks my clothes are dreadful. She's of the Boston school that goes out and buys something expensive but dowdy and then lets it sit in her closet for three years, just to be sure she can't be accused of being fashionable."

I had to laugh. After my mother's death, my father had been friendly for a few years with a lady professor of that ilk. She specialized in Anglo-Saxon literature and linguistics. I'm happy to say he never married her, and she moved to the Pacific Northwest. However, before she left, she was in the habit of inviting us over for boiled New England dinners, which were quite dreadful. I'm sure she would have disapproved of French food, but I doubt that she ever ate any. On the other hand, she might have liked the food provided by the tour.

Macauley shouted with laughter at the remarks on catching cold and her mother's taste in clothes and told Hester that she looked delectable. His wife Nedda didn't seem to appreciate the compliment, Hester blushed, and Jeremy gave Drummond a blank look, as if he wasn't sure what was meant by that remark or who the fellow was who had made it. Nonetheless, Jeremy allowed himself and Hester to be whisked away by the Drummonds. I noticed as they departed that Jeremy found himself paired with Nedda. Hester was back in her gaily-colored gypsy togs and listening to Macauley.

Robbie had also purchased a dashing lined cloak and looked the picture of fashion as we made our way to lunch. We hadn't been invited to join the Drummonds—their loss, because we found a delightful second-floor café whose upstairs dining room overlooked the harbor. What could be more wonderful? The company of two good friends, a cozy table by a window with a charming view, and a large crab with a salmon pink shell and flesh so tender and sweet that one didn't really need anything to dip it in. Which is not to say that I resisted the horseradish mayonnaise that came with the crab. The French have a way with mayonnaise. You can buy the most expensive mayonnaise in the States or you can make your own, but it will never match the richness of French mayonnaise.

We even saw a hint of blue sky as we ate. Of course, now that we were inside a dry, warm café, the rain had stopped, leaving the patterned stones that paved the streets glistening. What period was it, I wonder, when towns took the time and money to have their streets paved in, say, intersecting arcs, one of the designs I've seen in Europe? At home we look underfoot (or under tire) only when the pot-holes catch our attention.

"I'll bet Childeric pushed you," said Hugh. "Did he? He's probably getting back at me because he thinks I'm harassing him."

"I wouldn't put it past him," said Robbie.

Hugh and Jason were devouring large bowls of fish soup. "The man's nuts," said Hugh bitterly. "I almost wish I'd never let them put me up for dean."

"Don't even think about dropping out," said Robbie. "I don't want that old bastard to be the dean of my college."

"And I don't want you to be injured," said Hugh seriously.

Robbie laughed. "Sweetie, whoever pushed me in, what good did it do them? I was wet before I got dunked, and then those sweet sailors gave me a cheer when I climbed the rope ladder. I think the whole thing was a hoot."

"But you didn't see who pushed you?" Hugh asked.

"Sorry. The shove came from behind." Robbie was feeding herself and Hugh French fries with hungry gusto.

"Jason?" I asked. "Did you see who pushed her?"

He shrugged. "I was standing beside her. The Markarovs were beside me, so they couldn't have done it."

Did that rule out Ivan? I wondered. And anyway, why would he attack Robbie?

"Hey, don't worry about it, folks," said Robbie. "I'm fine."

"You could have drowned," cried Hugh.

"Not a chance," she replied.

"What if you'd hit your head on the way down and gone in unconscious?"

"Why, you'd have rescued me. Carolyn, pass that mayonnaise, will you? It's delicious on these fantastic fries. Don't tell me you can make stuff like this."

"Not if I can help it," I replied. "I write about food. I don't cook it."

"Alas," added Jason.

"Cheer up, love. You can have the rest of my crab." It really was large enough for two people, and I didn't want to make a pig of myself. I dipped a last French fry in mayonnaise, then pushed the plate across to my eager husband, who can eat two entrées without the least discomfort or weight gain. The fries are as good as the mayonnaise in France, I mused as I chewed. Imagine ordering them with mayonnaise at some hamburger joint in the States. You'd gag.

23
Is Cheese Disease Fatal?

Jason

This tour was a rotten idea. After lunch in Honfleur, which was excellent, both Carolyn's crab and my fish soup and fresh oysters, we realized we had lost track of Chris and Edie, I suppose because we were so shocked by Robbie's mishap at the wharf. We found the kids together in a souvenir store, eating street food, Chris being solicited for opinions on various T-shirts that appealed to Edie. Carolyn was furious with herself for forgetting them. Anna Thomas-Smith looked grim because she had started searching for Edie before we did, and the departure from Honfleur was delayed by their disappearance, innocent as it had been. They could hardly seduce one another at a counter that displayed miniature brass sailing ships and busts of Samuel de Champlain.

And then there was the attack on Robbie—not my favorite woman, but I wouldn't want to see her come to harm. A gaggle of academics being attacked by persons unknown? Extremely unlikely, I would have said. Now Hugh Fauree, who is as calm and rational a man as I've met during my years in science, was accusing a noted, if irritating, medieval scholar of pushing his girlfriend off a pier. Hugh was convinced he'd become involved in an escalating feud over the deanship. Carolyn was still asking people questions about Ivan Markarov, although why she'd think the Russian Mafia had an interest in Robbie was beyond me. And I, on the way to a Calvados distillery, was trying to plot a strategy to protect my wife from Childeric.

Sitting behind me on the bus, Estrella Markarov provided counterpoint to my thoughts by telling one and all about Saint Teresa of Lisieux, some poor child who received so much indoctrination from her parents that she went to Rome to badger the Pope for permission to enter the local convent. The girl took vows at fifteen, lived eleven more years, wrote an autobiography, and specialized in small duties and miracles. All this information was offered because Estrella wanted to visit the saint's basilica and Denis insisted that the tour called for stops at a cheese factory and a Calvados distillery.

Denis won, and poor Ivan was left to comfort his drearily devout wife. I couldn't imagine what he saw in her. Meanwhile, Carolyn, although not asleep, was unusually uncommunicative. Maybe she was still fretting over her failure to keep tabs on Edie and Chris. As for Childeric, I didn't have to worry about him that afternoon. While we were having lunch, he, having received no invitations to dine, informed Denis that he couldn't be bothered with distilleries and cheese factories; he'd find something more interesting to do and rejoin the group in Caen that evening. When Estrella suggested that she join him for a visit to

Saint Teresa's basilica, he refused; it was evidently too modern for his taste.

The Calvados distillery was actually fairly interesting, huge and smaller wooden vats banded with iron, a good explanation of the distillation process, and an amazingly primitive apple press in their museum. The size of a wooden screw incorporated in the apparatus was mind-boggling. Carolyn perked up and commented on the intriguing, musty smell of fermenting apples that pervaded the barnlike structure. Then we had a Calvados tasting. My wife tried all varieties and went back for seconds, which explained her long silences on the bus. She was in pain and admitted as much when I asked. Robbie provided more Tylenol, and other members of our group, who still blamed him for Carolyn's condition, made unfriendly comments about the absent Childeric. Another day of camaraderie on tour.

We went on to the cheese factory, which proved to be a large dairy farm with lathe and plaster buildings, a boarded-up estate château, and fields full of brown and white splotched cows with pendulous udders. Denis led us into a barn, where we watched from overhead as the cows jostled one another to get to the milking machines. It was a mildly entertaining exhibition, especially when one cow got its head stuck under the rails that separated its stall from the next. It shifted about uncomfortably, or so it seemed to me, the neighboring cow paid no attention whatever to the head protruding into its space, and Jensen speculated that mad cow disease might have infected the herd.

His remark was not well received. The company representative, who understood enough English to translate *mad cow disease,* became agitated. His exclamations in French resulted in an outcry among the employees supervising the mechanized milking operation, the gist of their remarks evidently being that there was no mad cow disease in their herd, nor in any cows of the Calvados district.

Before Jensen could get a conversation going with fellow bovine experts, Unsell approached the dairy representative and asked how the epidemic was affecting their business and that of French dairymen in general. Unpleasant remarks were made about Americans, and general ill will prevailed as we trailed after our flustered guide toward the cheese-making building. Evidently word of the American faux pas had spread there as well, for the explanation of the process was brusque.

When finally we attended the much-touted cheese tasting, the final break in international relations occurred. Several ladies refused the cheese samples for fear of contracting "the brain disease." No one could convince them that they would be safe. Edie announced loudly that she wasn't risking any fatal "cheese diseases," not after being exposed by Carolyn to "raw, mad-cow beef" in Paris.

A pretty young server, dressed quaintly as a milkmaid, burst into tears, and an older woman, possibly her mother, scolded Edie. Whatever she said, it must have been unpleasant because neither Denis nor Laura de Sorentino would translate. Unsell told his wife not to be a fool and to eat the "damn cheese."

"And have my grandchild catch some dangerous disease from me?" Grace demanded. "You eat my share if you think it's so safe, Manfred. Then you can stay away from our grandchild, just as you're ignoring her pregnant mother."

"Actually, Grace, the cheese isn't that good," whispered my wife. She had exhibited complete indifference to Edie's glares and complaints, inspired, no doubt, by the fact that Edie had not been allowed to sit with Chris after their Honfleur escapade. When offered cheese, Carolyn had shrugged, murmured "What the hell," and helped herself to four or five samples.

I assume that her uncharacteristic language devolved

from her generous sampling of the Calvados at our last stop. She'd certainly been circulating through the group, both here and in the milking barn, asking questions about who'd seen what when she went down in front of the bicycle and Robbie into the harbor.

When she got to the Drummonds, Macauley asked loudly, "Are you suggesting that I was responsible for your injuries yesterday, Carolyn? Getting a bit paranoid, are we? Maybe you and your friend Robbie just fell."

"We did not," Carolyn snapped. "We were pushed."

"Then don't let your medieval fetish convince you that the eminent Professor Childeric wasn't responsible."

Carolyn flushed, Drummond looked pleased with himself, and various members of the tour group treated my wife as if she'd accused each one of a crime.

I hurried to her side as she was popping another piece of cheese into her mouth. "Are you all right?" I asked solicitously.

"Of course, I'm all right," she retorted. "I just happen to prefer Brie."

French Bruschetta

I had the most delicious and astounding bruschetta at a restaurant in the Caribbean. One expects to find garlic and tomatoes on a bit of toasty bread when ordering bruschetta, and it's usually very good. This bruschetta consisted of two narrow ovals of sliced, toasted bread, perhaps six inches long. On the toast were bits of ripe tomato, spread with a creamy avocado paste, rather salty and flavored with garlic, and topped by a thin slice of Brie. The whole must have been run rapidly under the broiler because the Brie was soft—slightly melted, in fact—and just a bit browned at the edges.

The dish is wonderful and easy to make at home, in a

*smaller size as an hors d'oeuvre or, as it was served to me,
as a first course. What combination could be nicer? I do
love Brie and adore avocados. Even though the dish was
made by a Bahamian chef in a former English colony, this
recipe is a sort of French bruschetta, which, believe me,
is better than the French lasagna I had in Paris. It just goes
to prove that cuisine has become a truly international art.*

Carolyn Blue, "Have Fork Will Travel,"
Oklahoma City Plains Courant

24
Terrible Turkey

Peacock was a favorite meat during the Middle Ages,
goodness knows why. The author of a cookbook in
1420, Chiquart Amicco, advised overcoming the
toughness of peacock by boiling, larding, and roasting.
After that, he suggested slicing the cooked peacock
meat and allowing it to stand around for one or two
months, then scraping off the mold before serving. His
alternate suggestion was that the chef throw out the
peacock, keep the plumage, and use it to dress a roast
goose. Did gourmet noblemen realize that they were
eating meat from which mold had been removed?
When turkey was discovered in the New World and
brought back, peacock began to be supplanted. After
so many years, one would have expected the French
to come up with wonderful recipes for turkey.

However, while traveling in Normandy, I had the
worst turkey dinner imaginable. It featured the usual
things: turkey, dressing, gravy, and so forth, but it was
overcooked and thoroughly disappointing. Now, why

would a restaurant in France, a country noted for its wonderful food, serve such a meal? Were they trying to please American tourists by re-creating Thanksgiving in Caen? It was April when our tour group visited that city, not November. Or maybe the meal was meant to illustrate that our national cuisine leaves something to be desired. If so, I'd have preferred that they treat us to some marvelous turkey recipe that put traditional American holiday fare in the shade.

Such recipes are to be had, even in America. My mother had one that an aunt had clipped from the old *New York Herald Tribune*. It featured an exotic dressing of fruits, meats, and an expensive array of herbs and spices, not to mention searing the turkey in mustard paste and then basting it with cider. That recipe would be perfect for Normans, who are so proud of their apples and cider production. Maybe that turkey was a sort of culinary joke. If so, no one in our group was amused.

Carolyn Blue, "Have Fork, Will Travel,"
Naperville Voice

Carolyn

By the time we finished our dinner in Caen, our destination for day six, I had begun to see our group as a society in miniature on the very edge of disintegration. People were getting hurt, or at least being attacked. Robbie hadn't actually been injured, but I had—twice. Now I had not only the healing cuts from pot shards but also my bruises, aches, and pains, which had, happily, abated somewhat with another application of Calvados and acetaminophen. If I don't watch out, Jason is going to think me in danger of falling into alcoholism.

France, by the way, has quite a high alcoholism rate: five million heavy drinkers, two million alcoholics, and seventeen quarts of pure alcohol consumed per year per person. Gracious! In France, they sell wine at highway service stations; remember that if you're driving on their highways. And really keep your eyes open in Paris; in 1979 the police stopped administering Breathalyzer tests because restaurants protested that the practice was hurting business, not surprising in a department that was founded to protect citizens going out to dinner. But I digress from my sociological analysis of our group.

In our little society, acquaintances and colleagues were accusing one another of plots and violence, husbands and wives were snarling at each other, and there was a shunning movement afoot against Childeric. Not that I didn't think he deserved it. Being around him both scared me because of my injuries and embarrassed me when I remembered his awful assumptions when he visited my room. Jason absolutely insisted that I avoid Childeric at all costs, and I was happy to do so.

At dinner in the tour-chosen restaurant, Jason accomplished that very neatly. We were to sit in two large, four-sided wooden booths. These booths had only a small opening on one end through which the dinner guest could slide. All that scooting while seated was awkward, and if one was seated in the middle and wanted to visit the facilities, five people had to wrestle themselves out. Jason quickly directed traffic so that our booth contained the kids, separated; Hugh and Robbie; Ivan and Estrella; Jeremy and Hester (although Jeremy arranged their inclusion, to keep Hester away from the Drummonds, I think); and Janice Petar. Childeric had to sit with the Jensens, Unsells, Drummonds, de Sorentinos, and Anna, who looked quite unhappy about her companions.

I suppose she'd have preferred to sit with Janice, but since Janice disliked Childeric, it was probably for the

best. At least, the arrangement gave Anna a respite from
Edie. I would have liked one, too, but felt I had to keep an
eye on her. We could have sent Chris to the other table so
that Janice could sit with Anna, but then Chris probably
needed the respite from Childeric. Both of them had complained about the other to me. I was so incensed with
Childeric that I pretended I didn't hear him. Oh, it was so
complicated!

Anyway, some of the unfortunate things that happened
as a result of Jason's seating arrangements were the alter-
cations that ensued when Childeric wanted to find someone to share a bottle of wine with him. Unsell refused,
against Grace's wishes, because he wanted a whole bottle
to himself. The Jensens refused because they don't drink.
The Drummonds refused because Nedda announced that
they were over their budget and could only afford single
glasses, which infuriated Macauley. He said she could skip
wine, and he'd share with Childeric. Nedda retorted that
she had as much right to her glass of wine as he. I gather
they didn't speak to one another again that evening. But
the worst refusal came from Lorenzo de Sorentino, after
Laura generously offered to skip wine so Lorenzo and
Childeric could share.

Lorenzo said, "If you're capable of pushing the girlfriend of one rival into the harbor, Childeric, you're capable of poisoning my wine because my wife is up for that
job you obviously covet, out of all reason. After all, it's
just a deanship. Who the hell cares about something that
unimportant?"

Oh, my. Childeric was apoplectic. He shouted, loudly
enough to be heard in our booth, that he had not pushed
Robbie Hecht into the water.

Robbie muttered, "Much good it did you, you dirty old
man."

Oh lord, I thought. *She's going to tell everyone what*

happened. I sneaked a glance at Childeric, but he hadn't heard, and Robbie said nothing more, thank goodness.

Hugh murmured to Jason, "That man should be drummed out of the university. He's a menace!"

Childeric then, in what I considered an astonishing show of hypocrisy, gave a resounding peroration on the importance of deans and the necessity that they be eminent scholars and men of impeccable behavior. He mentioned the latter qualification while staring vindictively across the booth wall at Robbie and Hugh. Robbie gave him such a steely look that his eyes dropped and he flushed after glancing at me. However, Janice was the one who replied.

"Deans have to be men? Is that what you said, Childeric? Why not women? And any demand for impeccable behavior eliminates you, at least in my view."

Had Robbie told my story to Janice? Janice might well launch a feminist offensive on my behalf. Before she could say anything else, Laura tried to practice her peace-making talents, and Childeric told her brusquely that he didn't need any support from a rival candidate for dean, who, on the basis of recent attacks on his person, evidently did not wish him well. Then he harassed the waitress, a young girl who must have been new to her job. She did get the orders mixed up, and she brought him the wrong wine, and later she charged him for a bottle instead of two glasses. Each time he shouted at her, she became more incoherent, and the manager had to be called to adjudicate. It was a complete disintegration of civility. I imagine we would have been ejected from the restaurant if it weren't for Denis and the management's desire to secure returning tour business.

Of course, the dinner was practically inedible. Well, the salmon mousse with creamed lemon dill sauce was fair, the sauce a bit bland but the mousse quite good. While eating it, I had hopes that the next course would be acceptable. It wasn't. Turkey. The only thing that can be said for it is that it was probably better than peacock, its once popular pre-

decessor, which was evidently dreadful in every respect
but the feathers, which were put back on before serving.
Edie wouldn't eat her turkey, I left most of mine as did
Grace, but Hester, Robbie, and the men scarfed it down
with minor complaints.

There was a dessert buffet at which I hoped to make up
for missing the entrée, but we were slow getting there because it was so hard to exit the booths and I had to ma-
neuver to avoid Childeric. Why couldn't he have skipped
dinner as well as the Calvados and cheese tours? Surely, he
was embarrassed after his overtures to me.

The buffet, when I managed to reach it, had some
promising offerings, chocolate mousse, for instance. On
the other hand, the tarts were disgusting. Soggy pastry and
gelatinous fruit filling. Perhaps they had been made in the
morning, then overheated in a microwave, and finally left
to decompose on the table. I'm sure any Frenchwoman
who cooks or just likes good food would back me up about
that dinner. I'm not a Francophobe. I love French cooking,
but I intend to send a complaint to the tour company.

25
Warfare: Modern or Medieval?

Jason

When Carolyn and I returned to our room in Caen after
that contentious dinner (frankly, I thought Childeric was
losing it), we had a largely fruitless discussion of who
could have pushed Robbie off the wharf at Honfleur.

"Why Robbie?" Carolyn asked. "Why would anyone

push her into the water? A boat propeller could have started up and cut her to pieces. Or one of the boats could have heeled over and hit her. It was a dangerous thing to do."

In reply I put my arms comfortingly around her. At least I hoped it was a comfort. "Are you still aching?"

"Some," she replied. "Janice Petar was really snippy yesterday at lunch when Robbie wanted to switch rooms around so she and Hugh could share. You don't think Janice—well, was she near Robbie on the wharf?"

"I don't know, but my candidate would be Childeric," I replied. "He was furious when she doused him with water at Giverny. Maybe he wanted to do the same to her."

"Sometimes I think people are being attacked at random. And we don't know why."

"Childeric seems to be the only link. The most we can do is avoid him and keep our eyes open."

"Well, that's another thing. Tomorrow we have the choice of a half-day at the Normandy beaches and a half-day at Bayeux or a whole day at Bayeux. I imagine you and Chris will want to visit the beaches."

"I would like to see the invasion sites. My great-uncle died on—"

"Exactly, and I don't like those war sites, especially the modern ones, but I'd love to spend the day at Bayeux."

"I know, but Childeric—"

"Will be sure to choose Bayeux." She shuddered.

Although I hate to see Carolyn upset, I was relieved that she was taking seriously the danger inherent in associating with Childeric.

"Another problem is Chris and Edie. We should try to keep them apart. If they're on the same tour, even both of us—well, look what happened yesterday. Not that I blame Chris. She plucked him off the street, dragged him into a shop, and they had lost the others entirely by the time he managed to get back outside. She's a . . . a minx."

Clue List

Day	Place	Victim	Injury	Means
6	Honfleur	Robbie	fell in harbor	push

I had to laugh. "Aren't you ashamed for calling Judith Atwater's daughter a—"

"Not at all," Carolyn retorted. "I suppose I'll have to take Edie to Bayeux while you take Chris to the invasion beaches."

"But you're too soft-hearted to brush Childeric off," I protested.

"No, Jason, I'm not," she said.

"Admit it. You feel half sorry for the man, even though he pushed you into that bicycle's path."

"Whatever happened, I'm staying away from him," said my wife. "In fact, I'm going to enlist Anna to stick with Edie and me. She doesn't think much of him, and the two of us should be able to keep Edie in line."

"Anna's not going to agree to spend the day with you if it means Edie tagging along," I protested.

"Oh yes, she will." Carolyn seemed surprisingly sure of that. "In fact, I think I'll go talk to Anna right now."

"By yourself?" I didn't like the idea of Carolyn wandering around the hotel on her own, especially with everyone in such a nasty mood. "Call her. You don't want to broach this proposal with Edie listening, do you?"

Evidently Anna was sympathetic to the problem, once Carolyn had explained it, and agreed readily to join her in minding Edie and fending off Jean-Claude Childeric.

"She's a nice woman!" Carolyn said with satisfaction as she hung up. "By the way, she said I was very lucky to have such a protective husband. Which I am." Carolyn sat

Clue List

Present	Suspect(s)	Motive
everyone	Childeric	revenge
	Janice	affair with H.

up to give me a kiss. Too bad she was in no shape for anything more intimate.

Carolyn

Once Jason had plastered me with horse liniment, he went to sleep. I got up, wrote a column, and printed it out. I now have a small travel printer, which adds considerably to the weight of our luggage but makes Paul Fallon in New York happy; he doesn't like to receive faxes of handwritten columns. Having finished that chore, I pulled up my clue list and entered Robbie's mishap.

I looked over my list of suspects and couldn't see that Ivan would have any reason to attack Robbie, not if I was his target. And Hugh certainly hadn't, although Childeric had accused him of other attacks. Edie didn't seem a likely candidate; she seemed to approve of Robbie's affair with Hugh. I didn't think the de Sorentinos were a likely choice even if Childeric had once accused them of attacking him. That left Childeric, a target himself, Janice, or persons unknown. I shivered to think of the horrible things that could have happened to my friend while she was swimming to safety in that harbor full of boats. Then I shivered, remembering Childeric's visit to my room.

Anna, bless her, hadn't hesitated a moment to offer her assistance tomorrow. She hadn't even grumbled about Edie, although she had said that it would seem I hadn't told Jason about Childeric. Of course, I hadn't. We didn't need any additional anger erupting on this tour, and Jason would not be happy to hear about unwanted advances to his wife. No, I wouldn't tell Jason unless I had to, but I would have to figure out why these things were happening. The violence, not the amorous attack.

If there really was an administration spy on the tour and I knew who, I'd certainly be tempted to tell that person about Childeric. He didn't deserve to be dean. He'd probably make sexual advances to the women in the college, if he were appointed. Hints from Janice indicated that he'd done such things before, although she had never been specific. Surely, he hadn't tried anything with her! What a thought! She'd never have let it go the way I was doing. In fact, she'd be ashamed of me. On that thought I went to bed and slept badly, even though the liniment had eased my pain considerably.

Travel Journal
Day Six, Honfleur, Calvados, Caen

  Shoving Roberta Hecht into the water didn't help much. It certainly didn't frighten her into leaving the tour. Instead she swam around with her nipples showing through her wet shirt.
  Who'd have thought she could swim like that? Or row? Damn. She came out looking like a hero. Fauree's even more infatuated. Stupid fellow. Talking about dropping out of the race to keep his girlfriend safe. Can't have that. The fool will never be dean if he keeps sniffing after her.
  But people think C. pushed her in. And he made a complete jackass of himself at dinner. Treated everyone badly. So I'm getting to him. And he's alienating the rest. Good.
  I hope there is a spy from the selection committee with the tour. Someone to see what a bastard he is and report back.
  An entertaining dinner. Bad food, though. What did they do to the turkey?
  Blue won't let his wife near C. He can tell that C. wants to

*seduce her. And Carolyn's finally stopped feeling sorry for C.
Small wonder. She's still limping after his attentions.*

*De Sorentino. There's another woman who needs to
toughen up. She'll blow her chance at the position if she keeps
trying to intervene on C.'s behalf. Doesn't she see that a user
like C. doesn't deserve kindness?*

*Calvados tastes like fuel oil. And the cheese. I thought tast-
ings were supposed to be tasty.*

Only smart thing C.'s done is skip the afternoon.

But there's always tomorrow. I'll get him.

26
One-Upping a Philanderer

In 1809 white mushrooms were being cultivated in
quarry tunnels outside Paris. Perhaps the people who
now grow mushrooms in the multimillion-dollar tunnels originally built for a massive physics project in
Texas got the idea from the French. However, I don't
think the French taxpayer had to finance the mushroom tunnels. Does anyone know how much the
Texas mushrooms would cost per pound if the con-
gressional expenditure on tunnels was factored in?

An English botanist in the late sixteenth century
said of mushrooms ". . . fewe of them are good to be
eaten and most of them do suffocate and strangle the
eater." I like mushrooms myself, especially in an
omelet or buckwheat galette.

Carolyn Blue, "Have Fork, Will Travel,"
Evanston Observer

Carolyn

Laura told me to try the buckwheat galettes, one of the delights of Normandy and particularly good in Bayeux, so at lunch I ordered the Gruyère and champignon variety (that's cheese and mushroom for non–French speakers). They were wonderful. The galette is a very thin, crispy-around-the-edges, nonsweet crepe sort of thing made of buckwheat instead of white flour. Gruyère is a mild cheese that melts nicely, and mushrooms need no explanation.

We'd had a fine morning in Bayeux, even considering the rain. The seventy-six-yard tapestry tells the story of Harold of England and William of Normandy, whose battle at Hastings changed the history of England for all time. Happily, there is a complete English translation of the French signs beneath the display to explain every panel.

Actually, it's not a tapestry at all, but a crudely embroidered story, wool yarn on linen, and it wasn't embroidered by William's queen, as Denis had told us on the bus before he went off to the beaches of Normandy with the others. William's half-brother, the Bishop of Bayeux, commissioned the Bayeux tapestry. This from Professor Childeric, who spoke very loudly because no one was talking to him. I found it particularly interesting to see that piece of history from the French point of view.

After a lovely morning, spent dry and warm under roof, we ventured into the gale and arrived for lunch, pretty much soaked, at a creperie. It was then that Anna showed her mettle. She kept Edie and me from taking chairs until Childeric had been seated, the first person who was. Then she hustled us to another table under the puzzled eye of the waitress. The Drummonds and Foxcrofts sat with us, which left Childeric by himself. Shades of junior high school when cliques took joy in excluding lone students. I hate that sort of thing, but I wasn't going to sit with him myself. I needn't have worried. Before I could do anything to stop it, Edie got up and joined him.

I turned to Anna. "Should we—"

"He can't very well seduce the girl in a creperie under the eye of such a formidable proprietress," Anna murmured.

True. The black-clad woman at the cash register did look terrifying, and surely Childeric wouldn't even want to beguile Edie. "She's young enough to be his granddaughter," I remarked.

Evidently, Anna didn't think the age difference was a safeguard, but she did remark that Edie, being no part of the dean competition, shouldn't be in danger from another "accident." "And he'd be a fool to harm the only person in the group willing to sit with him," she added.

Meanwhile Edie was chattering merrily to Childeric, while casting competitive glances at me. That child was a ninny if she thought I'd be jealous. Such behavior makes one glad to have left the teenage years behind.

Nedda Drummond said to me, "Maybe you can explain, since you like medieval history, why they made Harold out to be the bad guy. After all, William invaded someone else's country, burning down cottages while women and children wept."

The weeping families were embroidered on one of the invasion panels.

"Harold even rescued a bunch of Normans when he was visiting William," Nedda continued. "At least, those are two stories the pictures told."

Professor Childeric heard and took it upon himself to answer. "That tapestry is the story of a broken oath. Harold took a sacred vow to support William's claim to the throne, which he broke when he ascended the throne himself upon the death of Edward the Confessor."

"Harold was tricked into the oath," I objected. "He didn't even know there was a sacred relic hidden—"

"Who cares, anyway?" Drummond interrupted.

"William the Conqueror was a great figure in history," Childeric proclaimed. "Harold was only—"

"—a guy who ended up with an arrow in his eye," Drummond finished.

"Harold might have won at Hastings if he hadn't had to march an exhausted army from a battle with the Vikings to face William," I murmured to Anna, as if she cared. I just couldn't let Childeric have the last word.

"Jeez," said Edie.

"I thought it was cunning—the way you could tell the Normans, who had funny hair, from the English, who had mustaches," Hester offered. "And all their heads were sort of skinny and lopsided."

"Absolutely," Drummond agreed. "And I rather enjoyed William's men rushing out of the coronation and setting fire to nearby houses. Not a very auspicious beginning."

"He was an excellent administrator and a great warrior," said Childeric testily.

"Who made the mistake of setting his sons against each other by dividing his lands between the two eldest, and giving the youngest only money." I just couldn't seem to resist one-upping Childeric.

"It was the custom of the time," said the professor haughtily.

"Too bad they didn't dramatize the story," said Nedda. "I'd teach a play like that, but I really detest those crude, farcical medieval church plays that—"

"Have you even read any of the great drama cycles of the Middle Ages?" Childeric demanded.

"Enough," Anna muttered.

Macauley Drummond, who had been whispering in Hester's ear, turned to Anna and asked, "What, Miss Smith-Thomas? Don't you home economists like academic debate? Too busy clipping recipes and making doilies?"

Reddening with anger, Anna gave him a look that would have cut steel, and I can't say that I blame her. Macauley Drummond had a penchant for gratuitous rudeness. Was he reacting to the stress of dangerous circumstances? I wondered. Or was he simply an unpleasant person?

"That's *Dr.* Thomas-Smith, not Smith-Thomas, and doilies are out of style, *Mr.* Drummond. Furthermore, my research is done in a laboratory, not in a kitchen," she retorted coldly.

And so it went. At least the lunch was tasty, although the cold and damp seemed to exacerbate my aches and pains. How I wished for Robbie and her bottle of Tylenol. I should have bought my own.

27
Watch Out for That Lunch Box

Carolyn

After lunch we wandered, guideless, toward the cathedral, where we were to meet those who had gone to the invasion beaches. Even in the rain, the cobbled streets and stone houses reinforced the atmosphere of ancient times. I particularly liked the old water mill site with flowers blooming in boxes on a stone wall. And the cathedral, originally built by the bishop to hold the tapestry, was an amazing conglomeration of styles and periods and alterations.

The original building, the west towers and the crypt with its rough carving and painted stone, the gorgeous fifteenth-century central tower, delicate with stone tracery but supporting a clumsy nineteenth-century top of the blob-and-spike variety, the Romanesque Norman sculpture of the eleven and twelve hundreds in the nave, Gothic influence in the chancel—I loved it all, took pictures, made notes, then watched with fascination a bit of contemporary byplay as workmen on scaffolding pulled to their high perches large iron pipes. What were the pipes for? Perhaps to drain off the pelting rain.

Later, the men hauled up, for their midday meal, heated pies and lunch boxes heavy enough to hold a four-course dinner. Jeremy, who had been sketching the round, arcaded façade and lawns outside, came in and stood gazing toward the workmen who were feasting above us. He looked wistful, as if he'd like to join them and see the church from their lofty heights.

Then we heard the voices of our party as they entered the church, greetings exchanged, the chatter of compared experience. Jeremy turned to watch them. Above, the workmen began to lower their oversized lunch chests on the ropes. French voices drifted down to us, but we were absorbed with our own group until a hoarse shout pierced my consciousness, if no one else's, certainly not Jeremy's. One of the boxes, descending on its rope, began to rotate as it fell. It swung in a widening, falling arc.

"Jeremy!" My warning came too late. The arc intersected his thigh with a sickening crack, and Jeremy cried out and fell. From all over the cathedral the hum of tourist chatter stilled, and people began to stream toward the ugly sound of injury and pain. I reached Jeremy as quickly as anyone, and the poor man lay on the cathedral stones, blood soaking his trouser leg. He couldn't rise. De Sorentino was called upon to investigate, but he was of lit-

tle use. Jensen, however, pronounced the leg as broken as
any cow's he'd ever seen.

Gendarmes and ambulances arrived, priests offered
prayers, gawkers pressed too close. All of us on the tour
shivered with new apprehension even as we tried to be
helpful to Hester, who was in tears, and Jeremy, who was
gray-white and sweating in an effort not to cry out again in
pain.

While Childeric declared to the police that the attack
had undoubtedly been meant for him, and Laura de
Sorentino told them in perfect French what had happened,
an unfortunate accident, preparations were made to take
Jeremy to a hospital. Soon he, Hester, and Denis were
gone, but not without Denis begging us to take care until
he could return.

"Hit by a lunch box!" Macauley Drummond exclaimed.
"Now there's an embarrassingly mundane injury for you. I
must remember to watch out for such sinister weapons.
Did it have Bugs Bunny painted on it? How did you manage that, Childeric? And what could you possibly have
against someone as innocuous as Foxcroft? Did you think
he was going to jump into the dean's race? Or support
someone else? Who would that be? Well, Laura perhaps.
She's prettier than you and not as alien to the arts as Fauree. And of course, she speaks better French."

Sharp words were exchanged between Drummond and
Childeric, and neither seemed to remember poor Jeremy.

I simply stopped listening because Jason was at my side
by then, encircling me in a protective arm, Chris in tow.
"You all right?" my husband asked.

"Yes, fine," I murmured back. "It wasn't me this time.
But poor Jeremy—did you hear the sound of his leg breaking?"

"Nothing else happened this morning?"

"Isn't that enough? Truly, I'm fine, Jason. And that had

to be a real accident, don't you think? How could anyone plan to hit Jeremy with a lunch box?"

"Well, maybe that's it for today," said Chris.

"Where's Edie?" I had a sudden fear that she had escaped and—but I was wrong. She was hanging on Childeric's arm.

And that was *not* it for the day, as my son had suggested. When we were descending a hill on slick cobblestones, Macauley Drummond slipped, bumping painfully and ignominiously from stone to stone for a good twelve yards. People jumped out of his way. He had to rescue himself, and when he did, he rose, reeling, and screamed up the hill at Childeric, "Don't think I don't know who gave me that shove."

"If you mean me, Drummond, you're quite mistaken," said Childeric with nervous dignity. "I do not—"

"Shove it, you asshole. You did it. And you'll be sorry. People don't screw with me and get away with it. I'll be watching every move you make. I don't need any poufy French police to defend me. I can beat you to a pulp with my bare—"

"For heaven's sake, Macauley," hissed his wife. "I didn't see him—"

"Shut up, Nedda."

"It's slick," she persisted. "You probably fell on—"

"I said, shut up! Don't you understand English?"

Childeric looked pleased at Drummond's redirection of his fury. Nedda turned her back and walked away. And I felt a shudder of apprehension pass through me. *Had* Childeric pushed him? I had been ahead of them and couldn't say. Slipping my hand into Jason's, I leaned against him. "This is . . . is—"

"Surreal," he finished for me.

28
Tripe à la Mode de Caen

Tripe. The light-colored, rubbery lining of the stomach of a cow or other ruminant, used as food. (American Heritage Dictionary)

Doesn't that sound tasty? In El Paso tripe is very popular. Mexican restaurants advertise the days on which they serve menudo, a tripe soup. Sunday is popular because menudo is rumored to cure the hangover from Saturday night festivities. And the use of tripe in Mexican cooking is not a modern taste. Bernal Diaz de Castillo, a Spanish conquistador, mentions tripe as one of many foodstuffs he saw for sale in the market of the Aztec capital. That would have been tripe from wild deer, the only ruminant available at that time and place.

My husband likes menudo, which I, too, have tried. It's made with the less exotic cow tripe, and the broth was delicious, but the tripe? I'd sooner attempt to eat an inner tube.

In Caen, France, the signature dish is Tripe à la Mode de Caen. A culinary tome I read advised that if you have to eat tripe, Caen's is the best. Faint praise, indeed. And with good reason. It's cooked in cider. Even my husband didn't like it, but then maybe the restaurant hadn't done it properly. The sauce was black, which the author said was not a good thing. I quite agree.

Carolyn Blue, "Have Fork, Will Travel,"
Syracuse Star-News

Carolyn

We all ate together at a place suggested by Denis. Possibly we felt there was safety in numbers. Certainly we wanted to hear news of Jeremy as soon as any arrived. I'm embarrassed to say that I encouraged Jason to have the local specialty, tripe, and he agreed readily. Poor man, it was awful. I gave him part of my beef Bourguignon, which is usually a safe choice and was in this instance. Childeric was not along, so we didn't have to make any effort to avoid him. Although he was being blamed for it, he couldn't have been responsible for Jeremy's accident. As for Drummond's ignominious slide downhill and his rude and profane reaction to it, Childeric might have been responsible for that, but Drummond had been so nasty to everyone, who could blame someone for giving him a shove?

Did I say that? Soon I'd be responding to aggravation and fear with violence. Not a happy thought. I like to see myself as more civilized. Indeed, I was beginning to feel that the whole trip was a nightmare for which none of us was to blame. Well, Childeric for pushing his way into my room and making a pass at me, as well as for his ludicrous declarations of affection and insulting assumption that I returned that interest. But enough of that. He'd stayed away from me since then.

Jason, however, brought up a matter that had been bothering me, too: the fact that our son was rooming with Childeric. I might be able to forget, if not forgive, Childeric's advances, or even my injuries in Rouen, especially because I wasn't hurting as much, but when it came to my son—well, I made no protest when Jason voiced his unease.

Chris shrugged. "I can take care of myself even if he is crazy, and believe me, he is. He never stops bitching"— Chris glanced at me guiltily—"complaining," he amended. "When I shave, I leave hair in the sink. I'm rumpled; I ought to iron my clothes. For Pete's sake. I'm living out of a suitcase. If he wants to iron *his* shirts, great. I'm not ironing mine. And he doesn't want me hanging out with Denis because Denis is a moron who doesn't know anything about French history. Like I care. He won't even let me listen to CNN on TV. He says in France, French is the language, so I should listen to French TV. Man, I've had it with him."

That was quite a long speech for Chris, who's not usually a complainer. My opinion of Dr. Childeric dropped even more. If he has children of his own, I feel sorry for them.

"Maybe we can make some other arrangement," Jason offered, although he didn't look very hopeful. Then he obviously had a thought. "If the Foxcrofts have to stay here in Caen or go home because of his leg, perhaps you could—"

"Listen, Dad, Denis has an extra bed in his room, and he says I'm welcome to it."

I looked a question at Jason while Chris said, "I've already told Childeric. He said, 'Good riddance.'"

Good riddance? That dreadful man! My son is a very nice young person. Professor Childeric should be so lucky as to have a son like Chris. "What do you think, Jason?" I asked, prepared to agree.

"It might be better," said my husband.

"I wish *I* could change rooms to someone more fun," said Edie, who was sharing the table with us. "In fact, I'd be more fun than Denis, Chris." She gave him what my grandmother would have called a come-hither look.

"This isn't a joking matter, Edie," I said.

"Who's joking?" she retorted.

"She's just putting you on, Mom."

"Okay," said Edie. "Maybe I'll move in with Professor Childeric."

Anna, who was sitting at the next table, leaned over and tapped Edie on the arm. "You are a shameless girl."

"And you're mean," Edie retorted.

"Edie," I scolded, "your mother would be—"

Anna, chin raised, said, "Carolyn, you really don't need to defend me from Edie. And anything her mother needs to be told, I can certainly do myself."

"Nobody likes a tattletale," said Edie.

Oh, my, I was so tired of angry people. I wanted to let my husband give me a good horse-liniment rubdown and then go to sleep in a quiet room. However, before I could fulfill my wish, I had to deal with Ingrid Jensen back at the hotel. Upon hearing Chris say that he'd go upstairs and move his belongings to Denis's room, she whispered to me, "You're not going to let your son room with that—that Denis, are you?"

"Why not?"

"Because he's a homosexual. I can always spot one. They prey on young boys, you know. Your son—"

"—isn't a young boy," I replied wearily, "and I believe homosexuals prefer to form liaisons with other homosexuals rather than approaching men who aren't of like mind. And furthermore, Ingrid, didn't I hear you telling your husband that you thought Janice and Anna were lovers? You really shouldn't spread rumors. People's feelings and reputations can be hurt."

"Well, I never!" Ingrid looked offended and flounced off.

Jason

We heard from Denis, before going to our room, that Jeremy would be in the hospital overnight, his leg definitely broken and already in a cast. The blood had been from a cut, not a compound fracture, which was good news. However, it occurred to me that the cut, even stitched, would be slow to heal under a cast. Perhaps I'd ask de Sorentino about that tomorrow. He'd been no help when Jeremy needed it, but he should at least be able to answer a question about the dangers of infection. Presumably Jeremy would be going home and Hester with him. Denis hadn't known any more than that Jeremy would be on crutches for some time, perhaps until the leg healed. Carolyn was very upset about his accident but had to agree that it *was* an accident. Neither of us could propose a scenario in which someone arranged for a workman's lunch box to strike a member of our tour group.

As for Drummond's fall, he said, as had others before him, including Carolyn, that he had been pushed, but by whom? Although he had accused Childeric, Carolyn pointed out quite rightly that the novelist seemed bent on offending everyone with whom he came in contact. Childeric was only the latest person he had attacked, but there were others who might have felt an overpowering urge to shove Drummond and had given in to the tenor of the times, as it were.

While I was preparing for bed and puzzling over the day's events, Carolyn was staring morosely at her "Clue List," something she'd started several days earlier in an attempt to track the series of attacks/accidents and come to some conclusion about the perpetrator. Finally, she closed her computer and said, "I can't tell what's happening. It could be anyone, or no one or everyone." Then she rose and said, "I'm going to brush my teeth."

When she returned, she'd had another idea: that someone might have a grudge against the tour company and be pursuing our group with the aim of ruining the company's reputation. "Look at the victims," she pointed out. "Childeric, me, Robbie, Jeremy, Drummond. How could one person have a grudge against all of us? And no one ever spots the person who does it. Maybe that's because it's someone none of us recognizes."

"And why would someone have a grudge against the tour company?" I asked for the sake of argument.

"The meals they provide certainly come to mind," Carolyn replied. "Remember the turkey? That was reason enough for just about any revenge."

"Granted," I replied, unable to suppress a grin. Most people wouldn't consider boring food cause for violence. "So the possibilities are that the tour has simply become a general free-for-all among a group of unpleasant and/or stressed-out people or that one stranger with a grudge against the tour company—"

"Unless it's Denis who's the target!" Carolyn exclaimed. "Remember. He told us to be careful in Rouen because he'd get in trouble if anyone were run down. Oh, Jason," she cried, "Chris is—"

"Denis himself hasn't been attacked. If we're postulating an attempt to get him fired, Chris should be safer in his company than elsewhere."

"Of course. Thank goodness." She gave me a hug. "There are certainly advantages to having someone around with an observant eye and a scientific mind."

"Glad you think so," I replied, "although I'd prefer that you loved me for my body."

"But I do, Jason. Both."

"So how are you feeling tonight?" I asked. "Any interest in—"

"Absolutely," said Carolyn, and slipped under the duvet.

Travel Journal
Day Seven, Bayeux, Caen

Worst piece of crap I've ever seen—that tapestry.

C. got blamed for the lunch box accident. Stupid, because it couldn't have been planned, but just what he deserves, the thief! Stealing my research.

*Then he got blamed for Drummond, while I had the plea-
sure of sending that arrogant piece of shit bumping down the
hill. I remember Mr. Bonheim, the father of a kid who never
got to play, calling my dad, the big football coach, an arrogant piece of shit, which he was.*

*And now C.'s lost his roommate. Let's see how he likes
being absolutely alone. Night after night. Like I've been.*

*Of course, the girl said she'd move in with him. Good idea.
It would ruin him.*

*He ruined me. She ruins him. I wouldn't mind some help in
that direction.*

*Doubt Carolyn would allow Edie to do it. That girl is a slut
in training. And rude.*

*Also, she's a wild card. Uncontrollable. My father would
have said, "Drop her from the team before she screws up an
important game."*

29
"Sweet Doggie"

Jason

On the eighth day of our tour, we left Caen and after a
stop at the World War II Battle Memorial and a cafeteria
lunch, headed for Saint-Malo, a seaport town in Brittany
built on an island of granite and joined to the mainland by
an old causeway.

Our hotel was far enough up a steep roadway to give us
a view of the town ramparts and the sea beginning its rush
toward the shore. Denis later told us that the ferocity and
power of the forty-meter tides were second only to those of

the Bay of Fundy, a rather frightening statistic. On our tour of the town we saw, of course, the cathedral; we admired the towers built by various rulers; we stared at the statue of a pirate/hero; and we walked the ramparts, some sections of which dated back nine centuries. It was a wind-and-water-buffeted place with, according to Denis, who is not always the most reliable source of information, a stirring history of privateers who preyed on British shipping in the seventeenth and eighteenth centuries and of warring nobles in earlier times.

Perhaps the most interesting tale was that of the English mastiffs, huge dogs that were kept penned and hungry until 10 P.M., then let loose to roam the streets attacking curfew breakers. In the morning the dogs were lured back and fed, if they were hungry. It seemed unlikely to me that either strangers or natives of the city would have been foolish enough to break curfew in those times. We were particularly lucky, Denis informed us, because there was actually a mastiff in residence, recently purchased by a history- and profit-minded citizen who kept the dog in his yard and allowed tourists to view the creature for a small fee, which Denis had arranged for the tour to pay.

So all of us crowded into the yard, standing back a respectful distance from the fence that separated Bishop Jean from the rest of the world. The dog was named after Bishop Jean de Chatillon, who, after taking refuge in Saint-Malo from unfriendly Normans, built the walls and cathedral in the twelfth century. Now, I had some notion of what an English mastiff looked like: square, dark, droopy face and powerful, short-furred body. But let me tell you, seeing a picture does not prepare you for this animal. He may not be as tall as a Saint Bernard or a Great Dane, but a full-grown male weighs more, 180 to 220 pounds, and he is very powerfully muscled.

His owner, Monsieur Broussais, a wizened little man wearing a beret and V-necked cardigan sweater, admitted proudly that he could not walk Bishop Jean on a leash unless he used a collar with spikes on the inside. Carolyn looked horrified. The owner, cackling, explained that the dog pulled him right off his feet and over the cobblestones without the proper collar, not that His Excellency was a mean dog, no indeed. He might be leery of strangers, but he was gentle with family and friends who were gentle with him.

Monsieur Broussais then went on to destroy that friend-of-the-family portrait with a history of the breed, which might have been brought to England by Phoenician sailors around 500 B.C. or bred by medieval lords to protect their forests and deer from hungry peasants. The breed had been used as war dogs by Roman armies and later human combatants and would die tearing an enemy apart in order to save their masters. During the Renaissance they participated in the notorious bull and bear baiting entertainments of England, but then what else could one expect of the thrice-damned English? asked the dog's owner rhetorically.

He concluded by assuring the ladies (and he claimed that Bishop Jean did love ladies) that a mastiff made a fine guard dog, was good with children, and in most cases would only clamp his jaws gently on the arm of an intruder or troublesome child. Watch the tail, the owner advised. Down, he's calm. Curved up, he's excited. Not that we'd see him on the streets tonight in either state, for Monsieur Broussais had his dinner at six and went to bed at seven, and Bishop Jean did the same. All this was said to us in a heavy French accent, but we did get the point. As we learned about him, the mastiff sat on his haunches studying us as if he were getting a lecture on humans.

"He looks like a nice enough dog," said Carolyn.

"Especially behind the fence," I replied, noting that when his mouth was closed, his teeth didn't show, which was a point in his favor.

Robbie was evidently enchanted, for she sidled up to the fence and began to speak to the dog—"Is he my sweet Bishy-wishy?" and other such endearments—while Hugh whispered urgent pleas for her to back up. She didn't; she extended her fingers through the gate. The dog stared, rose ponderously, and sidled toward her, watching the hand and listening to the voice. The rest of us held our breath, imagining the horror if he clamped those powerful teeth on her slender fingers with their brightly painted nails. Instead, he drooled on her.

"Oh, sweet doggie," she cooed. Bishop Jean rubbed his huge head against her hand. She had seduced the canine warrior even faster than she seduced poor Hugh Fauree.

The dog was our last stop on the walking tour; we then covered the short distance to our hotel and met Hester coming up the hill, all smiles and fluttering, brightly colored skirts.

"Ah, Madame Foxcroft, how is your husband?" Denis asked.

"Very well, thank you—considering. He has a huge cast on his leg, but still he got on the plane home with very little trouble. They have wheelchairs and people to carry you, and they even gave him an empty seat in first class. Wasn't that nice? And the construction company that was working on the cathedral paid for everything."

"You let him go by himself?" exclaimed Estrella.

"My mother's meeting him at the other end. He's taking her a picture of me in my new black dress." Delighted laughter bubbled from Hester, who evidently took an adolescent pleasure in tweaking her mother's conservative Boston sensibilities. "She loves to take care of people and boss them around. She's driving Jeremy straight home to Dedham, and then I'll meet him at the Boston airport after the tour ends to take him home with me, and—"

"He's your husband!" Estrella exclaimed. "It's your duty to take care of him yourself."

"But Jeremy's already seen France," Hester replied, astonished. "I haven't." Seeming sure that Estrella or anyone else would understand her point, she turned to Denis and said, "The clerk at the hotel told me you were going to see a huge, ferocious dog that used to eat people on the streets at night."

"Ah, but we have already been there, madame," said Denis apologetically.

Hester looked very disappointed. "Couldn't I go on my own?"

"I could not allow that, dear lady. Christopher and I will escort you."

And so the three of them went back up the hill, while Edie looked furious and Estrella muttered, "Just what you'd expect of a woman who'd leave her poor, injured husband to fend for himself. She can hardly wait to see a vicious dog."

"It was nice of Jeremy to insist that she complete the tour, don't you think?" Carolyn whispered to me. "Come along, Edie. You don't want to see that dog again."

"How do you know he insisted?" I asked. "Maybe she insisted."

"Don't be a pig," Carolyn whispered. "Did you notice that Professor Childeric hasn't said a word all afternoon? Not even to correct Denis, who undoubtedly made lots of mistakes, although I don't know what they were."

"A welcome silence," I responded as we climbed the stairs to avoid the rickety elevator. I've observed that many French elevators seem to be antiques, probably valued by the natives for their historical interest, as opposed to those of us, Philistines all, who would choose safety over history if given the choice. "Denis says we're eating at that fancy hotel down the street. Maybe we'll get a decent meal tonight."

"The Chateaubriand?" Carolyn's eyes lit up. "Do you think it's called that because their signature dish is a tenderloin of beef for two surrounded by delicious vegetables?"

"No, I think it's named for one of the city fathers."

"Is that the man who was ambassador to the court of Saint James and had the beef tenderloin dish named after him?"

"I have no idea, sweetheart. Why not ask Denis?"

"Now, that would be a waste of time. I wonder if I can work in a nap before dinner."

My wife does like to nap in the afternoon. She claims she got in the habit when the children were babies. While they napped, she napped to prepare herself for being awakened in the middle of the night. You'd think, to hear her tell it, that I never got up with the babies, yet I can remember several occasions when I did. I fell asleep in a faculty meeting, not a good idea for a new assistant professor, as a result of one such nocturnal fatherly stint. It must have been Gwen I walked the floor with. Lord, that child had a pair of lungs! No wonder she can make herself heard, without amplification, at the back of a large auditorium (a plus for a drama student). She began practicing early.

30
Finally a Good Meal

Carolyn

Maybe Denis had relayed the grumbling about the food because the restaurant in which we ate that night was regally appointed with linen tablecloths and chandeliers. It even had its namesake, chateaubriand, on the menu, along with other tempting beef dishes.

Manfred Unsell, having been reminded of beef, remarked that the American Red Cross had announced a ban on blood donations from people who had spent ten of the last twenty years living in or traveling to Spain or Portugal. The ban related to putative exposure to mad cow disease. Dr. Unsell was not giving us a health warning; he was bemoaning what the news would do to the European economy, to American holders of European stocks, and to world trade in general. I just wished people would stop talking about it; I'd have loved a tasty piece of beef tenderloin in béarnaise sauce, not that we were offered that for dinner.

Still, our meal was quite acceptable: a crepe stuffed with seafood and cheese (no sand), chicken rolled in herbs with a rich gravy, lovely little green beans, potato galettes, and a chocolate éclair. Jason ordered a good light burgundy, and we were quite happy with our dining experience in Saint-Malo. That is pronounced "Sanmaloo," according to Denis.

Unfortunately, the company at dinner was not so pleasant. Macauley Drummond seated Hester between himself and his wife and talked only to Hester. Not surprisingly, Nedda took offense, while Hester seemed oblivious. She was too busy telling them both what a source of inspiration Bishop Jean was; she planned to do a glass sculpture, nonrepresentational, of course, showing the dog in his warrior role, maybe even a piece depicting a bull baiting with mastiffs on the attack. She asked the table at large if pictures of those events were available in old books.

Before anyone could answer, and Professor Childeric seemed to be the only person inclined to, Nedda observed that Hester might find more customers for her sculptures if she produced something pretty instead of pursuing the macabre.

"Pretty!" hooted Macauley Drummond. "Since when have you turned into a stuffy, English professor type,

Nedda? Pretty is not avant garde. Pretty is Philistine. No wonder you only teach drama up to George Bernard Shaw. What about the theater of the absurd? What about—"

"Shut up, Macauley. You don't know anything about drama. You're too wrapped up in your own novels to read anything you haven't written yourself," his wife retorted.

"Next you'll be pushing your syllabus back into the Middle Ages. You'll be consulting Childeric about *Gammer Gurton's Needle* and the like."

"An excellent idea!" said Childeric. "Although I'd call that play Renaissance. However, Professor Drummond couldn't do better than to solicit my input on medieval drama."

"*Dr.* Drummond," Nedda snapped. "To distinguish me from my *husband,* who never *got* his doctorate. The committee didn't understand his novel and turned him down." She cast her husband a malicious look.

"Which reflects badly on them, not me," he retorted.

"Goodness, I didn't mean to start a fight," said Hester. "It's just that I like red glass." Her eyes turned dreamy. "Drops of blood on fawn and black. Maybe flowing around the form."

Anna excused herself and headed toward the ladies'. I might have followed, but I hadn't yet been served my chocolate éclair and was afraid the waiter might skip me if I wasn't there. I do love chocolate éclairs, even those that contain pudding instead of cream, although at that moment I didn't yet know this one would.

"Perhaps we could agree that we all have different tastes," said Laura quietly, "and arguing about taste rarely changes anyone's mind."

"Ah, my wife, the peacemaker," said Lorenzo.

"After dinner, let's take an evening stroll on the ramparts," Laura suggested as if her husband had never spoken. "I've read that it is a thrilling sight—the waves breaking against the walls, especially when the moon—"

"There you go, Childeric," Lorenzo interrupted. "You've nothing to worry about from Laura. She's much too *nice* to be a dean. *Niceness* seems to be a genetic female trait that keeps womankind from accomplishing—"

"By God, Lorenzo," exclaimed Janice. "You really are a pig, as in male chauvinist. Females can be as aggressive and underhanded as men if they have to, and the accomplishments of women in the twentieth century have been . . ."

The arrival of dessert cut into the quarrel. Then Anna returned, but after so long a time that I asked discreetly if she was ill. She had pushed away her éclair as soon as she sat down, and she looked flushed.

"Too much rich food," she murmured. "I think I'll have an early night. If anything's planned for later, you'll see to Edie?"

"Of course," I replied. "Is there anything I can do for you? I think I have some Tums. They're good for both one's digestion and one's bones."

"And I, being postmenopausal, have to worry about my bones?" Anna asked dryly.

"I didn't mean—"

"It's quite all right. Very kind of you to offer. In return, let me suggest that Chris might eat a lower-fat diet. It prevents prostate cancer in later life."

I was quite taken aback. One never thinks of prostate cancer in terms of one's son, or even one's husband, if the thought can be avoided.

"I'm afraid I've upset you," Anna murmured. "Nutritionists should learn to keep their mouths shut, especially during meals. I'm as bad as those who were discussing mad cow disease while you were eating beef tartare."

"Don't think I didn't take that to heart," I responded. "I had a nightmare about my brain getting all spongy and full of holes, and Jason saying something about science being the guide to a good memory, only I couldn't remember his name. It was awful." I had fished the Tums from my purse and now held them out to her.

"It sounds awful," Anna agreed. "The dream. And put your Tums away. I'll be fine after a good night's sleep."

"But Nedda," Hester was saying, "I thought you *loved* Macauley's novels. *I* thought the one about the man who beheaded his mother and sent her head to New Guinea to be shriveled was amazing."

"I'll bet you did!" Nedda replied, rising from the table and leaving. She didn't even finish her éclair, although it was quite tasty for one with pudding inside. Maybe it was the chocolate flavor of the pudding that won me over.

Hester looked confused and stricken, Macauley told her to pay no attention, and Estrella whispered to Ivan, "*Menage à trois.*"

He laughed. "Only if all of *trois* stay around, my pretty borscht beet. I think wife go to her room, maybe lock her door, and leave husband in hall."

Once the meal was over, we milled around outside the restaurant, discussing what route we'd take to the ramparts. Anna stayed with us that long, speaking to various people, which was a relief to me. She looked a bit better; nonetheless, she did start toward our hotel, and I suggested that Jason or Chris see her back, to which she replied, "Nonsense. It's just up the street."

Walking the ramparts was exciting. The half-moon silvered the tops of the waves, and the roar and swish of the breakers, rolling to the very walls and foaming white below us, was magical. However, a stiff wind, blowing like ice off the sea, soon turned us toward home. Although we had meant to walk the whole circuit of the walls, we were soon back on the cobblestone street climbing toward the hotel.

Jason was talking science to Ivan again, so the de Sorentinos invited me to walk with them. Given Lorenzo's remarks about women in general and his wife in particular,

I'd have refused had Laura not been so eager for my company. I went for her sake, talked only to her, and even managed to maintain my sense of humor when he suggested that a laser peal might take care of the fine lines on my face.

What fine lines? I said, rather politely I thought, "If I *have* any lines, they are badges earned in the lists of motherhood, and I'll just keep them, thank you."

Before he could urge some other operation on me, Bishop Jean, the English mastiff, suddenly loomed in the pool of light under an antique street lantern. He was unaccompanied! And he looked hungry!

31
Bad Doggie

Carolyn

If the dog is loose, it must be after curfew. No. What am I thinking? That was centuries ago. Mastiffs no longer patrol the streets of Saint-Malo. Yet, there he is. My heart speeded up frantically when he produced a great, deep woof. Women screamed. Men shouted. Someone ran. The mastiff, mouth open, teeth displayed menacingly, sprang straight toward us. I was momentarily paralyzed with fear, yet my mind continued to function. Into my head popped an odd conversation with my postman, who often has to fend off unfriendly dogs. It seemed a flimsy weapon against such a huge creature, but I opened my umbrella in Bishop Jean's face.

He halted immediately. He whined and looked con-

fused—I think. Dogs' expressions are not easy to interpret.
Laura had gasped and cowered toward her husband. The
dog raised his nose in the air, sniffed, gave a lower, but still
frightening woof, and wheeled in another direction. Within
seconds, Lorenzo was setting his wife on her feet, and the
mastiff was thrusting his broad face at Childeric. The medievalist roared with fear and punched Bishop Jean in the
nose. Tail curving promptly upward, the dog clamped his
teeth on the professor's arm.

Oh lord, I thought. *The tail's up. That means he's agitated.* Childeric was caterwauling, "Help! Help!" He was
agitated too.

"Shut up," Robbie hissed. She had dropped Hugh's arm
and rushed toward dog and professor. Bishop Jean's ears
twitched at the sound of her voice, and he turned his head
toward her, widely set legs still braced against any move
Childeric might make, the professor's arm still impris-
oned.

"Sweet dog," she crooned, smoothing the mastiff's
wrinkled brow.

"What do you mean, *sweet dog*?" Childeric moaned.
"He's trying to eat my arm."

"Do be quiet, Professor," she cooed, looking into the
dog's eyes, but speaking to Childeric. "Let go, Bishop.
Umm. Let go of the nasty man's arm, little Jeanie Weenie."
She leaned down to kiss the dog's ear.

I could see that Childeric was close to total panic. Sweat
glistened on his forehead. "Don't move, Professor," she
singsonged in a sweet voice. "Let go. Good dog. Good,
sweet puppy dog."

The smitten mastiff rumbled, dropped Childeric's arm,
and leaned against Robbie adoringly. Hugh had to shore
her up to keep her from falling over. "Take off my shawl,
Hugh," she murmured. "Good dog. Sweet puppy." Bishop
Jean jumped up, paws on her shoulders, and licked her
face. Robbie and Hugh both staggered, but Hugh managed

to grab the scarf. "Hold me up, for God's sake, Hugh," she whispered soothingly.

"Can't you make him get down?" Hugh asked in a shaky voice.

Robbie rubbed her silky shawl against the dog's ears, then twisted it and tied it around his neck. The two were nose to nose as she did this, and I, for one, was terrified. What if he turned on her? What if Childeric did something stupid and irritated the dog again? What if—

She issued a command in French, and the dog, to the mystification of all, dropped his paws from her shoulders and allowed her to coax him, tied to the end of her silk shawl, toward his backyard enclosure. He listened to her cajoling as if she were a Siren luring him, a willing sailor, onto the rocks.

"We can't let her go alone," I whispered to Jason, who had hurried to my side when the dog appeared.

"Hugh's following behind, for all the good that will do," Jason replied quietly. "She's the one the dog likes. Anyone else might set him off again."

Our group, coming out of shock, began to stir. "I thought they weren't supposed to roam the streets anymore. How did it get loose?" asked Grace Unsell quite calmly.

"My God, he could have killed someone. That dog should be put down," said Macauley Drummond.

"He didn't hurt anyone. Not really," Hester protested. There was more excitement than fear in her voice.

"Carolyn, how did you know to put up your umbrella?" asked Laura. "I think you saved my life."

"My postman told me about it," I replied in a shaky voice.

"Don't think the dog meant any harm," said Carl Jensen. "Didn't seem dangerous until Childeric hit him on the nose. That's when the tail went up. Owner told us about the tail. Anyone'd looked at the tail first off would know he didn't mean any harm."

"You're saying it's my fault he tried to bite my arm off?" Childeric demanded.

"Haven't got any bite marks, have you?" Jensen asked. "Just a bit of drool on your sports jacket. Drool won't hurt you. Many a cow has—"

"But it wasn't a cow, Carl," his wife protested. "It was a huge, mean dog with big teeth. Cows aren't mean. But that dog—well, I wouldn't want him living on my street."

"The Chamber of Commerce should put a stop to such things," said Manfred Unsell. "Killer dogs roaming the streets after dark may make a good story to tell the tourists, but the effect on tourism of the actuality is definitely poor economics."

"Oh, do be quiet, Manfred," said his wife. "You're so insensitive. We've all had a terrible fright, and here you're worrying about the gross national product or—"

"I didn't mention the gross national product," Unsell retorted. "If you'd been listening—"

"If I may be so bold as to point out who that dog went for," said Childeric. "The intended victims were Dr. de Sorentino and myself. Two dean candidates. You notice the dog wasn't interested in Fauree. That certainly tells us something about who was responsible for this vicious attack."

"For God's sake, Childeric," said Jason, "you're the one who provoked the dog. Roberta and Hugh rescued you."

"Indeed, which makes the ploy that much more clever. Who would suspect them of plotting against me when they are the ones who called the dog off? Utterly Machiavellian. But I am no fool. And Mrs. Blue, I must thank you for your quick thinking. You saved Dr. de Sorentino. Although your actions caused the dog to turn on me, I certainly don't blame you for putting me at risk." He gave me an unctuous smile, which I did not return.

"Perhaps you, Dr. Lorenzo de Sorentino, should rethink your remarks on the female sex. It was this fine, gallant woman, not you, who rescued your wife. If I should be so fortunate as to become dean, I certainly intend to show my esteem for our female faculty."

"I'll believe that when I see it," muttered Janice, "and I hope I don't have to."

We all, much shaken, resumed our walk toward the hotel. Jason put his arm around me. Chris took my hand, and Edie headed off to comfort Dr. Childeric, with many a resentful glance at us. "My lord, I was scared when I saw that dog heading for you," said Jason. "And me, off talking science with—"

"Let's not discuss it." I was shivering. "No one got hurt, and—"

"So speaks my cool-headed wife. I can't believe you fended him off with an umbrella."

I didn't tell Jason that I'd fended off worse opponents with an umbrella. I did explain the theory. "The postman told me that if you open a black umbrella in a dog's face, he gets confused because he thinks he's gone blind."

"Thank God it worked."

I could hear Hester asking Professor Childeric if there were any good medieval statues or paintings coming up. Estrella, overhearing, asked if Hester was Catholic.

"No," Hester replied cheerfully. "I just like those grisly crucifixions and saints being tortured. I did a prize-winning glass sculpture after spending a couple of hours in a Catholic church in Boston. It was the first prize I ever won."

Estrella looked dumbfounded at this revelation. "That's—that's sacrilegious."

"I beg to differ, Mrs. Markarov," Drummond put in. "Since Hester has no religion, how can anything she say be sacrilegious? At the least, it's an interesting philosophical point. Jean-Paul Sartre—"

At that point we reached the hotel and didn't have to hear what Jean-Paul Sartre would have said. Hugh and Robbie returned, and she announced, "The doggie's back at Mr. Broussais's, so all's well, although he wasn't too happy to be awakened or to hear that someone let the dog loose."

"Oh, indeed," snapped Childeric. "We can see why you'd think that all is well, having orchestrated the attack on myself and Mrs. de Sorentino."

"Dr.," said Laura.

"You, Fauree, and your hulking girlfriend—"

"What's that supposed to mean?" Hugh demanded. "You're blaming me? How the devil could I have orchestrated that if I'd had it in mind, which I didn't? You're dead crazy, Childeric."

"Hulking?" exclaimed Robbie.

"For heaven's sake, let's go upstairs," I whispered. "Thank goodness, you're no longer rooming with the professor, Chris. Edie, come along." She was still clinging to Childeric's arm. "We'll walk you to your room."

"You don't need to walk *me*," said Edie. "Dr. Childeric will do that, won't you?" She fluttered her eyelashes at him and, before I could intervene, dragged him off toward the balcony that looked out on the town. "First," she said, "let's check to be sure that mean old dog is really back in his dog house. What if he got into the hotel? It gives me the shivers, doesn't it you, Professor . . ."

I knew that I should go after her, but the thought of being on a balcony with Jean-Claude Childeric, even with Edie present, made me more nervous than the thought of Bishop Jean getting into the hotel. Instead of doing my duty, I dropped into a chair. I'd wait until she came back and see her safely to her room. When I told Jason, he offered to visit the bar and bring me back a snifter of Cointreau, which sounded like just what I needed.

32
That Nasty Old Man

Jason

The bar was more crowded that I'd expected; it must have been five minutes before I returned to the lobby where Carolyn had dropped, as if shot, onto the hotel's green brocade sofa. Other tour members were draped on the chairs in one of those "conversation groups" of furniture, talking about the mastiff attack. Robbie objected to the term *attack* as I handed the snifter of Cointreau to Carolyn.

"He may be a sweet dog, as you say, Robbie, but he certainly scared me," Carolyn murmured.

"You didn't act scared," Robbie retorted.

"Well, I was." Carolyn smiled her thanks to me and sipped some of the orange liqueur. "When you want a drink because you're upset or frightened or sad, is that a sign of alcoholism?" Carolyn mused.

"I don't think you need to worry, Caro," I assured her. "Now, if you were drinking in the daytime—"

"What about lunch after I got hit by the bicycle, and at the Calvados tasting? I don't even like Calvados, but . . ."

I'm not sure what my wife said after that because Edie appeared at the French doors that led to the hotel's scenic-view balcony. The first thing that caught my eye, oddly enough, was her navel. I hadn't noticed before that she was wearing a pair of slacks—more like tights—the waistband of which dipped below her belly button. Her top, some sort of snug-fitting knitted thing, was cut off several inches above that navel. A strange style. I remembered seeing coeds in such outfits, some with their navels pierced by rings. Edie didn't have a ring, but I thought the outfit unsuitable for a sixteen-year-old.

The second thing I noticed—the girl was crying. Carolyn evidently spotted that first because she rose from the sofa, pushing her snifter onto an end table. "What's wrong?" Carolyn asked. By then Edie had collapsed, weeping, into my wife's arms. "Edie? What happened?"

"He's . . . he's . . . disgusting," the girl hiccuped.

"Who?" My wife wore an expression—well, almost of dread. "Edie, what happened?" She had one arm around the weeping girl and patted her shoulder.

"He . . . he . . . that nasty old man . . . he—"

"Young woman, that's quite enough of that."

We turned toward Jean-Claude Childeric, who strode up, looking much more flustered than he sounded. My wife eyed him over Edie's shoulder with a dislike that would have withered a less self-important male. "What did you do to this child?" she demanded.

"Nothing. Believe me—"

"He kissed me," Edie wailed. "It was disgusting."

"I did not. I—I just patted her on the—the shoulder. As you're doing."

"Why were *you* patting her?" Carolyn asked through gritted teeth.

"She—we were supposed to be looking for the dog— and suddenly the girl just—just launched herself at me, babbling about how frightened she'd been—and—and what was I supposed to do? I tried to reassure her."

"How?" said Carolyn coldly.

"He hugged me," sniffled Edie. "Tight."

"I did not."

"Then what *did* you do when she—how did you put

it?—launched herself at you?" my wife persisted. She sounded like a district attorney. Evidently her mothering instincts had kicked in on Edie's behalf, although I myself tended to take the girl's story with a grain of salt.

"Well, I may have—I mean I suppose I put my arms around her," stammered Childeric, "and gave her a—a pat or two—as I said. In a fatherly way."

"You kissed me on the mouth!" Edie peered at him accusingly from the safety of Carolyn's arms.

"I did no such—"

"You're saying you didn't kiss her?" Carolyn persisted.

"You don't believe me, do you, M-Mrs. Blue?" Edie stopped sniffling and burst into a fresh bout of hard crying.

"Yes, Edie, I do," said Carolyn.

She sounded quite grim, and I was rather surprised at her easy acceptance of the girl's story. I myself was still dubious. It had, after all, been Edie who dragged Childeric off to the balcony.

"So Professor Childeric, did you kiss this girl or not?"

"Well, I—I may have— Really, my dear Carolyn—"

"I am not your dear Carolyn," my wife snapped back. "I want to know exactly what happened out there."

"I—I may have brushed my lips against her forehead— but—but only as a—as a gesture of sympath—"

"My father never kisses me on the mouth. There's nothing—s-sympathetic or f-fatherly about being kissed on the mouth by a disgusting old man who—who smells like wine and—and dog spit," Edie wailed. "He had his arm around my neck, and I could smell where the dog slobbered on his coat sleeve."

Childeric turned pale. The rest of the group stared at him with amazement and distaste. My wife said, "Professor, you should be ashamed of yourself."

"But I didn't . . ." His voice trailed away as Carolyn, Edie clasped firmly in the curve of her arm, led the girl toward the elevator, murmuring to her in a motherly fashion.

I would have followed them, but Carolyn shook her head, and I backed off.

As there was only one elevator, the rest of us headed for the stairs, leaving Childeric, looking distraught, in the lobby. *Good lord,* I thought. The fool actually made a pass at a sixteen-year-old girl? I couldn't think of any more repugnant and self-destructive action in an educator. And how had Carolyn known that Edie was telling the truth? I suppose women have an instinct for that kind of thing.

33
Protecting Lolita

Carolyn

Edie was knuckling her eyes like a five-year-old as the elevator door closed. "Thank you for b-b-believing me," she said.

"You're welcome," I replied. I was experiencing a rush of guilt. If I hadn't been too embarrassed to tell anyone but Anna and Robbie about my own experience with Childeric, this might not have happened to Edie. "Anna's going to hear about this," I said gently. "Do you want to tell her, or shall I?"

"You." Edie began to cry again. "She won't believe you, though. She doesn't like me."

"I think she'll believe us. Now don't cry." I handed her a travel pack of Kleenex.

"No, she won't." Edie blew her nose but continued to weep as we stepped off the elevator. She hung back when I started toward their room.

"Come along." I took her hand. "You need a good night's sleep, and for that you have to go to bed." Edie followed obediently. "And Edie, tomorrow, and for the rest of the trip, please stay close to me." *If Childeric is exacting revenge for what he sees as dangers to his person, his reputation, and his chances at being dean, he'll see Edie as a threat after that scene downstairs,* I thought. *And he doesn't seem to be a man who accepts responsibility for his own actions.* "I can't protect you if you keep disappearing."

"I th-thought you didn't like me," she whimpered.

I sighed. "Why don't we start over?" I gave her a hug before I knocked at Anna's door. Edie hugged back.

"Thanks, Mrs. B. For sticking up for me with—with him. I hate him."

I almost said, "I know what you mean." Instead, I advised, "Best to stay away from him."

Edie nodded, not at all the rebellious girl she'd been through most of the trip.

At that instant, Anna, wearing a seersucker robe and a hair net, opened the door. "How are you feeling, Anna?" I asked. She looked pale.

"Tired," she replied, "but I'll survive. How was the walk on the ramparts?"

"You won't believe what happened," said Edie in a subdued tone.

"Have you been crying, child?" Anna asked.

Edie immediately began to weep again, and I told her to get ready for bed. With the girl in the bathroom, I told the story.

"Stupid child," Anna muttered. "Why did she throw herself at him out there?"

"I suppose she was frightened by the dog attack." Then I had to tell Anna that story, adding that I'd been pretty frightened myself.

"So he used the poor girl's fright to take advantage of

her? Well, we shouldn't be surprised, should we? The man is completely without scruples."

"If only I hadn't been such a wimp when he grabbed me—"

"Don't blame yourself, Carolyn," said Anna. "You didn't do anything that any decent man would have taken as encouragement, any more than he can be excused for taking Edie's immature flirting as an invitation. The girl's only sixteen. And not that bright."

Edie appeared in the bathroom door, wearing a baby-doll nightie, all ruffles, bare legs, and shoulders. "I'm not dumb," she said resentfully. "I make good grades."

"Then show some intelligence when it comes to the male of the species," said Anna. "You can't go around flirting indiscriminately and expect that your age will protect your from a response you didn't anticipate."

"I told you she'd blame me," said Edie bitterly.

"Then you were wrong," Anna snapped back. "There's no excuse whatever for that miserable lecher's actions, and don't let him, or anyone, tell you there is. On the other hand, stay away from him, and everyone else in trousers."

"Mrs. Blue wears trousers," Edie ventured, trying to smile.

"And don't get smart with me," Anna retorted.

Edie flounced into bed and pulled the sheet over her head.

I could have wished that Anna had been a bit easier on the girl, but still, some things need to be said.

I was trudging back to my room when Hester Foxcroft stopped me in the hall. "I have something Jeremy wanted me to give you," she said.

Tired after a frightening evening, baffled at the idea that Jeremy, injured and on his way back to the States, had left a present for me—or was it a message? Or what?—I stared blankly at Hester.

"It's a drawing he did of Jason. In the Rodin gardens in

Paris. You were so kind to him when that lunch box hit him, he wanted you to have it. If you want it. You don't have to—"

My eyes filled with tears. "That's so nice," I mumbled. "And poor Jeremy was so badly hurt. I'm surprised he thought of—"

"Oh, Jeremy's like that. He's as sweet as they come," said Hester. "And they'd given him lots of painkillers by the time he told me to give you the sketch. I had to tear it out of his sketchbook right there at the hospital. Do you want it?"

"Of course I want it." I gave her a hug, and she gave me a large manila envelope, then headed off to her own room. I walked to mine, double-locked the door behind me and, remembering the mastiff attack, asked my husband, "Was that dangerous, or not?"

"A man his age coming on to a girl Edie's age? I'd certainly—"

"I didn't mean that. I hope word gets back to the university and he gets sacked."

"Carolyn, have you been crying?"

"Oh, not really. I was just so touched—"

"By what?" asked my husband, astonished. "I can't think of anything touching that happened this evening, unless you're thinking of dinner. It was pretty good."

"Hester Foxcroft just gave me that sketch Jeremy did of you. He wanted us to have it." I set the envelope down on the bed. "In fact, I'm going to tell Judith what Childeric did. But I was talking about the dog before. I can't decide whether we were in danger or not. What do you think?"

"No idea," said Jason. "It certainly seemed dangerous at the time."

"And could someone have planned it?"

"I don't know how."

I nodded my agreement, unwound the cord that held the envelope flap, and pulled out the sketch. "Oh, my good-

Clue List

Day	Place	Victim	Injury	Means
8	Saint-Malo	Childeric	arm chomped	by dog
		Laura	attack	dog
		Me	attack	dog
8	Saint-Malo	Edie	attack	sexual

ness. It's wonderful. Look at that." I held it out to my husband. Jeremy had caught Jason perfectly: the beard, the expression of excitement on his face—that was when he was talking about toxicity in paint, one hand raised to make his point, the other draped casually where his ankle rested on his knee, and behind him the vague outlines of the lovely garden. "I didn't even know he did portraits. I'm going to have this framed. Where shall we hang it?"

My husband admitted that it was a good likeness, said he was glad Jeremy had skipped the phase when he was fidgeting and feeling like a fool, and suggested that the Chemistry Department might like to hang it outside his office.

"Oh, go to bed," I said, laughing. "I think I'll have copies made for the children, too. And your mother. She'd—"

"I think I'll go to bed before you've got this sketch posted on the Internet and offered to the *Journal of the American Chemical Society*."

Jason climbed in bed, laughing, and I put the sketch safely in my hard-sided, wheeled computer case and sat down to access my clue list, to which I added the day's events.

Clue List

Present	Suspect(s)	Motive
everyone	Fauree	deanship
	Fauree	deanship
		couldn't have been planned
no one	Childeric	philanderer

I looked over my list. Who would have reason to sic the mastiff on Childeric, Laura, and me? Or since I just happened to be by Laura, perhaps I could discount myself as a target, in which case, Laura and Childeric, being dean candidates—well, that left Hugh, but he had been with us, and Robbie had led the dog away. Of course, Hugh might have figured she'd be able to, so no harm would be done except a bad fright to Childeric and Laura. And Childeric had certainly made a fool of himself. And then gone himself one better by making a stupid, unconscionable pass at Edie, which couldn't help but make Hugh look like a more respectable candidate.

Oh me, Jason would be very unhappy if he knew that I was actually looking at Hugh as a possible culprit. And I had no idea how he, or anyone, could have arranged the dog incident.

Conclusions: (1) I'm no detective. (2) This tour is not only scary, but also an enigma. (3) There was nothing for it but to go to bed.

Travel Journal
Day Eight, Saint-Malo

Not a bad dinner, and the chef was very cooperative about giving me raw meat chunks for my dog. The French love dogs. Someone's always letting his dog poop on the street. Or bringing a dog into a restaurant, making you think there's probably dog hair in the food.

Who'd have thought it would be so easy to slip the meat into the pockets of Childeric and Lorenzo de Sorentino? Who doesn't think his wife is fit to be dean.

No problem to let the dog loose either and set him off in the right direction. Too bad Laura saw fit to walk with her husband, and that Carolyn saw fit to save his hide. I was hoping he'd be so frightened by the dog that he'd leave the tour before he could slander a perfectly good dean candidate again.

And C. No harm done, unfortunately, but again he made an ass of himself. Accusing Fauree. Too bad the dog didn't break skin. Or bone. Too bad C. didn't pee his pants. Dad used to say the cowards always did. Guess he was wrong. No big surprise there. He was just a loud-mouthed bully. Probably a coward himself. Had about the same opinion of women as de Sorentino.

And C. making his speech about supporting women. Then putting a move on Edie. Now that, if it gets back home, should really screw him out of the dean's position. Must be sure the girl's parents hear about it.

Contumacious conduct. Trying to seduce a sixteen-year-old faculty daughter would count as contumacious conduct. And even a tenured professor can be dumped for that.

I'm definitely going to ruin the slimy bastard's life. And when he's out on his ass, I'll send him a letter, so he knows who did it.

Can't think of when I've had more fun. Probably never. Not in years anyway. Not since C. screwed up my life.

So what shall I do tomorrow? Seize the moment, I guess.

*That's what C. used to say, Carpe deum. He carpe deumed me
out of a couple of years of research. It was all downhill after
that. No full professorship. No family. There's nothing like
being an aging, single nobody to make you invisible. Though
invisibility has its uses. Carpe deum.*

34
Mont-Saint-Michel

Savory Beans of Brittany

*The salt marshes of Brittany and Normandy produce an
excellent lamb, rarely available in the United States. Still,
we can prepare a tasty bean dish in the fashion of the region to go with our own legs of lamb.*

• Heat *3 tbs. butter* in a frying pan and brown *1
chopped onion*, stirring frequently.

• Add *4 minced cloves of garlic*, *¼ cup tomato puree*,
4 ripe chopped tomatoes that have been peeled and
seeded, *salt and pepper* to taste. Stir and simmer for 30
minutes before adding to *1 pound of canned flageolets
or white northern beans*. Reheat and sprinkle with *1½
tbs. chopped parsley*.

• Serve with roast leg of lamb and gravy.

Carolyn Blue, "Have Fork, Will Travel,"
Tuscaloosa Weekly Register

Carolyn

Day nine contained the excursion to which I had most looked forward: Mont-Saint-Michel, that towering monastery and fortification thrusting up on a rocky promontory off the French coast. It embodies all the branches of medieval architecture from the Romanesque of the early Middle Ages to the Flamboyant Gothic as the era drew to a close, all the miracles a good Christian could imagine, and all the warfare any general or admiral could wish to relive in imagination. Until that day I had seen it only in pictures, but I loved it before I ever arrived over the causeway in a bus peopled by wrangling academics, a very subdued sixteen-year-old girl sitting beside me.

Two discoveries had been made the night before by Jean-Claude Childeric and Lorenzo de Sorentino, discoveries that explained the canine bishop's attraction to these particular people (evidently Laura and I hadn't been under attack). Each man found a piece of raw meat in his pocket when he arrived in his hotel room. The questions were: How did the meat get there? Placed by whom? Obtained from whom? Accusations flew. Childeric again accused Fauree. Lorenzo accused Childeric, without being able to explain why Childeric had the same irresistible item in his own pocket.

Maybe, I speculated, Childeric had meant to put the meat in Fauree's pocket and been unable to do that or to get rid of it before the dog arrived, nose on the scent. Janice Petar doubled over with laughter and was accused by both men. No one could explain how the dog had gotten loose, but Robbie said the gate to the enclosure was wide open, the owner asleep, and Bishop Jean perfectly amenable, after his brief adventure, to being returned. Hugh and Robbie insisted that they had closed that gate, not opened it, and they'd had no raw meat available as bait.

"Wonder if a dog can catch mad cow disease by eating

beef?" mused Jensen. "Was it beef?" He addressed the latter question to Lorenzo.

"How the hell would I know?" Lorenzo snapped. "Ask Childeric. Maybe he tried it."

"I flushed it down the toilet," said Childeric angrily.

"That explains the plumbing problems this morning," said Grace Unsell. "The variety of things a person can reasonably flush down a toilet is limited, you know. I'm sure you inconvenienced not only the management but also many of us guests. I, for one, hate beginning my day with backed-up plumbing."

"I didn't have any trouble," said Hester. "How big was the piece of meat? Was it bloody?"

She pulled out a notebook and began to sketch as Lorenzo described his doggie treat, likening it to various human organs, which, as a plastic surgeon, he never had to deal with, thank God.

That was the gist of the conversation at breakfast and on the bus.

At least the wonders of Mont-Saint-Michel followed. Denis was particularly interested in the miracles associated with the island. Early Christian hermits had lit fires to signal the mainland when they needed supplies, which were then loaded by devout peasants onto a donkey. God directed the donkey to the island and the waiting hermits. When a wolf ate the donkey, so Denis's tale went, the wolf had to haul the supplies for the rest of his life. Then, there was the building of the first church on Mont Tombe, as the island was then known. Bishop Aubert had the church constructed at the request of the archangel himself, who appeared in a dream and later returned to remind the skeptical and/or dilatory cleric by poking an angelic finger into his forehead. Further miracles included the choice of the very site on which to build because the spot remained dry when dew covered the rest of the area; the removal of a large boulder by a toddler, who pushed it away with his foot; and the discovery of a freshwater spring at the foot of the boulder.

"Do you think those things really happened?" Edie whispered to me.

"I have no idea, Edie," I replied. "I just enjoy the stories and leave the question of authenticity to the theologians."

Estrella was ecstatic at these revelations; my son was highly amused, especially about the hungry wolf and the hole in Aubert's skull, still there when his bones were miraculously rediscovered. Chris's favorite was the stolen bull that miraculously appeared on top of Mont Tombe. My son said that wasn't a miracle; that was the ultimate fraternity prank.

Amid various disastrous collapses, the monastery was built, modified, added to, fortified, and even rebuilt by abbots, dukes, and kings until it became a huge labyrinthine complex of many layers that are a joy to explore. For me, at least. Edie wasn't that fascinated, although she did try to listen. It seems that the monks, too, were given to falling into decay, spiritual and intellectual in their case, and had to be expelled or reformed or educated from time to time, until finally they were ejected after the French Revolution and Mont-Saint-Michel became a prison. In our time the monks have returned, the monks and the tourists.

Pilgrims were coming to Mont-Saint-Michel as early as 860. Imagine! In the Middle Ages they walked across at low tide to expiate their sins, and children's crusades set off from as far away as Southern France to reach the archangel's citadel. Edie thought the children must have had a good time, roaming the countryside on their own. Lest she decide to follow their example, I remarked that most of them had died of disease, exposure, and hunger.

The island was also attacked by Vikings, then supported by their descendants, the Normans. Here the three sons of William the Conqueror faced one another over the water;

Henry Beauclerc (later Henry I of England) holed up there while his brothers' armies waited ashore to starve him out. William Rufus, King of England, was touched to his chivalric soul (chivalry being one of his few virtues) by Henry's request to cross in surrender at low tide with his banners flying, so all ended well, although Henry later supplanted both brothers and took over Normandy and England.

During the Hundred Years' War, Mont-Saint-Michel fought off the English and provided sanctuary to those who remained true to France. In fact, at one point, a Breton fleet from Saint-Malo had to sail off to defend the citadel and drive away the pesky English ships. "That's where we're staying," Edie whispered.

"The very same." She was finally beginning to appreciate the delights of history.

"So the pirates sailed over to help the monks?"

"Even pirates were religious in the old days," I replied. A simplistic answer, but she seemed taken with the idea of pious pirates.

We did have a wonderful morning, following Denis from room to room, stair to stair. Then we went into the town for lunch, where we Blues and Edie consumed delicious omelets at Hotel Poullard. Mère Poullard was the mother of tourism at the site, for she sold her famous omelets to visitors once the island prison was closed in the early 1900s. I must say, Edie had been a model of propriety and good humor. She'd asked questions during Denis's lectures; she ate her lunch without complaint; and although she may have looked a bit sullen when Anna was within arm's length, she wasn't rude to her roommate. She didn't even ask for wine or flirt with Chris at the table, and we all stayed well away from Professor Childeric.

Although I had entertained the fantasy that he would be embarrassed enough to avoid the tour entirely, that proved to be too much to hope for. He was, after all, a dedicated medievalist. Even with Childeric tagging along, it was one of the best mornings we'd had. No one was hurt. Perhaps the culprit, or culprits, would finally be satisfied with all the fear and humiliation visited upon us and leave us alone.

35
Mont Tombe

Carolyn

After lunch we could wander at will, and the tour group was soon scattered by the complexity of the structure. I saw and took pictures of everything from the Artichoke House in town to the cannons left by the English. Once I had lost track of Chris and Jason, I explored with Edie, and in the company of whomever we met, the towers and ramparts, the soaring nave, crypts, cloisters, gardens high in the air, long stairways, chapels, refectories, halls built for great nobles and poor pilgrims, and the quarters of the monks, which were highest in the structure. Edie didn't see why the monks should get the best views since they were supposed to spend their time praying, not looking at the scenery.

"It was symbolic of the social order in the Middle Ages," I explained. "The religious orders were closest to heaven and God, the nobility next, then the peasants."

"I thought the poor were supposed to inherit the kingdom of heaven," she said. "That's what our minister says. Not that anyone I know wants to be poor."

"I think you've just put your finger on one of the paradoxes of Christianity, Edie." I hoped that I wouldn't be

getting any irate telephones calls from her mother some-
time in the future.

"I guess you mean we're all hypocrites," she said.

She'd been right last night when she told Anna that she
wasn't dumb, and I decided to change the subject. "We
haven't seen the great wheel yet. It was powered by serfs
plodding around and around and was used to draw up supplies from sea level."

"Gross," said Edie. And somehow I lost her between the
monks' quarters and the wheel. I did look for her. And I
told others I came across, one of them Anna, to keep an eye
out for Edie.

"Flown the coop again, has she?" said Anna and shook
her head. She was sitting on a stone bench and didn't seem
moved to rise and search for Edie.

The exploration of Mont-Saint-Michel was a breathtak-
ing experience, literally (all those stairs) and figuratively,
which left me once again at the lower levels, sans husband,
son, and Edie, and gazing wistfully at the beaches as I
imagined myself riding (not that I like horses) with Henry
Beauclerc in the eleventh century to meet his brothers,
Robert Curthose, Duke of Normandy, and William the Red
of England.

"We should walk the beaches," said Macauley Drummond, who appeared unexpectedly at my side with Hester
in tow.

"Oh, let's do," cried Hester. "I hate the Midwest.
There's no sea."

"Wouldn't it be dangerous?" I asked, both yearning to
go, even in his unpleasant company, yet wary after all the
misfortune that had befallen the group.

"Not at all," Jean-Claude Childeric answered, having
joined us. "The tide is receding. Forgotten who told me,
but there's nothing to worry about. Can't you imagine the
sons of William facing one another across the marshes?"
He addressed this to me.

He'd read my mind, which did not please me. I didn't want to talk to him or be in his company. "I've just been thinking of that," I mumbled reluctantly, unable to stifle an honest reply, "of when Rufus allowed Henry to leave the island with all battle honors."

"Ah, those were honorable days," said Childeric wistfully.

I wanted to retort that he was a fine one to talk about honor, but then William Rufus had been a pretty disreputable character himself, although not where women were concerned. His romantic interests had evidently lain elsewhere.

"If you folks are thinking of walking out a bit, I'll join you," said Carl Jensen, who had entered our circle. "Like to see those salt marsh sheep."

"Well, let's go before it's time to catch the bus," said Drummond impatiently. "You better not bring down disaster on us, Childeric."

"Don't be a fool. I'm not responsible for anything that's happened. It's Fauree."

"I imagine they carried swords and lances," said Hester, "those sons of the king."

"Indeed," Childeric assured her and led the way. I hung back, but in the end I couldn't resist joining the group.

"The salt marsh sheep are famous," Jensen told me. "You'll want to taste those. Supposed to be the best lamb you ever ate."

"I've read about them. Will we see any?"

"Hope so," replied Jensen. "Sheep aren't the smartest of God's creatures. Like to see how they manage in a marsh."

Soon we were strolling on the hard-packed sand, staring back at the abbey, which loomed above us. Then we walked for a bit toward the mainland, and we could see sheep grazing, as well as cars and buses on the causeway and the little chapel of Saint Aubert with its stone stair and walkway, separated by water at high tide from the abbey.

Childeric, who was behind me, complained of all
Denis's misinformation, Macauley chatted with Hester,
who seemed oblivious to his interest, and Jensen wondered
if the sheep "out there a ways" were subject to the scrapies
that resulted in mad cow disease. "Doubt they're using
sheep that popular for feed," he added.

I nodded absently, for I was recalling favorite bits of
history as they came to mind. My pleasant musings were
interrupted when Childeric suddenly appeared at my side
and murmured, "Carolyn, I really would like a word with
you, if you don't mind."

I looked around for Jensen, but he had stopped to in-
spect a weedy clump growing in the sand. Then he bent
over, plucked a blade, and chewed on it thoughtfully, as if
it were some delectable tidbit offered for gourmet consideration. "I do mind," I said to Childeric, silently berating
my own foolishness for walking out here. I increased my
pace, hoping to get away from him.

"Believe me, I would never—never have declared myself had I known you wouldn't be receptive." His voice
was low and urgent. "I misread the signs. Unforgivable, I
know, but, Carolyn, I didn't mean to offend you. I hope
you won't—"

"What? Tell other people? Isn't it a bit late to worry
about that after you made advances last night to Edie? I really can't forgive—"

"It wasn't at all what she made it out to be. I assure
you—"

"What the hell!" cried Macauley Drummond, interrupting a conversation I desperately wanted to escape. We
looked back to see that water was swirling around his feet
and Hester's.

"I thought you said it was low tide, Childeric," shrieked
Drummond.

"I was—I asked and was told—" He stopped, frightened because the tide was now at his feet and mine and

frothing around the shins of Hester and Macauley. Jensen, in between the four of us, stared down as if flummoxed by this unusual situation.

We all looked desperately toward the mainland, which was closer than we'd meant to go but still farther than Mont—Tombe. It used to be called Mont Tombe!

"Best head toward the monastery," said Jensen. "It's closer."

"But the tide—it's coming from that direction," Childeric protested.

I ignored him and waded after Dr. Jensen toward the island beach, which was disappearing before my eyes as the water swelled around us.

"You idiot," screamed Macauley.

I glanced up in time to see him swept from his feet and grabbing for Hester, who cried, "I can swim. I can swim. Save yourself, Macauley."

"Thirteen miles an hour; that's how fast the tide comes in here," called Jensen. "Best hustle, folks."

I was off my feet and trying to keep afloat among seemingly conflicting tides. Nor was I doing well. I wasn't used to swimming in anything more troubled than a crowded pool or a lake whose surface was now and then disturbed by the wake of a boat.

"Help!" cried Childeric. He caught up with me and proceeded to pull me under.

I fought my way to the surface. "Can't you swim?" I gasped. He threw both arms around my neck, and I went down, seeing, before the water closed over me, people on the shore, shouting. I was coughing up water when I resurfaced and whacked the struggling medievalist with my handbag. He let go, went under, and I managed to grasp his collar, determined that if he pulled me under again, I'd leave him to drown. Silly thought. We'd all drown.

"Childeric?" Jensen had slowed his efficient crawl and allowed the tide to wash him in our direction, while Drum-

mond, with Hester following, swam ahead. I turned on my
back to catch my breath, but waves broke over me, and
Childeric's weight, suspended from my hand, pulled at me.
"Think—I—knocked him—out," I gasped.

Jensen chuckled, took in a mouthful of water, sputtered,
dove down, and brought Childeric up by the other arm.

"Boat," Hester called to us. She angled toward a rowboat, manned by two men, which, as I tried to keep it in
view, seemed to go back as much as forward in the churn-
ing waters that had now obscured the beach.

"Just stay afloat, Miz Blue," said Jensen. "I'll tow
Childeric along."

I tried, but the water kept breaking over my head.
Childeric's head I couldn't see at all, although I still had
him by the collar and tried to keep him above water.

"I've got him," Jensen gasped. "Let go. Use both arms."

I'm ashamed to say that I obeyed, much good it did me.
I was sucked under, holding my breath, what little there
was, for dear life, no idea how to fight free of a force I
didn't understand. Mont Tombe! I was terrified. Sure I was
about to drown.

36
Down the Abbot's Staircase

Jason

We were all to meet at the bus below the town at four.
Somehow Chris and I had lost both Edie and Carolyn, who
tends to stay looking at things without mentioning her in-
tention. She, of course, maintains that it's the business of

the person ahead to be sure that those trailing aren't left behind. Losing Edie was never a hard thing to do. If Chris wasn't paying enough attention to her, she tended to scamper off, usually in a huff. Neither of us was quite sure when she disappeared. Perhaps on the western side of the structure among the gloomy eleventh- and twelfth-century, barrel-vaulted rooms. Perhaps she had gone off with Carolyn, although I doubted it.

We noticed her absence several stories down where Chris discovered the "two twins," small dungeons that could be accessed only through holes in the pavement. Denis had told us dreary stories about occupants, one of whom, he had insisted, was a beautiful noblewoman whose husband didn't trust her and therefore left her in the care of the monks during the Hundred Years' War. As it turned out, Tiphaine, the lady in question, had her own house in the town. Chris decided that Edie could probably be found in a T-shirt shop in the town.

When we reached the bus, neither Edie nor Carolyn was there. Various people reported talking to Carolyn, so we assumed that she was still exploring, enraptured with Mont-Saint-Michel and forgetful of the time. Edie was another matter. Carolyn had asked other people to keep an eye out for the girl, but no one had seen her for some time. Denis muttered that those who were so rude as to be late should be left behind. Grace Unsell told him in no uncertain terms that any tour director irresponsible enough to suggest leaving a young girl behind in a strange country should be reported to his company.

Denis relented. Given the continuing problems that plagued his tour, he had probably been worried about losing his job before Edie disappeared. With various volunteers from the group, we searched the tourist area of the town, looking in shops, asking people if they had seen her. Our efforts were hampered by the lack of a photograph and the fact that no one could remember what picture had been printed on her T-shirt. She wasn't found.

Several of the women were now worried because no one thought Edie was so interested in Mont-Saint-Michel as to lose track of time. "I imagine she got lost," said Unsell. "Women get lost all the time."

"Maybe she met an attractive young man," suggested Laura de Sorentino. "Have you been avoiding her, Chris?" She smiled at Chris, who smiled back and said, "No, ma'am. I just try to hang out with my parents for protection."

"Where's Childeric?" demanded Janice Petar suspiciously.

We were all embarrassed to be reminded of events the night before, but no one had seen him either.

"Speaking of parents," I murmured to Chris, "your mother is still missing. Maybe she's found Edie and is regaling her with historical facts." Carolyn *would* lose track of time under those circumstances.

"Let's hope she's with Carolyn," said Anna. "Maybe we should see who else is missing."

"Professors Childeric, Foxcroft, and Drummond," said Denis.

Estrella nodded as if she had just discovered something significant. "Nedda, have you seen your husband with any of—"

"I lost track of him hours ago," Nedda snapped.

"Carl is missing, too," said Ingrid Jensen. "Now where did I see him? On one of those balconies that look out over the sea."

"Yes, he was talking about the sheep that feed in the salt marshes," said Unsell. "I remember asking if they are a popular French export, but he didn't seem to be interested in anything but the effect of marsh grass on the flavor of the meat. Tell me, Denis, has the tour planned to see that we sample this Norman delicacy?"

Denis looked uneasy, and I assumed that if we were to try salt marsh sheep, which Carolyn had mentioned, we'd have to pay for our own. The chicken and turkey we'd been fed heretofore were, no doubt, cheaper.

"We'll have to search the monastery," said Grace. "We can't let that child wander around on her own. She's too irresponsible."

"Grace, she's not *our* responsibility," her husband protested.

"What if she were your granddaughter, Manfred? Would you still—"

"She's not my granddaughter, thank God. I want to get back to the hotel. Denis, can't you send us back on the bus and—"

"I'm not leaving without Carl," said Ingrid. "What if some French criminal attacked him? In fact, the whole missing group may be terrorist hostages. Denis, you should contact the authorities."

Denis sighed. "There is a waiting period for missing persons before they are searched for. At worst, when the gates close for the day, they will have to leave. In the meantime, if some of you would be willing to help me . . ."

And so we spread out, searching the thinning crowds, stopping tourists who spoke English to ask if they'd seen Edie, keeping our eyes open for the adults. An hour later, Chris and I and Janice Petar found the girl at the bottom of a stone staircase that had, we later ascertained, been the entrance to the monastery in the twelfth century. Edie had obviously fallen, for she was bruised and unconscious, her head bleeding.

"She must have been with Childeric," said Chris. "When people get hurt, they're either Childeric or with him. And Mom's missing."

"Chris, can you find your way to the entrance?" I asked quickly.

"Of course," he replied, insulted that I'd think he was lost.

"Go for help. If you find an official before you reach the town, send him here." Fortunately, Janice had a guide-book, so we were able to tell him where we were exactly, the Abbot's Staircase. Chris loped off, taking the steps two at a time. "Be careful," I called after him.

Janice Petar, although almost as abrasive as my mother, was also as efficient. She took the girl's pulse, listened to her heart, lifted her eyelids, took off her shoes, and poked her feet and knees.

"Concussion. Probably no paralysis, definitely uncon-scious, maybe in a coma. Cover her central body with your coat, will you? I'll put my jacket over her legs. We don't want to move her at all."

"I wish I knew where my wife is," I mumbled unhap-pily, then felt abashed that I was worrying about Carolyn, who was probably fine, while this girl, who was more or less in our care, had been injured.

"If you're feeling guilty about Edie, don't," said Janice. "No one's been able to keep track of her since we left. No reason you should have any more luck than anyone else, especially since she resents being denied private access to your son."

Janice tucked my jacket about Edie's body and spread hers over the girl's legs. "She'll probably end up pregnant and puzzled about it before she ever graduates from high school. She's one of these hapless females who think, be-cause they're pretty, bad things can't happen to them no matter what they do." Janice took the girl's pulse again. "You'd think her experience last night with Childeric would have taught her a thing or two. In fact, maybe we should ask ourselves whether he pushed her down these stairs. He was beside himself when she let everyone know what he'd been up to."

Surely the man hadn't—well, I wasn't guessing what

anyone would or wouldn't do. Not anymore. We sat on the steps beside the unconscious girl, answering questions from the only two people who passed and wondering how long Edie had lain there unconscious. Finally, Chris returned with Denis and a French policeman. Denis said medical personnel would follow. I can't say that I've ever seen the ebullient Denis look more distressed, as well he might. Here we had yet another injury on his tour.

"Dad, listen," said Chris, drawing me aside. "People are saying two women and three men were caught in the incoming tide. A boat went after them, but no one seems to know—"

"Oh, my God." I don't think I've ever felt such dread. Besides Edie, five people had been missing from our group, Carolyn and Childeric among them. Wherever that pompous bastard went, disaster followed. She couldn't have taken a chance—who were the others mentioned before we went hunting Edie? Drummond. He would be too self-involved to help anyone but himself. Childeric, too.

Hester? A New Englander, but was she a strong enough swimmer to fight a riptide or a whirlpool, both reported to be features of the huge seas in the area?

Oh God, Carolyn couldn't have—wait, Jensen. He was missing. Ingrid had refused to leave without him. Jensen was a sensible man, but I had no idea whether he knew how to swim. Carolyn did, but—but it would be no ordinary situation out there.

I remembered one of Denis's stories. The pregnant peasant girl, who got caught in the tide and gave birth. It took a miracle to save her. Why would any of them have walked out—then I remembered. The sheep. Ingrid had mentioned her husband's interest in salt marsh sheep.

Surely, he wasn't foolish enough to—surely, Carolyn wouldn't have been interested in an expedition to look at—

"Dad?" Chris said sharply. "Dad? You're white as a sheet."

"She loves lamb," I mumbled, grabbed his arm, and headed up the stairs. "We've got to find your mother."

37
Bailing

Carolyn

The boat wasn't big enough for the five of us. They dragged me in and then Childeric. He had to be revived, no easy matter in the bottom of a boat. I was coughing up water as one of the fishermen pulled Hester in. She immediately turned Childeric over and pumped him, while Drummond demanded to be taken aboard next. As I hung over the side of the boat, still coughing and vomiting, Jensen was treading water and suggesting to the fishermen that they throw him a life preserver and let him cling to the stern. They didn't understand English. What a good man— even if he was obsessed with mad cow disease. He'd dived after me when I was being pulled down, dragged me up, and gone after Childeric.

Managing to edge away from the fisherman who was using oars in an attempt to keep the boat in place before it was driven away from those still in the water, I held a hand out to Jensen. Drummond tried to push him aside, but I withdrew my hand, for which I was roundly cursed. "You translate, Drummond," I ordered and grasped Carl's wrist. I wasn't saving Drummond. He hadn't done a thing for anyone but himself. Lucky that Hester was a good swimmer. He'd have let her drown.

"He's breathing," she said and propped Childeric up. He was also vomiting.

Drummond screamed broken phrases in French, clinging to a rope that Hester threw to him. Evidently he got some of the message across because the second fisherman gave me a life preserver and a rope for Carl, and I managed to get him tied. Meanwhile, Drummond shrieked, "Now, take me in."

Hester threw him a life preserver. "There's not enough room, Macauley. Hang on."

He shouted curses at her and at me. I slumped against the boat and sent a weak smile toward the oarsman. *"Merci. Merci,"* I whispered. They had given the only two life preservers to the men in the water. God help us all if the boat swamped. We were being buffeted by the waves and pulled this way and that by conflicting tides. The second fisherman, mumbling to himself, handed me a bucket, and took up the second pair of oars.

Hester was already bailing when I gathered almost nonexistent strength and wielded the bucket, keeping my eye on Carl, poor man. I don't know how he managed to get enough air to exist in those terrible seas, and I was terrified that the knot with which I had tied his preserver to the boat would give way and leave him stranded. A square knot. My father had taught me as a child to tie them, very impatient because I was so slow to learn. I remember a mathematician at a cocktail party. He studied knots, but in DNA rather than rope, and never when he was in danger of drowning. I was so frightened. And the boat seemed to take on more water than Hester and I could scoop out one-handed. I clung to the seat with the other hand.

38
Who Was Saved?

Jason

When Chris and I arrived in the town, we went straight to the bus. Carolyn wasn't there. Nor were any of those missing before we began to search for Edie. "Maybe they're in town having a drink," said Chris, who looked frightened.

"We'll find the police station," I responded, heading away from the parking lot.

Before we got there, we were hailed by members of our group who were sitting in a sidewalk café drinking Campari, Unsell among them. "Did you hear?" he called. "We think some of our people had to be rescued by local fishermen."

"Who?" I demanded, heart in my mouth.

"That's right. Your wife is among the missing. Now mine seems to be. Haven't seen her since she went off looking for that Atwater girl. Damned silly—"

"Who—was—rescued?" I demanded.

"No need to snap at me, Blue. We don't know. The boat headed in on the tide toward the mainland."

"How many were out there? How many were picked up?"

"Five," said Nedda Drummond sourly.

I breathed a sigh of relief. "Thank God."

"There were five on the beach. My husband and Hester. Your wife, I suppose. Childeric. Jensen."

"I can't believe Carl would be so foolish," said Ingrid plaintively. "But he *is* a strong swimmer."

"And they were all pulled in?" Chris asked, anxious for reassurance.

"Well, we don't know that, do we?" said Unsell. "Won't know until Denis lets us take the bus back to the mainland. I hope you found that silly girl so we can—"

"How can you not know whether they were rescued?" I demanded.

"The fishermen didn't come back here," Ingrid explained, "and none of us saw the rescue."

Chris and I exchanged agonized looks. "Let's try the police station," said Chris. "Dr. de Sorentino, could you ask someone where it is?"

"My wife's the French speaker, not I," said the plastic surgeon, waving to the waiter for a refill.

"Where's Robbie?" I asked. "And Hugh?"

"I think Dr. Fauree is still looking for the girl," said Ingrid, "and"—she sniffed disdainfully—"and Dr. Hecht came back here, heard about the tide catching Carl and the others, and went looking for news of your wife."

"We'll see if we can find Robbie," I said to Chris.

"Maybe you'd be so good as to tell me where my wife is before you leave," said Unsell.

"And Edie," added Anna.

"Fell down some stairs. An ambulance is coming for her," I called over my shoulder. "She's unconscious."

We met Robbie by the third gate. "No one knows who was picked up and taken to the mainland," she said. "Jason, what if she—well, she just has to be okay. I've asked everyone I could get to stop. I asked at the police station. There's just no news."

"Then we have to drive back. I'll drive the bus myself, if I have to."

"Good idea, but I can do it," said Robbie. "I drove a school bus when I was a graduate student. Anything to make money. I even tried topless dancing." She laughed, then said, "Sorry. Not funny. I'm whistling in the dark. Scared to death. Let's go."

39
Police Interrogations

Jason

The ambulance was gone, carrying Edie and Grace Unsell, who insisted on accompanying Edie. Grace had been an emergency room nurse before she married. Neither her husband nor the French ambulance attendants could convince her to stay behind. At Denis's insistence, the rest of us had to wait for the last of the searchers to straggle in. I kept Roberta on the telephone trying to get information from French bureaucrats on shore about the fate of the boat from Mont-Saint-Michel.

Even when the bus finally reached shore, there was no word. Police were there to interview us about Edie's accident but denied knowledge of a boat rescue. Not their business, I gathered. Try the coast guard, they said. But we couldn't try because we were not allowed to leave the police station. I did manage to get interviewed first, Chris and I separately, because we had found the "victim." Translators had to be found. Members of our own group could not be trusted to substitute, evidently.

Janice, furious when Laura's offer of help was turned down, launched into a diatribe on the French treatment of

women, which she insisted that Laura translate. Laura evidently put the matter in such a way that the confused po-
licemen misunderstood. They apologized profusely to the
frustrated Janice, whom they thought wished to be questioned by a woman. Then they produced a policewoman,
who not only had a marginal understanding of English but
also provided a box of Kleenex to Janice and kept patting
her on the shoulder as she escorted her away.

Then while I was being questioned, the cell phone
given to me by Grace Unsell rang. When she insisted on
accompanying the unconscious girl to the hospital, she had
left the phone with me as the only person left of the couple charged with Edie's welfare.

"Word of Miss Atwater," I said to the protesting inter-
rogator, who wanted to confiscate the phone. I backed
away from him. The translator translated. "How is Edie?"
I asked.

"Unconscious," Grace replied, "but they expect her to
recover. I thought you'd want to know that the rest of our
party is here."

"In the hospital? Carolyn?" The last was asked with
both hope and dread.

"She's wet, frightened, and exhausted, but she's fine,
Jason, and asking the doctors to let her see you."

I clicked off and rose to leave immediately. The inter-
rogation officer tried to stop me. The translator tried to explain, presumably, my over-the-shoulder cry that my wife
was in the hospital. On orders, a gendarme stopped me in
the reception area. My fellow tour members stared as I
tried to shake the policeman off, all the while bellowing,
"Chris, they've found your mother."

Chris appeared at another door, trailing his own ques-
tioner and translator. General pandemonium ensued, but I
did manage to convey the news that Edie was going to be
all right and could be asked what had happened to her,
something I did not know to be true.

A compromise was reached under which Chris and I were escorted to the hospital by our respective interrogators, while the other tour members remained behind protesting, especially Mrs. Jensen. I did notice that Nedda Drummond showed no interest in visiting her husband. In fact, I hadn't asked about the others. I simply said a fervent thanks to Grace and hung up. Carolyn would say that I should have been more thoughtful. However, panic and its sudden relief will overcome ordinary consideration for others. I was sorry, but I was also frantic to get to my wife.

40
French Health Care

Carolyn

Chris and Jason barged into the curtained-off room where I sat shivering in a hospital gown while a doctor applied a freezing stethoscope to my back and babbled from time to time in French.

"Carolyn!" Jason cried and embraced me.

"Monsieur," the doctor protested, trying to extract his stethoscope from under my husband's tight grasp.

"Are you all right?" Jason asked.

I burst into tears. It was the first time I had done so since the water engulfed me, and it was a relief to cry. With one arm around Jason's neck and one hand clasped by my son, who looked pale and distraught, I sobbed, "It was Childeric's f-f-fault." My teeth had started to chatter.

"It was not," cried a voice from another cubicle.

"He s-s-said it was safe."

"Anna said it was," protested the voice.

"That's Ch-Ch-Childeric. He p-pulled me under when I tried to r-r-rescue him."

"Oh, sweetheart." Jason tightened his hold on me.

The doctor protested in French. A nurse bustled in and tried to remove Jason. She was young and pretty, so Chris said, "Hi, there."

She replied, "Eye, Yan-kee," and tossed her head.

"Dr. Jensen s-s-saved me," I chattered.

"For God's sake, can't someone get her a blanket?" Jason demanded. "She's freezing."

"I was so f-f-frightened," I sobbed. The nurse and Chris wrapped a blanket around me. The doctor snarled at her. French was tossed about. "Then two f-f-fishermen picked us up. J-J-Jensen and Drummond had to be dragged behind because there wasn't r-r-room in the b-b-boat."

"My God," said Jason.

"Drummond w-wanted to get in."

"I'll bet," said Chris. He was gazing at the young nurse while the doctor lectured her. Evidently there was some French hospital rule against wrapping freezing, traumatized victims of accidents at sea in warm blankets.

"What took you so long to get here?" I must have sounded weak-kneed and pathetic because my poor husband actually stammered out his explanation about Edie's disappearance and fall and the subsequent hunt for her.

"Oh, Jason. Is she all right?" I asked, now guilt-ridden because I was the one who had lost her.

"Unconscious in this hospital. She should recover."

"If you'd been looking after her as you were supposed to," croaked Childeric from beyond the curtain that separated us, "this wouldn't have happened."

Jason had to restrain me. I think I had in mind to stalk next door and attack that horrible man. At the risk of my own, I'd helped save his life, and he wasn't showing the least appreciation. "Too bad you didn't drown," I muttered.

Chris looked shocked. Childeric shouted that he'd heard me.

"You probably pushed Edie yourself to keep her from telling her mother what you did to her," I called back. "You're a nasty old man."

"He pushed Edie and almost drowned you?" Chris dropped my hand and started around the curtain.

"I was with your mother. How could I have done anything to that girl?" Childeric quavered.

"That's right. You tried to drown me," I said.

"Help!" Childeric wailed.

"Chris, come back here," said Jason and kissed my forehead. "Don't get yourself upset, sweetheart. I'll take care of Childeric later."

The young nurse tossed the folds of her nurse's headdress and went after my son, saying something like, "*Non, Yan-kee,*" and other things in French. The doctor shouted at her, then at Chris, and finally at me, because I wouldn't let him remove my nice, warm blanket.

"I want to go home," I sniffled.

"To El Paso?" Jason asked. "Well, maybe we can leave tomorrow with Chris from Tours."

"Actually, I meant to Saint-Malo. Which reminds me"—I was beginning to feel better—well, warm at least—"I met a lady from Seattle in the Crypt of the Mighty Pillars. She told me that Saint-Malo has a wonderful dining room in a small hotel—I wrote down the name, but I suppose my note got all wet. Anyway, they serve Coquille Saint-Jacques. I'd like to go there for dinner."

"I think Mom's feeling better," said Chris.

41
Accusations

Carolyn

At last I was released from the hospital, dressed in my saltwater clothes, which Chris's nurse friend had put through a dryer. I'm sure I looked a fright, but we five survivors of the tide boarded the bus with the rest of the group and drove back to Saint-Malo. Childeric stopped by my seat and apologized for shouting at me in the hospital.

"I was distraught," he admitted. "And I hope that I didn't endanger you. If I did, my apologies."

His clothes were still soggy. I was pleased to see it, and I didn't forgive him, either. I was still distraught myself. Jason told him to leave me alone.

Looking chastened, the professor started farther back in the bus. People who were sitting alone moved to aisle seats to prevent him from sitting down by them. He didn't appear at dinner that night. Nor did he thank Professor Jensen or me for saving his life. Possibly he didn't remember much about what happened.

When he passed Drummond, the novelist said, "You might thank Hester for reviving you once they dragged you into the boat, taking up so much space that Jensen and I—"

"Don't apologize on my account, Childeric," interrupted Carl Jensen. "I'm none the worse for the dunking.

A man needs a bit of excitement now and then. Can't spend a whole life with the cows."

"Excitement!" cried his wife. "I was terrified when I discovered you missing. I want to go home."

"We're on the way, Ingrid," said Jensen and readdressed himself to Childeric. "Glad to drag you up, Childeric, after Carolyn, here, had to hit you with her purse."

"Hit me with her purse?" Childeric looked dumbfounded and turned toward me.

"You were dragging her under after the water hit," said Jensen. "Some folks just naturally panic when they think they're going to drown."

"You hit me with your purse?"

"I hear he accused me of misleading him about the tides," Anna remarked from her place beside Janice at the front of the bus. "I distinctly heard Denis telling everyone to stay away from the water because of the tides." She turned to Childeric. "You were there, Professor. You must have heard him, too."

"I—I don't remember—"

"You were probably spouting some dull bit of medieval trivia," said Janice. "I've noticed that you rarely listen to anyone but yourself."

That was certainly the truth, I thought, but not as angrily as before, for I was so tired. I just wanted them to stop talking so that I could take a nap during the trip back.

"Professor Thomas-Smith *did* tell me that it was low tide that afternoon," said Childeric defensively. "I'd never have suggested walking out if I hadn't—"

Janice stood up and faced him. "Drummond says you claimed *someone* told you it was low tide. How is it that you've now decided it was Anna?"

"Well, I—" He looked toward Anna. "Anna, didn't you—"

Anna said quietly, "Professor Childeric, I knew the tide was coming in. Denis told us that."

"That's right, he did," said Nedda, who was not sitting with her husband. "Which makes me wonder why my husband was so stupid as to take Childeric's word for something so important."

"I'm the one who was nearly killed," snarled Drummond. "And I didn't hear Denis say anything about—"

"I told you all to stay off the beaches at high tide," Denis interrupted. "I told you the story of the pregnant peasant girl who—"

"Given the rank inaccuracy of everything you say," Childeric snapped, "you can hardly expect us to pay any attention to—"

"So you admit that you weren't paying any attention," Janice interrupted. "Then why should we believe you when you say Anna misled you? Why would she do that? And why would you listen to anything she said, given your attitude toward statements other than your own?"

"I wonder, Professor Childeric, whether Edie Atwater was with you when she came to grief," Anna asked softly. "Isn't it enough that you made advances to the poor child yesterday? Perhaps you were angry because she rejected you and embarrassed you in front of the others."

"You're saying I had something to do with her fall?" Childeric flushed red over his soggy woolen jacket with its puckered suede elbow patches. "On top of insinuating that there was something unseemly between that girl and myself? Her accusation was a lie. A vicious lie." He saw the disgust in the eyes of his fellow travelers and amended his accusation. "To put the best face on her story, she may have mistaken the kindness of an older man for . . ."

Wearily, I watched him working himself into a state of self-righteous indignation.

". . . and I don't have to put up with accusations of this sort. I was told that the tide was going out, whoever said it, and I did not try to drown Mrs. Blue, although she evidently tried to drown me by hitting me while I was struggling in the water. I don't, in fact, remember anything about that until I regained consciousness in the boat. And my relationship with Edie Atwater is entirely that of mentor to student. I thought the child had an interest in medieval history, which I've now begun to doubt. No matter what she or anyone else says, I have done nothing to be ashamed of. Nothing. If Miss Atwater is continuing to slander me—"

"She's unconscious," said Hester. "In the hospital unconscious."

"Took a terrible fall down some stairs," Janice added. "So how did that happen?"

"I was on the beach," said Childeric desperately.

"How convenient," Janice replied.

I didn't want to think about all the frightening things that had happened or who might be responsible. Rather than tax my poor, tired brain, I closed my eyes, and the clamor died away as the bus rolled toward Saint-Malo. I dreamed of a terrifying figure chasing me toward a restaurant where scallops were served in a delicious sauce. *If only I can get there before he catches me,* I thought. *I'm so hungry, and I don't want to die.* I woke feeling for my umbrella to defend myself. Jason was telling me that we'd arrived.

42
Exodus Dawning

Jason

Less than half of us ate dinner that night in the dining
room about which Carolyn had heard from another tourist:
the de Lorenzos, the Jensens, the Markarovs, a very sulky
Unsell, Chris, Carolyn, and myself. Carolyn ordered not
just one plate of Coquille Saint-Jacques but two. I didn't
say a word, although I did wonder if she'd be surprised
when the second order arrived.

I had the salt marsh lamb, which caused my wife to look
distressed. I can't imagine why; she loves lamb, but she
wouldn't even sample an offered bite when it came, and
she evidently hadn't made a mistake in her order because
she polished off both plates without comment. Of course,
there were only two oyster shells per plate. She did try the
Bretonne beans that came with my dinner and said that if
she'd had the energy, she'd have asked for a recipe. However, the proprietress didn't look that friendly, and Carolyn
didn't feel like an argument.

Not that Carolyn's reluctance prevented others from
quarreling. First, Ingrid Jensen reiterated her desire to
leave this "terrifying tour" and go home.

"Now Ingrid," said Jensen, his mouth full of fish in
white sauce. "I'm the fellow who had the scare, not you.
We paid a bundle for this vacation, and we're seeing it
through. All those fancy châteaux. I know for a fact you

want to see them." Ingrid subsided, but she was not a happy woman.

Then Lorenzo de Sorentino announced that he and Laura were leaving as soon as he could book a flight out.

"Why?" his wife asked mildly.

"Because it's foolish to expose oneself to danger."

"See there, Carl. *He* doesn't want to get *his* wife killed," said Ingrid.

"Phooey," said Carl. "You're not gonna get killed, Ingrid."

"Well, *we* can certainly afford to skip the rest of the tour," de Sorentino continued. "Not that I see any reason to lose money. I intend to demand that the company, which obviously cannot protect us, return a portion of our payment."

"Whatever you plan to demand in return, Lorenzo," said his wife, "cut that in half, because I'm not going."

"Of course you are."

"No, I'm not!" She took a sip of the Château la Tour he'd ordered with great fanfare and set her goblet down. "I am not fleeing. Is that tough enough for a dean candidate, or do you want me to go out and punch someone?"

"Don't be ridiculous," he snapped.

A shocked Estrella Markarov whispered in Laura's ear, "It's a wife's duty to cleave to her husband."

"Is that in general or while on vacation?" Laura asked.

"At all times," said Estrella, forgetting to whisper.

At that moment the Unsells' telephone, which was still in my pocket, rang, and I answered. "Is that my cell phone?" Unsell demanded. He reached for it.

I waved him off. Grace was telling me that Edie had awakened and seemed to be progressing nicely. I relayed the news to the others. "But the poor child has amnesia. She can't remember how she came to fall down the stairs," said Grace. I passed that on. Unsell tried to get the telephone away from me again, but Grace mentioned Carolyn, so I held on tight. "Tell Carolyn not to worry about Edie," Grace said. "I'll stay here and take her home. She should be ready to travel tomorrow or the next day."

When I told Carolyn, Unsell shouted, "What? Give me that phone," and he knocked over Lorenzo's wine goblet yanking it away from me.

"You come straight back here, Grace," he ordered. "That girl's not your responsibility . . . Then let the tour company take care of her . . . Insensitive? The devil I am. You get yourself back here by tomorrow morning or I'll . . . Don't tell me that. Maddie always thinks she's about to deliver." Then he held the cell phone away and stared at it. "She hung up on me," he said, astounded. "She's worse over this grandchild than she was when she was carrying Maddie."

"I'm so sorry to hear that your wife won't be rejoining you, Professor Unsell," said Estrella Markarov, "but the coming of a child is a blessed event. Perhaps you should consider—"

"Mind your own business," muttered Unsell, his red nose shining like a beacon in the candlelight.

"Not talk to my sweet potato like that," said Ivan. "Is sweet potato right? Orange potato with sweet gummies melted on?"

"You're so smart, Ivan," said Estrella, beaming. "What a command of English! Our child will be trilingual. Isn't that exciting?"

"*You're* expecting a child?" said Unsell, looking at her with patent disbelief. "It's probably menopause."

"It is not," cried Estrella. "I'm pregnant." Laura, too, looked surprised. Estrella cried, "Well, I am, aren't I, Ivan?"

"You say baby coming. I celebrate. No cigars, but we drink toast to baby, no?"

"No," said Estrella. "Alcohol causes birth defects."

"Okay," he agreed. "I drink toast."

"You needn't look like that," Estrella said to Laura de Sorentino. "Maybe if you were a more dutiful wife and a better Christian, you could have a baby."

"Maybe if my husband had wanted a baby, I'd have had one," said Laura.

I could see that our group was moving from quarreling to exodus and wondered if Carolyn and I shouldn't leave tomorrow night with Chris.

Carolyn ordered a chocolate gateau.

43
Could It Be Lorenzo?

Jason

Carolyn was too tired to write a column that night, but she did pull up her clue list and add Edie's fall. As a suspect she typed in Childeric, although I pointed out that Edie could have tripped. "He had reason to wish her harm," Carolyn replied. "He could be dropped from the dean's race or even fired for what he did to her yesterday."

"True, but I don't see that hurting Edie would help him. Everyone heard what she said. He's only off the hook if she decides not to tell her parents and no one else tells tales. And he was out on the beach with you. My God, Carolyn, how could you—"

"Are you blaming me because I nearly drowned?"

"No, but—"

"There were four other people, and we all thought it was safe. I suppose someone could have given him misinformation deliberately, but it seems more likely that he asked a question and didn't bother to listen to the answer. Men do that."

"I don't think I can be accused of not listening to you. I—"

"The really awful thing is that he panicked and nearly drowned me trying to save himself. And I was trying to help him. He didn't even say thank you."

"You want me to punch him?"

"Oh, don't be silly, Jason," she mumbled.

"I'm serious, Carolyn. I don't like the man, and I don't like the fact that he spent so much time hanging around you earlier in the tour, and I certainly don't like the fact that he could have killed you. I'll be glad to punch him in the nose."

"Oh, Jason." My wife started to giggle. "Professors don't punch each other."

"On this tour, I wouldn't be surprised to see it happen. I could give him a jab, and it would probably precipitate a free-for-all. No one would even notice I started it."

"I would, so don't do it." She then fell silent for a moment, looking thoughtful, and added, "It is strange that we never see who did any of these things. It's as if we have an invisible nemesis. One person hurt this afternoon and five of us in dire straits. Eleven incidents before that. I think." She glanced at her computer screen.

Later before we went to bed, Carolyn asked, "Why would Lorenzo de Sorentino decide to leave?" She was rubbing cream into her face.

"Maybe he was frightened by the dog last night."

"He didn't seem frightened. I wonder if he's the one causing all these *accidents*."

"Why would he?" I couldn't fathom her line of reasoning.

"I think he was around every time something happened. He could have pushed Edie. He wasn't with the five of us on the beach."

"Neither was I, Carolyn," I pointed out. I had been lying in bed, reading an article on toxicology, which mentioned that French bakers in the nineteenth century used copper sulfate and alum to whiten bread. Copper sulfate is highly poisonous and alum moderately toxic. I rolled sideways to tell Carolyn since the information intersected with her interests.

"I hope you're not saying that we can't eat white bread in France," my wife replied. "Surely, their Food and Drug Administration wouldn't let the bakers use poisons in this day and age."

"We don't know if they have an FDA. Don't the French still allow the sale of absinthe? That's poisonous."

"Do they? I remember thinking I'd like to try an absinthe frappe when we were in New Orleans. Of course, they weren't available." She then returned to her new theory that Lorenzo de Sorentino might be the tour terrorist. "He could have been the one who told Childeric that it was low tide. Childeric obviously has no idea who said that. If anyone did."

"But why would Lorenzo—"

"I don't know, Jason, but the thought is especially dreadful since he's an M.D. He took an oath to do no harm."

"Doctors do harm all the time. Just putting someone in a hospital often does them harm. That's where the worst antibiotic-resistant bacteria reside. Did you read the statistics about—"

"No, and I don't think I want to hear them." Then she eyed me with new alarm. "Are you saying I might have picked up a fatal disease because they took me to that hospital today?"

"Of course not. You didn't have any invasive procedures. A lot of the infections—"

"Maybe Lorenzo's doing these things to control Laura. To make her go home when she wants to stay."

"Come to bed, sweetheart."

Carolyn removed the cream she'd applied to her face, turned out the light, and slid into bed beside me. "He definitely doesn't want her to be dean," she said, her voice drowsy.

"Then making Childeric look bad wouldn't be a good move." I could have saved my breath. Carolyn had fallen asleep. She didn't even wake up when Chris came by to suggest that it would be a good idea if we left France tomorrow with him, even though our spring break allowed us to finish the tour.

"And if we don't, you might have to sit with de Sorentino on the way home," I said dryly. "He'll tell you about the plastic surgery you'll be needing in twenty years or so."

"Great. Mom told me that Professor Thomas-Smith said I should cut down on fats so I won't get prostrate cancer."

"Prostate," I corrected.

"And Mrs. Jensen said I shouldn't room with Denis because he's queer. Of course, she thinks half the world is. When I didn't pay any attention, she looked at me like I was."

I'm afraid I chuckled at my son's complaints. And it was a relief to hear about problems that evoked laughter instead of dread.

"I'll tell you, Dad, it'll be good to get back to the fraternity: no high school girls and no advice from weird adults."

Travel Journal
Day Nine, Mount St. Michael

Dark and dank. Stone and stairs and dungeons. Perfect setting for skulking around, setting people up.

So Laura de Sorentino's husband's leaving? Good. He was ruining her chances of beating out C. for dean.

And Edie Atwater. Not my favorite person. Now people are

whispering that C. might have pushed her. Wouldn't surprise me. No question he's scared the story about him and Edie will get around back home. So he should be. If no one else spreads it, I will.

And C. so panicked in the water he almost drowned Carolyn Blue. Good again. Now everyone's scared of him.

No one sat with him on the bus. No one ate dinner with him.

Let him see how it feels to be alone. A nobody in a crowd.

44
A Reading over Croissants

Carolyn

Still wobble-kneed on my way to breakfast the next morning and having forgotten to put my bag out the night before, for which I think I can be forgiven under the circumstances, I ran into Ingrid Jensen and told her how much I appreciated her husband's bravery yesterday afternoon. She told me that she'd heard Chris come to our room last night and commiserated with me over the reason. I must have looked blank.

"Well," she said, a bit huffy, "you don't have to tell me if you don't want to."

"Tell you what?"

"Obviously, Denis made a pass at him. I did warn you not to let him room with that man."

"Chris didn't—"

"Didn't tell you? I suppose he was embarrassed to

admit such a thing to his mother. You'll find he told Jason. Unless, of course, he didn't mind."

I was beginning to take offense. "If Chris told Jason something while I was asleep, Jason would have told me this morning. And what do you mean about not minding? If you're implying that Chris is—not that there's anything wrong with that—"

"Nothing wrong?" Ingrid looked shocked. "It's against God's—"

"—but it happens that my son likes girls," I continued before she could say anything more irritating.

"Yes, I noticed him pursuing that little high school girl. I've heard some people go both ways, as they say."

"He doesn't—he didn't—"

"I wonder if he got her pregnant? That would explain her timely fall down the stairs. She probably miscarried last night at that French hospital."

"Have you ever considered writing for soap operas, Ingrid?" I asked and headed for the breakfast room. To think I had started the conversation by saying something nice.

Having collected my croissant, coffee, and fruit juice, I had no more than sat down beside Jason, bent on telling him about Ingrid Jensen's penchant for gossip, when Nedda Drummond spotted her husband entering the breakfast room behind Hester Foxcroft. "Well, the errant lovers show up for breakfast after a night of wild, illicit sex," Nedda said. Everyone gaped. Some even slopped coffee into their saucers.

"If you're addressing me, Nedda, you're talking absolute rot," said Drummond as he mixed coffee and hot milk in his cup.

Nedda stood up, her hand closed so tightly around her juice glass that the knuckles were white. I waited for her to hurl the glass at him, if it didn't break in her hand first. "You weren't in *our* room last night," she said.

"What if I wasn't?" he retorted.

"Well, he wasn't in mine," Hester added. She had been contemplating the croissants as if she thought something different might appear if she waited. "I'm sleeping in Hugh's—"

Estrella had just entered and gasped.

"—single," Hester continued, "so he and Robbie can have my double now that Jeremy's gone home."

"Not that you can't have fun in the single," added Robbie, laughing. "We put it to good use. Of course, I'm not accusing anyone—" Everyone was glaring at her now. "Oh, poof!" she said and sat down.

"By the way, if anyone cares, Jeremy's doctor in Boston says his leg is healing nicely, and he should be out of the cast in two months," said Hester, her tone that of a woman mildly offended by the preceding remarks, "and I've never been unfaithful to Jeremy, so you have nothing to worry about, Nedda. At least, not where I'm concerned."

"While I," said Macauley Drummond, "do not appreciate having my comings and goings monitored as if I were some schoolboy. A man without freedom is a man whose marriage has become an impediment to his creative expression."

"Really?" His wife pulled a shirt box from under her chair. "Creative expression? While I was waiting for you to show up last night, Macauley, I entertained myself with your latest effort at creative expression. Not quite up to your usual obscure standards, but I'm sure our fellow travelers would be delighted to hear a reading."

Drummond shrugged. "Don't be a fool, Nedda. No one wants to hear a first draft." He sat down across the table and reached to take the manuscript from her.

She jerked it away. "Don't be modest, Macauley. People love to recognize themselves in a novel, especially by such a *famous* writer." Backing away from his grasp, she ran her eyes around the table that seated our group, what was left of it. Three had already departed. "He's writing a

novel about the tour," she said. "I thought I'd share some
of it with you before I leave this evening on the plane from
Tours."

Macauley looked shocked, then readjusted his expression to one of amusement. "You're doing no such thing,"
he said. "Don't be a fool."

"Leaving you is the least foolish thing I've ever proposed in my life," she replied and began to thumb through
the manuscript after putting on her reading glasses. "Let's
see. Here's a passage that just has to refer to Dr. de
Sorentino, the medical one: 'The aging Pygmalion, whose
power over his creation was fading with his virility, turned
to the woman he referred to as Brillo-Head'—that's me,
wouldn't you say?—'and thrust the dull blade of his wit
into her ill-defended ego.' My ego's in better shape than
you might think, Macauley . . . Ah, here's another. It's
about the lovely Estrella, I'd say. 'She wanted a child as a
boa constrictor lusts after a tasty rabbit or a young goat, so
that she could consume it utterly.' "

Estrella began to cry and had to be led from the room
by her husband, who could be heard saying in the hall, "Is
nothing to cry on. He have no baby to see that is baby eating mother, not mother eating . . ." Estrella wailed with anguish at that piece of presumably well-meant, if ill-stated,
consolation.

"Goodness, Macauley, that one didn't go over very
well," said Nedda to her stone-faced husband. "Well,
here's a nice scene. The character says, 'Look at that cow!
Got an udder that makes a man's hands itch to grab it.' The
character's wife says, 'I wish you'd spend as much time
looking at my udders as you do at . . .' and so forth. I won't
trouble you with the boring and pornographic witticisms
that follow or the peculiar comparison to the begetting of
the Minotaur."

Not surprisingly, more people began to leave. As Jason
and I dragged Chris out, Nedda was saying, "Goodness,

Macauley, you seem to be losing your audience, not that you ever had a very big one. How many copies did your last book sell? Fifteen hundred? Well, let's hope this one does better because I'm hoping to get the royalties in the divorce settlement."

Hester murmured, "That's not nearly as good as your last book, Macauley."

"See, even your newest bimbo doesn't like it," Nedda exclaimed. "Let me read what he has to say about you, Hester. I believe he calls you an 'oversexed, bloody-minded pseudo artist.'"

Hester laughed. "Bostonians are never oversexed. So I guess your—well, your soon-to-be ex—has an overactive fantasy life." Then she looked thoughtful. "I wonder what the id would look like in glass."

45
Launched by Bubbles

Carolyn

No one spoke to Macauley Drummond on the bus that day, and Nedda refused to give back his manuscript. Instead she perched by various people and read choice bits to them. Before long, no one was speaking to her either. The last person to do so was Laura de Sorentino, who, unwilling to sit with her husband, had joined Anna. Having leafed through the manuscript to another flagged passage, Nedda stopped by Anna to say, "He calls you the 'portly virgin, patron saint of sexually deprived homemakers.' He's got you trying out one of those shake mixers as a—"

Laura leaned forward and cut off the rest. "Nedda," she said quietly, "put that spiteful manuscript away. You have a good reputation in the college. Don't ruin things for yourself because you married the wrong man. Lots of us make that mistake."

Nedda looked startled. Then she walked up the aisle and dropped the manuscript on her husband's lap, from which it slipped and spread out on the bus floor. Turning, kicking a few pages aside, and walking over others, Nedda returned to sit beside Janice Petar. "Now about this feminist point of view . . ." she said, and they fell into conversation.

The last thing I heard before I dozed off was Childeric saying, "You two are plotting against me, aren't you?" He had risen and leaned forward between Laura and Anna. They ignored him, but from behind came Janice's amused declaration, "No, but Nedda and I are." I carried that voice and the dread it caused into sleep, for it reminded me that Janice, who made no secret of her dislike for Childeric, was someone else whom I had suspected.

This uneasy premonition was still with me when we reached our destination, the château of Angers, part fortification built by Saint Louis to hold off the English, part pleasure palace of the Dukes of Anjou, and most interesting, home of the Tapestry of the Apocalypse. Since Denis had warned that some climbing was involved, Jason asked if I really felt up to this exploration. However, I was inspired by the great castle with its eighteen round towers and my somewhat morbid desire to see the famous tapestry depicting the last great battle of good and evil. I insisted on going, even though I was, in fact, exhausted from the struggle in the tide the day before and still experiencing pain from my collision with the bicycle in Rouen.

After the escalation of violence and the bickering that characterized this tour of seemingly ordinary people, the tapestry affected me with admiration as well as trepidation. Finished in 1382, it had survived all these years, a huge work of art both grim and glorious, as had been the vision of Saint John, who wrote the biblical book from which the tapestry was taken. Some parts were gone, some damaged, but the original bold colors still survived on the back, which had been lined.

And the scenes were amazing: the graceful, flowing robes of the Four Winds, the decorative beauty of the trees with their individual leaves, the simple lines of the palaces, and the horror engendered by such figures as skeletal death riding his pale horse against a blood red background with lovely trees whose leaves are beginning to wither; the bat-winged Angel of the Abyss riding a mailed horse with a king's head and scorpion's tail; the contrast of the hideous little demon with the graceful angel in the panel depicting the overflow of the wine press. So many visions of evil. In the end I was glad to get away from this vivid medieval depiction of the struggle between God and Satan, but I think Hester had found her favorite work of art. She had to be coaxed away by poor Denis, who wasn't nearly as sprightly as he had once been.

We stopped at a patisserie for lunch, mushroom quiche and a lovely chocolate-covered cigar shape filled with a pistachio-coconut filling for me. In a stab at normality I took notes and planned a column. After lunch, the visit to a Saumur vineyard and winery was an anticlimax—steel towers, oak vats, automated wine racks that flipped a half-turn a day until all the sediment had gathered in a metal cap, freezing to blow off cap and sediment, two infusions of bubbles, and voilà! Sparkling whites, rosés, and reds. The owner explained the modern processes and equipment to us with great pride. His was the winery of the future.

I don't suppose the man expected that a cap would actually blow off during his speech, but it did and hit Childeric in the forehead, both cap and wine sludge, which ran down his face. Comic relief. Childeric was unhurt but also unamused. Hester, to whom he had been chatting about the ugly tapestry images of evil, started to giggle. Drummond seemed to have deserted her in an attempt to attract the interest of Laura de Sorentino. Although Laura listened to him politely, probably as a means of ignoring her husband's mutters and glares, she was obviously unimpressed with her new admirer.

Meanwhile, Childeric decided that the wine cap incident had been a planned attack on him and ranted about it during the wine tasting that followed. No one listened. Unfortunately, the high-tech wine of the future was only fair. We sipped politely while Denis went from tourist to tourist dithering nervously. The explosive wine bottle was evidently the last straw for him, although hardly the worst thing that had happened. Still, who could blame him?

Then we moved on to Tours, where Chris would fly home, not to mention Lorenzo de Sorentino and Nedda Drummond. By tomorrow we would be missing six of the original twenty-two, with Chris's early departure the only one planned in advance of the tour.

46
Edie's Message

Carolyn

We traveled to Tours beside the Loire River through a pretty green countryside with odd dwellings built into the tufu stone of hillsides. The hotel in Tours, a Best Western, sounded reassuringly like home, and our room was larger than those we had been assigned in past days. It had floor space. It had the toilet in one room and the sink and shower in another. There was an armoire and desk and a ceiling that curved down to a white, leaf-carved molding. Although the weather had turned cold and the sky filled with dark clouds, it was not raining. All in all I felt more comfortable than I had all day.

Although the tour company was to provide dinner in the hotel, which did not augur well, Jason suggested that our meals would probably improve because the company would want to leave us with a good impression. Remembering the meal at the Chateaubriand in Saint-Malo, I again wondered if Denis had heeded our complaints or, perhaps, noticed me taking notes and ascertained that I was a food columnist. Whatever the reason, another good meal would be welcome. That chocolate-coconut-pistachio cigar at lunch had cheered me up.

I was just settling down for a before-dinner nap when the telephone rang. I stared at it, astonished. The only telephone ringing for us since we arrived in France had been Grace Unsell's cell phone, and we no longer had that. What if our daughter was ill? Or our maid was calling to say that it had actually rained in El Paso and our roof had collapsed. Gingerly, I picked up the receiver. Had Jason not been downstairs with Ivan and Hugh, I'd have made him pick it up.

"Carolyn? Is this Carolyn?"

"Yes," I said cautiously.

"This is Grace Unsell."

"Oh dear, has Edie taken a turn for the—"

"No, no. She's fine. We're in Chicago waiting for her parents to arrive. She's claiming to have regained her memory."

"Oh? Oh my goodness, does she remember who pushed her?" Now that the information might be at hand, I was afraid to hear it. "Or did she simply fall?"

"She says not."

"Then who—who did she say—"

"Well, first she said it was Professor Childeric."

I sighed. "I was afraid of that, Grace. After the scene in Saint-Malo, and given how much he has to lose—"

"But, Carolyn, he was out in the bay with you. The five of you almost drowned."

"Yes, but he could have pushed her before that, Grace. Maybe he went out on the beach to get away from—from the scene of his crime."

"Well, I didn't think of that, and I doubt that it was the case. At any rate, I pointed out to her that he himself had been in danger elsewhere."

"And what did she say?"

"She said that maybe it was Anna, that she'd seen Anna."

"Anna? You can't be serious."

"My reaction exactly, but Edie insisted when I expressed doubt. She was looking a bit confused, but she said, 'I'm sure it was Anna. I saw her. She doesn't like me,' and more of that sort of thing."

Of all the people I might have guessed, Anna would be a last choice, although it was true that the two hadn't gotten along. However, if one, indeed, had pushed the other down a flight of stairs, it seemed more likely that it would have been Edie pushing Anna. "I can't believe that," I said to Grace.

"Exactly. The girl is obviously lying, but what if she tells that story to her parents? She's probably trying to head off anything Anna might report about her—the flirtation with your boy, throwing herself at Professor Childeric, not that her behavior excuses his. Anyway, I thought I should warn you about what she's saying." There was a silence while I tried to take it in. Then Grace continued rather sadly, "And I missed the birth of my grandchild."

"Oh, Grace, I'm so sorry. I know how much you wanted to be there. Did everything go well?"

"Yes, it did. In fact, I was talking to Maddie when the

baby crowned and she had to hang up. I bought another
cell phone in Paris when we were changing planes. Manfred won't be pleased. Not that I care. Maddie had a little
girl. Six and a half pounds, twenty inches. As pretty as her
mother, my son-in-law tells me. You might pass the news
on to Manfred if he seems interested."

We rang off with promises to keep in touch, and I forced
myself to consider the implications of Edie's claim. Was
she speaking out of vindictiveness or confusion? Well, I
had to warn Anna. I couldn't let her go home unprepared
for such a damaging accusation. Good grief, the Atwaters
might actually believe Edie and contact the French police.
I took off my robe, dressed for dinner, and called Anna to
tell her we needed to talk. She was surprised, but she gave
me her room number.

After I'd explained the situation, Anna sighed. "What's
that saying about good deeds coming back to haunt you? If
I'd never tried to keep track of her and had managed to
farm her off as a roommate to someone else, I suppose she
wouldn't have come to hate me so much. Not that I like
her, but I did pity her, especially after the incident with
Childeric."

"Anna, I'm so sorry. I'm the one who lost track of her
at Mont-Saint-Michel. If I'd been a better minder and kept
up with her, she could never have blamed you for anything. For that matter, I'd never have been out on that
beach."

"Actually, she was with me for a while and completely
uninterested in sightseeing, but she got away, so you needn't
blame yourself, Carolyn. She was probably running head-
long down some staircase, trying to find a T-shirt shop, and
fell over her own feet."

"Well, anyway, I thought I should warn you about what
she's saying. Of course, Grace doesn't believe her, and neither do I. I'm sure nothing will come of it, but if—well—"

I smiled at her, embarrassed. "You can always call on me as a character witness."

My goodness. Our first course was a lovely, light puff pastry filled with creamed asparagus, and the entrée was Coq au Vin, very good too, followed by a cheese plate and pears poached in wine. Only two unpleasant notes were struck during dinner. The first was the acidic carafe of gamay we ordered; it was so nasty that Jason wouldn't drink it. I did. I do like wine with dinner and sipped my way through the half-liter with no effect whatever. It must have been watered. Jason ordered beer and complained to the headwaiter about the wine. The management did try to make amends. We found a half-carafe of a good local red when we returned to our room from the airport, but by then it was time for bed and we left it on the dresser, tasted but not drunk.

The second source of unpleasantness came from Lorenzo de Sorentino. Laura was ignoring him, and Macauley Drummond was still trying to attract her attention when I heard Lorenzo hiss into her ear, "My leaving is not meant as an invitation to take up with Drummond, Laura."

She replied, "Don't be ridiculous, Lorenzo," and went to her room instead of seeing him off at the airport.

47
Farewells

Jason

For the first time in my life I was glad to send my son away. I know that Carolyn was reassured by a relatively uneventful day, a good dinner, and the prospect of less marital turmoil tomorrow when the two bitterest couples were separated—quite possibly for good, although only Estrella Markarov was obsessing over that. Chris seemed torn between a desire to get back to school and the feeling that I needed him here to protect his mother. He also seemed worried about Edie Atwater, for he asked if any word of her condition had been received.

"I imagine she's back with her family even as we speak, Chris," his mother replied. "And having been able to make the trip home, she's evidently on the road to recovery."

"I'm really sorry that I didn't handle the situation with her better, Mom." Chris shifted self-consciously and readjusted his backpack. "If I'd told her to knock off the flirting and kept a better eye on her," he mumbled, " I expect she wouldn't have had that trouble with Childeric or even fallen down the stairs and hurt herself. All in all, it must have been a pretty miserable trip for her."

My wife sighed. "Don't blame yourself, Chris. I lost track of her after you last saw her. Even Anna did. Edie's going through that confused, rebellious stage."

Chris grinned. "Who isn't at sixteen? Anyway, Mom,

I'm sorry your vacation was spoiled by all this." I noticed that he gave Carolyn an extralong hug before boarding his plane, and Carolyn, as always, cried. She used to cry when one of the children went away to camp, even if it was only for a week. Yet she seems to enjoy the traveling and the time alone we now have. I certainly do. Well, what man can understand women?

I heard an offer that should prove my point about the mysterious nature of women. Lorenzo de Sorentino was giving Nedda Drummond (neither of their spouses came to see them off) advice about her hair and suggesting that he could improve her looks "one hundred percent if you let me do a nose job on you."

Instead of biting his head off, as I would have expected, she said, "Fine. I'll use the royalties from Macauley's book, from all his books, plus the alimony I plan to get in the divorce settlement. If he coughs up enough money, I won't even have to ask you for a tour discount."

De Sorentino laughed and took her arm as they boarded. Maybe he thought she was kidding. If his departure meant an end to the accidents and injuries, so much the better. Carolyn would be delighted to have the latest of her theories proved right, and I could enjoy a carefree and safe end-of-tour with my wife.

As we turned to leave the airport, we were caught by surprise at the sight of Professor Childeric, who hadn't appeared at dinner, walking away from an arrival gate accompanied by a stocky woman with black hair braided around her head.

"Ah, Dr. Blue, and Mrs. Blue, let me introduce you to my wife, Astarte."

Astarte? Wasn't that some prehistoric moon goddess? I'd have to ask Carolyn, who is the family keeper of arcane information. In her full-cut, no-nonsense suit and sensible heels, this woman did not look like a goddess. I remember Carolyn describing that shoe type as "a court pump." Mrs.

Childeric didn't look like a courtier either, or whatever the female of courtier is. Both Carolyn and Childeric would know that. Actually, Mrs. Childeric looked like an uncompromising battle-ax.

"My dear wife has been so kind as to join me for the last days of the tour. One does miss the companionship of one's spouse, doesn't one?" said Childeric.

Mrs. Childeric looked rather surprised and suspicious to hear this paean to her company. "Well, you know I wouldn't have come, Jean-Claude, if I hadn't played that ace of diamonds and dropped myself right out of contention. My opponent, the dummy hand actually, knocked his coffee into my lap or I'd never have made that mistake. I did complain to the judges, but—"

"Yes, yes," said Childeric. "Most unfortunate, but still it gave me the pleasure of your companionship, my dear." Again she looked at him askance. "And I know that you'll enjoy seeing the châteaux of the Loire Valley. Shall we share a taxi to the hotel?"

The last was addressed to us, and I'd rather not have, but it would have been rude to refuse in front of his wife, who, after all, hadn't tried to drown mine at Mont-Saint-Michel.

"You'll love the hotel, my dear," he said to the doughty Astarte.

That's what she looked like. A Wagnerian soprano.

"Excellent woodwork in the rooms," Childeric chatted on.

I think he was afraid that we'd do just what I wanted to do, refuse to ride with them, if we managed to get a word in.

"Well, I hope we're not paying extra for the woodwork," said Mrs. Childeric. "Last-minute tickets to Europe are expensive, you know."

"But worth every penny," said Childeric.

"Jean-Claude." She eyed him suspiciously. "Is something wrong with you?"

"Nothing that your company won't remedy, my dear."

Once in our room, Carolyn remarked that Childeric must have been very unhappy about being treated as a pariah by the tour group. "Now he'll have someone to talk to."

I shrugged and climbed into bed. "At least he can't lure anyone into danger or try to seduce any teenaged girls if his wife's with him."

"A comforting thought," Carolyn agreed. "Perhaps tomorrow will be a trouble-free day. I, for one, would welcome a bit of peaceful touring. And do you know, I'm not aching as much as I was? I only took four pills today. Maybe there's hope for my liver, after all."

"That wine you drank tonight would put holes in any liver, much less one already weakened by several days of acetaminophen. Still, if you're feeling better—"

"Yes," said Carolyn. "Let's," and she scooted over to my side of the bed.

Travel Journal
Day Ten, Tours

I actually enjoyed dinner tonight. The food was good, and C. had made a fool of himself over a flying wine cap. Everyone decided by the time we left Saumur that the bastard's paranoid, as well as dangerous and immoral.

He didn't even show up for dinner, which made it the best meal of the tour. I thought I'd succeeded. Isolated him, and no one the wiser.

Should have known better. He brought his wife in to keep him company. I'd almost forgotten about her. He's married. If Edie keeps her mouth shut, he's still got it all, spouse, reputation, a full professorship. Maybe even the deanship. He could

*be appointed before we get back and I can spread rumors
about him. God, I hate him.*

*And I've got to get him. While there's still time. All the
other things I did—they weren't enough. Not nearly enough.*

48
A Birth Announcement

Carolyn

At breakfast on the eleventh day, we were a subdued
group. Six of our number had left the tour, two injured, two
willingly, two in a snit. That left seventeen, since Mrs.
Childeric had joined us. She and her husband had a peculiar relationship in that they talked to each other but usually speaking at the same time, neither listening to or even
interested in what the other had to say. She described
bridge hands and strategies, and that morning he held forth
on Renaissance French history as it related to the châteaux
we were about to visit, Chenonceau, Azay le Rideau, and
the gardens at Villandry. I wonder if she knew what he'd
been up to in her absence. And if she noticed that people
on the tour were avoiding him. Her arrival was certainly a
relief to me.

This attention to the Renaissance was motivated by
Childeric's desire to point out Denis's mistakes when the
guide attempted to give us pretour information. Usually
quite immune to such carping insistence on accuracy,
Denis on this day gave up with hardly a fight. He had been
accused in the lobby before breakfast of causing Chris's
abrupt departure, the accuser Ingrid Jensen, who men-

tioned "unnatural attentions" and "unchristian perversions." At least, she was fairly discreet. I wouldn't have heard the beginning if I hadn't been at the front desk asking to have extra towels left in my room so that I could wash my hair when I returned from the day's activities. Denis was confused by her lecture at first. To me she seemed intent on converting him to heterosexuality. Finally, he caught on, went very pale, and broke into a stream of French invective.

Everyone heard what followed. "He's saying, in essence, that you are a woman with a nasty mind and slanderous tongue," Robbie translated for Ingrid, who had backed away when Denis took her remarks amiss. "Not to mention a liar for calling into question the manhood of one who has enjoyed many women and no men in sexual liaisons. Am I getting that right, Laura?"

"I think this is a subject best dropped," said Laura.

"Mon Dieu!" Denis exclaimed. "My honor has been—" Flushed, he turned to us. "Has your son—"

"Not at all," said Jason hastily. "Chris is not gay, and he has not accused you of anything, Denis. He went home because his spring break is over." To Ingrid, Jason said, "We've already told you that, Ingrid. Please, don't make accusations of this sort again."

"Don't know why you get these bees in your bonnet, Ingrid," said Carl.

"I told you we should go home," retorted his wife, now as flushed and angry as Denis. "Decent people shouldn't have to—"

"That's enough, Ingrid. I want my breakfast, not some big to-do that's likely to gave me pains in the gut, maybe even the trots."

"Carl, how can you mention your bowels in public?" Her voice was by then almost inaudible because her husband had hustled her away to the breakfast room.

That morning no one sat with the Jensens, and I felt the

demise of hopes that this might prove to be a less contentious segment of the tour. Most people in our group
were embarrassed enough to keep their eyes on their croissants and their mouths shut at the table, except for Janice,
who was excited about the visit to Chenonceau. According
to her, the château had been the home of many strong and
influential women. "Admittedly, they prostituted themselves through marriage and—"

"What?" Estrella looked horrified. "Marriage is a Holy
Sacrament of the Church, not—"

"Maybe you should read some Roman Catholic history," Janice interrupted dryly. "The Church didn't always
approve of married sex. Priests didn't even perform the
ceremonies for some time—before the tenth century, I believe."

"There's some truth in that," Childeric agreed but was
drowned out by his wife, who thought we might like to
hear interesting statistics on the success in tournament
bridge of married partners as opposed to unmarried partners.

"As I was saying," Janice cut in, "Chenonceau was
ruled by mistresses, wives, and widows, and although they
may have used sexual favors as stepping-stones to power,
they were, at least, women of intelligence."

As Janice talked, my eyes wandered from face to face,
thinking of all the people I had suspected of the violence
that plagued our group: Ivan, whom I had thought might be
a Russian hit man out to get me or Jason; Janice, who
hated Childeric (she seemed to think him guilty of crimes
against women, and I now understood why); Childeric
himself (he certainly had put me in danger more than
once); Hester, who seemed to have an unnatural interest in
violent art; Macauley Drummond, who was unpleasant by
nature; and Lorenzo de Sorentino, who was now gone. Oh
goodness, I really had no idea what was going on. I could
only hope that it stopped.

"By the way, Dr. Unsell," I said during a break in Janice's lecture, "congratulations on being a grandfather."

Unsell looked at me with real dislike. Was he the attacker? I wondered.

"May I ask why you think that my grandchild has been born?" he demanded.

"Grace told me last night." Had Grace asked me to tell him? I had been so upset about the accusations Edie made against Anna that I couldn't remember.

"She called *you* with the news instead of me!" The man's face turned as red as his nose.

"Actually, she called on another matter." I glanced nervously at Anna. "Of a more personal nature," I mumbled.

"What could be more personal than the birth of my grandchild? Possibly Grace was trying to call me and failing to reach me, called you to relay the message, after which you picked the most embarrassing time and manner possible to—"

"Look, Dr. Unsell, Grace called about something else and mentioned the baby, and now I remember. She said to tell you if you seemed interested, which obviously you're not. You haven't even asked the sex of the child, or whether mother and daughter are doing well. So please don't raise your voice to me."

Jason was tapping my hand, presumably to get my attention, when Laura broke in, "A granddaughter. How lovely. Congratulations, Dr. Unsell. I'm sure you'll want to go call Grace. What luck that you still have the cell phone."

Now there, I thought, *is a diplomatic woman. She not only headed him off but also reminded him in a subtle way that he had a cell phone, the number of which his wife knew, so that Grace could have called him if she'd really wanted to.* In deference to Laura's exercise in tact, I restrained myself. I must admit that I had been quite irritated with Dr. Unsell for yelling at me and not caring about—

well. I took a deep breath and glanced sideways at Jason. That rat. He had his hand over his mouth, and his shoulders were shaking. "Stop that," I whispered and gave him a poke.

"You're so cute when you're mad," he whispered back, starting to laugh again.

"Women my age aren't cute," I murmured. "We can be charming or handsome or well preserved or—" Now I had to suppress my own laughter, and both of us were getting disapproving looks from our fellow tour members, not the least of whom was Manfred Unsell, who gave me an absolutely vicious glare as he left the room.

Then I noticed that Anna had risen to leave. I jumped up and followed her into the lobby to assure her that I would not be mentioning Edie or Grace or the conversation we'd had the night before.

She nodded. "Very kind of you, Carolyn. Given the unpleasant mood everyone seems to be in, I'd hate to become the focus of their ill will."

I sighed. "I've obviously managed to enrage Dr. Unsell, although I didn't mean to. I expected that he'd have talked to Grace by now. Why wouldn't he?"

Anna shrugged. She seemed distracted.

"The tour today should be interesting, don't you think? All those 'Amazons,' as Janice called them."

"Yes, I'll be sorry to miss it," said Anna.

"You're not going?" She'd caught me by surprise. "But—"

"I'm afraid all this rich French food is catching up with me again," she said ruefully. "My stomach was happier when the offerings were plain and boring."

"Oh, Anna, I'm so sorry. Is there anything I can do for you?"

"Enjoy the tour and tell me all about it at dinner," she replied. "A day of rest and simple food should revive me. Then I can enjoy Chartres tomorrow. Janice tells me she was there in the spring once and saw flowers growing out of the stones high on the cathedral walls. That would be something to see."

"Oh, it is," I replied. "They looked like daisies." She sounded almost wistful, as if afraid she might not be well enough to see Chartres either.

Later, when I told Janice that Anna had stayed behind because she felt ill, Janice said that the tour had been very stressful for Anna. *As it has for us all,* I thought, although I was very sorry that the stress had made Anna sick, and very resentful against whoever was causing all this misery. I myself, rather than the rich food, might be responsible for Anna's illness. Perhaps I shouldn't have told her about Edie. Still, I couldn't let her be caught unprepared by Edie's accusation. Such a situation could ruin a career if the girl's parents believed it. Poor Anna. And Edie—was it confusion resulting from the fall or resentment against Anna that had triggered that allegation?

49
Le Château des Dames

Artichokes

The great châteaux of the Loire are known for both their architectural beauty and their gardens. Chenonceau, for instance, was first provided with an elaborate Renaissance garden by Diane de Poitiers, famous beauty and mistress of Henri II. These gardens featured flowers, shrubs, and trees, as well as orchards, fruits, and vegetables. Diane received as gifts rare melons and artichokes.

One wonders if they were considered ornamentals, as potatoes had been. Or perhaps her chef prepared them as hors d'oeuvres for the nobility while they drank champagne at the festive parties.

Did the king demand that his queen, Catherine de Medici, who not surprisingly hated her rival, provide prosciutto from her native Italy to wrap the melon slices? Maybe the artichokes were served with melted Norman butter. Incidentally, Pliny the Elder in his natural history called artichokes a monstrosity, but the Roman nobility loved them. Small wonder. Today's Romans fix the world's most delicious artichokes. For those of us less talented, artichokes are still an easy first course to prepare:

- Cut off the tough part of the artichoke stem.

- Strip away the tough outer leaves.

- Shear the sharp tips.

- Boil, covered, in lemon-flavored water for 40 minutes.

- Drain and chill.

- Serve one per diner with melted butter or mayonnaise for dipping.

Not only did the royal mistress, Diane de Poitiers, have exotic edibles in her garden. She had an interesting beauty regime. It seems to have worked amazingly well since she managed to hold, until his death in a tournament, the affections of a king twenty years her junior, and she was reputed to have been as beautiful as ever when she died at the age of sixty-seven. Here is the lady's beauty recipe:

Recipe for Enduring Beauty

- Rise early.

- Bathe in cold water.

- Go for a brisk horseback ride.

- Then retire and sleep until noon.

- Never wear makeup.

It probably helps to start out beautiful, as well.

Carolyn Blue, "Have Fork, Will Travel,"
St. Paul Star-Register

Jason

The more I see of Ivan and Estrella, the less I understand how he could have married the woman. If he didn't seem so smitten, I'd have guessed that the marriage was a ploy to avoid deportation. Be that as it may, our day exploring châteaux should have been very pleasant. Although I'm not necessarily a fan of elaborate country houses and mind-boggling gardens, the goings-on in these places over the centuries were enough to keep society in a state of continual overstimulation.

Our group paid closer attention to the remarks of the guide, who was a graduate student in history, than they ever had to Denis. Carolyn wondered in my ear if Denis had called the fellow in to relieve himself from another day of Childeric corrections. After ten days of shepherding our group, Denis was probably reconsidering his choice of profession.

First, we admired Chenonceau from afar. It bridged a

river with forests on one side and gardens on the other—
Frank Lloyd Wright's "Falling Water" on a much grander
and more traditional scale. The new guide, Maurice, called
Chenonceau *le château des dames,* and explained that a
mill and keep owned since the Middle Ages by the lords of
Marques had to be sold for debt. The new owner left his
wife Catherine Briconnet, the first *dame* of Chenonceau, to
build the château beginning in 1521 while he flitted around
France and Europe on the king's business.

Manfred Unsell remarked gloomily that bankruptcy had
a long history, but none so unscrupulous as contemporary
bankruptcies, whose losses were imposed on businessmen
by laws that allowed ordinary people to run up huge debts
and then wriggle out of them with no damage, except to
their credit ratings. Evidently, there were no bankrupts
among us because no one took offense, although Carolyn
whispered to me that the European nobility had, for centuries, been in the habit of running up debts with trades-
men, which could never be collected.

Unfortunately for the Briconnet family, Frances I
liked Catherine's château so much that as soon as she and
her husband died, the king announced that royal funds
had been mismanaged by the late Collector of Taxes; accordingly, the Briconnet son and heir was forced to hand
over Chenonceau in lieu of paying a huge fine for his father's alleged embezzlement, and Frances became the
owner of an estate he had coveted. The second dame,
Diane de Poitiers, took over in 1547 when Frances's son
Henri II came to the throne and gave his mistress the
château.

Carl Jensen was pleased at a description of Diane's interest in agriculture and said he liked to see land put to
good use. Ingrid was less pleased with the life of the royal
mistress; however, the thought of the king and Diane living in sin, and in such luxurious surroundings, was more
than Estrella Markarov could stomach. She compared the

beautiful Diane to Robbie. Robbie thanked her for the compliment. Estrella retorted that she had meant no compliment, that the comparison was between couples living in sin.

Ivan laughed, cuddled his wife affectionately, and said, "Sin—it can be much funs, no, my little samovar?"

His wife pulled away, eyed him with disappointment, and told him that as an expectant father, he was obligated to take a strong moral stance against sin and sinners. Robbie then told Estrella to mind her own business, and Estrella told Robbie that her seduction of Hugh and blatant sexual misconduct were ruining his chances of becoming dean, to which Robbie retorted, "Bull!"

"Obviously," Estrella continued, "a college cannot afford to have an immoral dean." Hand in hand with his legal spouse, Childeric had listened to this interplay with smug satisfaction while nodding his head in agreement.

Robbie began to laugh. "Well, you're in the College of Education, Estrella, and education professors are either stupid or dorky or both, so you'd probably be right if we were talking about deans of education."

Maurice, the new guide, had been staring open-mouthed during this argument but then recollected his duties and said, "The sublime Diane commissioned the bridge that links the château designed by Catherine Briconnet with the woods across the River Cher. After that, the court spent more and more time at this beautiful place. Shall we look at—"

"Sublime?" exclaimed Estrella. "That is a word better used for angels and saints, not—not—women of ill repute. This *Poitiers* person was a courtesan and an adulteress. Marriage vows are sacred."

"She was a widow, Estrella," murmured Laura. Perhaps she thought that would pacify the education professor.

"A widow? My goodness, I suppose you think that makes everything all right. Well, I was a widow before I married my dear Ivan, and I assure you that I did not become anyone's mistress. And the king was married—to someone or other."

"Catherine de Medici," said Childeric helpfully. I imagine he wanted to keep the skirmish going as long as possible now that Estrella seemed ready to attack a second runner in the race for dean.

"They were committing adultery." She glared at Laura. "A woman's place is by her husband, not in someone else's bed."

Laura's eyebrows lifted inquiringly. "If you're insinuating that, because my husband has gone back home, I am jumping into some other man's bed, Estrella, you're quite wrong."

"And I'm not either," said Hester, "if you've got me in mind. And I'm not a widow. Jeremy is definitely alive and in a walking cast now. And I am not sleeping with Macauley. Laura isn't either, are you, Laura?"

Laura looked somewhat embarrassed, but Macauley Drummond jumped in with relish. "Ladies, pay no attention to this woman. Professors of education have very small minds in matters both social and intellectual."

"But bigging tummies," Ivan chimed in, patting his wife where their child was presumably growing. I could tell that my friend had missed the point of Macauley's insult. Estrella had not. She scowled at Macauley, then at her husband, and poor Ivan looked crestfallen.

Maurice led us hurriedly toward the bedroom of Louise de Lorraine, perhaps thinking to pacify Estrella. Louise had received Chenonceau from her mother-in-law, Catherine de Medici, after her marriage to Catherine's son Henri III, and retired to that bedroom when an assassin killed her husband.

"Of course," said Carolyn, pink with excitement. "He was assassinated in the great market, Les Halles, while trapped between two overturned vegetable carts. The market was founded by Phillip the Fat centuries earlier."

"Henri III, while besieging Paris, was assassinated by a Jacobin friar," said Childeric. "Where in the world did you get that bizarre idea about food carts and Les Halles?"

"From a book about food," said Carolyn, crestfallen.

"Pardon, madame," said Maurice politely. "You are thinking of Henri IV, who had been King Henri III of Navarre before he became King of France. *He* was killed in the food market. Now back to Henri III."

Then Maurice told us that Queen Louise was so grief stricken at the death of her husband that she spent the rest of her life wearing mourning white and living in that bedroom, which she draped in black velvet and decorated with silver tears.

"An excellent example of a woman who *honored* her vows," said Estrella.

"Unlike you," snapped Robbie. "When your first husband got clubbed, you kept right on preaching bilingual education and snagged Ivan, right?"

Estrella burst into tears. Ivan said, "Is nice she choose me instead of black room."

By the time Maurice mentioned the second-to-last dame, the intellectual Madame Dupin, none of us had much to say. Things livened up a bit when Denis returned to the group and, seeing the grim faces, entertained us as we explored the gallery over the river with the exploits of Catherine de Medici who, once her husband Henri II died, was able to wrest Chenonceau and a quantity of jewels from her rival Diane and then rule France during the reigns of three sons.

I, for one, was interested to learn that young, bare-breasted noblewomen served refreshments at Catherine's balls, posed on the riverbanks singing, and sold their "favors" on spying missions for the Queen Mother. Estrella demanded that Ivan take her back to Tours before any more scandalous stories were told, so the Markarovs missed Azay-le-Rideau and Villandry, where Carolyn was interested in the decorative cabbages that filled the vegetable gardens.

"They look like posies," she said. "I wonder if they're edible, and if they were served during the Renaissance. Cabbage, even pretty cabbage, doesn't sound like food for a royal feast."

Thank God, there had been no incidents of violence, other than verbal, during the day, and my wife was back to thinking about food. She did ask, once we were seated in the bus returning to Tours, whether I thought Estrella could be the spy sent by the selection committee to check out the dean candidates.

"What spy?" I asked.

"People are saying there is one. I thought maybe it was Anna, but now—well, if it's Estrella, I'm afraid Hugh and Laura are out of the running. Professor Childeric *appears* to be the only candidate left who's not living in sin or failing to cling to his spouse. I hope Estrella hasn't forgotten his conduct with Edie." Carolyn looked quite upset at the thought of Childeric becoming dean.

"Be a pity if he got the post," I replied, glancing at Childeric. He was sitting by his wife, looking self-satisfied, and talking in counterpoint to her bridge tales.

50
Duck À L'Orange

Duck À L'Orange

A favorite meat in Normandy is duck, and a duck raised in Normandy is a treat indeed. Take that Norman duck and treat it Provençal style (Canard à l'Orange), and you have a culinary delight. Here is a recipe:

• Remove anything found in the cavity of a *duckling*, and cut away excess fat inside and at the neck and tail; bind the wings, legs, and neck skin to the body with kitchen *twine or skewers;* and prick the skin here and there to let the extra fat seep out while the duck is cooking.

• Paint the skin very lightly with *butter*, and roast to medium rare: 15 minutes per pound at 450° F.

• Do not salt the uncooked duck. Do *salt* the cooking juices and baste often with them.

• In the meantime, peel the zest (only the colored part) from *2 tart oranges and 1 lemon*, cut julienne style, cook 1 minute in boiling water, and drain.

• Reduce *3 tbs. wine vinegar* with *2 tsp. sugar* in a small pan until caramelization begins.

• Add juices of the oranges and lemon, reduce a bit, and add zest.

• Place the roasted duck on a heated platter, drain the fat from the roasting pan, and dissolve the brown juices with a little *Cointreau or brandy.*

• Add this to the sauce and simmer for several minutes.

• Garnish the duck with *orange slices* and serve the sauce separately.

• Serves 4 or 5 people.

Carolyn Blue, "Have Fork, Will Travel,"
Biloxi News-Courant

Carolyn

At last, a day without physical violence, and soon we would be flying home—not even on the same plane with these people. I understood that the tour had been difficult for everyone, frightening, in fact. But I don't see that anyone else had been in more danger than I had, and I didn't indulge in rude remarks. Well, perhaps about Professor Childeric, but he deserved them.

Although the tour was not providing dinner that night, Denis had suggested that we meet in the lobby so that he could suggest several restaurants that were both excellent and reasonable in price. I, for one, would have been happy to ignore our guide's restaurant suggestions, but Jason liked the sound of "reasonable in price."

"I have not yet provided you with the opportunity to sample the delicious *canard* of Normandy," Denis told us. "Therefore I offer two suggestions. One café has in Tours the best *canard à la rouennaise.*"

My gourmet sensibilities sharpened with interest, for I

had read that *canard à la rouennaise* is the very best way
to cook duck. Since I had not had the opportunity to sample this delicacy in Rouen, I nudged Jason and nodded, as
if to say, "That's what we want to try."

"The second café offers a sumptuous *canard à l'orange,* one the finest dishes of Provence. I leave it to you."
Denis gave us his winning smile.

"Why don't we vote?" suggested Carl Jensen. Alas,
they went with the dish they'd heard of, rather than the one
I tried to recommend. I suppose Jason and I could have refused to surrender ourselves to the democratic process and
gone off on our own in a show of elitist rebellion, but Jason
said, "Well, that's settled."

Once in the café, a long, narrow, noisy place with wall
benches and rush-bottomed chairs, we all ordered duck à
l'orange, like so many ducklings, waddling mindlessly
after Mama. Since I happen to like duck à l'orange and this
might be my only chance to sample the local duck, I too
acquiesced. It was, in fact, delicious, the dark, rich meat
contrasting nicely with the tart-sweet, orange-flavored
sauce and the fruit slices.

Surprisingly oranges from Seville are favored for this
dish. Jason and I once picked an orange from one of the
beautiful trees that grow everywhere in that lovely An-
dalusian city. My goodness, it was sour. Maybe we had
taken up orange theft in the wrong season, although our
choice certainly looked round, colorful, and tasty.

The surprise of a wonderful meal seemed to quell the
animosity that had plagued our group for days. People
were generally polite, sometimes even friendly to one another, and when tempers flared, Laura jumped in with
diplomatic words to turn the would-be attacker's wrath
aside. Diners less historically and religiously inclined listened with tolerance when Denis told us how Saint Martin,
then a young soldier in a Roman legion, cut his cape in half
to share with a beggar, after which, seeing Christ in a

dream clothed in the half-cloak, Martin sought baptism and began his holy life. Estrella offered the story of the transport of Saint Martin's corpse by river to Tours and the greening of the trees out of season as he passed.

Drummond, for once, managed to repress his usual offensive remarks, and Janice refrained from denouncing the patriarchal ways of the Church. When Childeric described in detail the Viking depredations in Tours, no one protested, and Hester showed an interest in the arson and slaughter.

Many of us asked solicitously after Anna's health and described the sights of the day to her, leaving out the arguments that had darkened the beauty of the tour. Anna said she felt much better, and she certainly looked better. That morning she had seemed ill and uncharacteristically nervous. Now there was color in her face, and she ate her duck with appetite. I didn't have the heart to suggest that, if rich food had been her problem, duck à l'orange was not a good choice. She seemed so calm, even peaceful, although when Childeric held forth, talking over the interruptions of his wife, Anna eyed them both coldly.

I couldn't blame her. I was heartily tired of the man myself, and his wife was simply a tiresome person of another color. Playing bridge can be entertaining, but surely she had some other interest she could talk about.

When dinner was over and even the grumpiest among us were mellow with good food and wine, Denis announced that he had a surprise; he hoped that we'd all follow him to see it. Janice said that she'd have to forgo the surprise since she was expecting a call from the States. She suggested that she and Anna walk back to the hotel together. Still becalmed on some mental island, Anna murmured that she thought she'd go along for the surprise. Although Janice seemed taken aback at the refusal, and I'm sure that I heard Ingrid make a tasteless remark about "trouble in fairyland," most of us paid our bills and trailed away after Denis through quiet, dark streets.

"Are you ready for the surprise?" our guide called gaily. We saw nothing but one more shadowed street. Then suddenly he waved us around a corner, and looming ahead was a magnificent cathedral, glowing in the darkness.

I swear that it looked like a magical vision floating in the night air, all ornate tracery and mellow stone with lovely stone lanterns topping its twin spires. Flamboyant Gothic architecture at its most glorious. It was so beautiful a sight that, for a moment, I could hardly breathe and wished that I had brought my camera.

Denis said triumphantly, "Cathedrale Saint Gatien!"

"Ah," said Professor Childeric, "a Gallo-Roman foundation, a Romanesque thirteenth-century base with a chancel designed, in all probability, by the genius of Sainte-Chapelle in Paris, stained glass of the same period, and upon the Roman wall the elaborate decoration of—"

"I do believe that cathedral was pictured on the decks of cards we used at a tournament in Cleveland," said Mrs. Childeric.

"—and topping this fine example of flamboyant Gothic, the charming Renaissance lantern domes that signal the church's completion in the sixteenth century."

"Yes, I'm sure it's the very same cathedral," said Mrs. Childeric. "I bid and made an amazing six clubs at that tournament. Everyone was quite impressed."

"Although Saint Gatien's is a cathedral of the second rank, still I find it very pleasing," said Professor Childeric. "Most graceful and—"

"*Anna!*" I cried. We were scattered in a loose group with the golden light of the church falling on us. By that light I saw something I could hardly believe: Anna Thomas-Smith had pulled a pistol from her purse and, holding it in both hands, was moving forward. "Anna!

What are you doing?" She continued quite steadily, quite calmly toward the Childerics.

51
Murder at a Cathedral

Jason

When Carolyn cried out, my attention was diverted from the cathedral, a very impressive sight, to Anna Thomas-Smith, a sight that made me question my vision. The woman had a pistol in her hand. Had someone threatened her? And if so, where had she gotten the pistol? One can't bring weapons on board a plane. And I doubted that a pistol would be easy to buy, especially in a foreign country, especially by a middle-aged home economist or whatever she was, an unmarried, middle-aged—well, I was struck dumb, frozen in my tracks when I saw the gun in Anna's hand.

Hugh had been beside Anna when Carolyn called out. He turned and, seeing the weapon, reached toward her, crying, "My God, she's got a gun!"

Anna pulled away from him and fired. Stunned silence fell over our group. "I missed," Anna said, her tone one of shocked lament.

Thank God! I thought as I lurched, belatedly, in her direction. Hugh actually got a hand on her arm, but she now held the weapon tighter, still in both hands, and fired a second time. As I grasped her left arm, I heard Professor Childeric wail, "I've been shot!" as he crumpled to the ground, blood spreading in rosy blossom on his pant leg.

Hugh and I immobilized Anna and wrestled the gun from her, as Childeric, trying to stem the flow of blood from his leg, screamed, "You tried to kill me, Fauree, but it won't help you get the deanship. I'm still alive, and I know you—"

"You stupid bastard," Hugh shouted back. "This isn't my gun." He waved it at Childeric.

"Give it to me," I said. "It may have more bullets in it."

"He's still alive?" Anna was shivering uncontrollably in our grasp. "Give the gun back." We didn't, of course, and she burst into tears, saying, "I can't seem to do anything right."

I shoved the revolver into my pocket and tightened my grasp on Anna who, although I could hardly believe it, had evidently meant to kill Childeric. Carl Jensen left the shocked crowd and attempted to stanch the flow of blood from the medievalist's leg. After commandeering neckties from all of us, Jensen balled several up, pressed them against the wound, and used the rest to tie the packing in place. "Well, that's better," said Jensen. "Now stop jerking around, Childeric. You'll dislodge the bandage."

A good man, Jensen, I thought. *Quicker thinking than the rest of us.* I'd have to remember to thank him again for saving Carolyn from the tides off Mont-Saint-Michel.

"Anna, what were you thinking of? Why would you—" My wife was now standing beside Hugh and our prisoner. Anna continued to weep.

"Anna?" Carolyn touched her cheek. "What happened?"

Anna sniffled, her attention caught by my wife's gentle words. "Oh, it happened years ago. If he just hadn't come on this trip. If I hadn't had to see him and listen to him every day."

"Anna, you shot me?" Childeric whined. "I thought we were—"

"Friends?" she asked bitterly. "In love? That's what I thought, Jean-Claude. That's what you told me."

"But that was years ago," he protested. "I mean . . ." He looked around at the staring crowd. "I mean you obviously misinterpreted some little—"

"I just wanted to ruin your life, Jean-Claude. The way you ruined mine. But I couldn't even manage that."

"Robbie, do you think you could call the police?" Hugh whispered to his lover.

"And before everyone gets going again with the re-criminations, someone should look at Mrs. Childeric. She hasn't moved at all," said Hester. "I think something might be wrong with her."

Jensen looked around, spotted Mrs. Childeric lying, face up, on the cobblestones of the open area in front of the cathedral, and ordered his wife to keep pressure on the professor's wound. Childeric was keening to himself when Ingrid took over while Jensen knelt beside Astarte Childeric. He lifted her eyelid, then felt the artery in her neck.

"Mad cow disease?" asked Macauley Drummond sardonically.

"Dead," said Jensen. "Bullet in the chest. Better get an ambulance, too, Ms. Hecht," he called after Robbie, who had found a telephone and was making the call to the police. She held up her hand to indicate that she had heard.

Anna's legs had given way when she heard that Childeric's wife was dead. "That's not what I meant to do," she mumbled. Since she seemed unable to stand, we lowered her to the cobblestones.

Carolyn sat down beside her, legs tucked neatly to the side. I'll never know how women manage such things in skirts, especially narrow skirts like the one my wife was wearing.

"Anna, you must still be sick," Carolyn suggested.

"I wasn't sick," Anna replied wearily. "I was out buying

a gun. It's hard to do when you don't speak much French. And very costly."

"But why would you—"

"I don't want to talk about it, Carolyn. I'm sorry you had to see this. You're a nice woman. And I'm sorry you got caught in the cross-fire."

"I didn't." Carolyn looked surprised. "I wasn't hit."

"Bad choice of words. The push in Rouen was meant for him." She nodded toward Childeric. "And the tide thing—I never dreamed you'd walk out on that beach with him, not after—"

"It was stupid," Carolyn agreed. "I was caught up in the romance of the Middle Ages—Henry, William Rufus, Robert of Normandy—well, it was stupid of me. The police will be coming, Anna. Do you want me to go with you?"

"I can't believe you said that, Carolyn," Childeric cried. He had raised his head and caught the end of the conversation. "I'm the one who was shot, and she's the one who shot me. Why are you being so nice to her? I can understand that Janice Petar hates me, although she has no reason except that she hates all men, but you! I had a tender regard for you. I—"

"Dr. Childeric, you've been shot," said Carolyn. "Just shot. That's all."

"All?"

"Your wife is dead, or doesn't that matter to you?"

Childeric looked at Carolyn with puzzlement, then glanced aside and noticed, evidently for the first time, the body of his wife. "Astarte?"

The police and hospital vans, sirens blaring, arrived at the same time. Childeric, while being placed on a stretcher, saw his wife's body covered with a blanket and said, "Oh, my God," as if he'd just realized she was actually dead. After listening to an explanation in their native language from Laura, the police took charge of Anna. Again my wife offered to go along.

"I think I'd be of more use, Carolyn," said Laura. "She'll need a translator."

"There's a journal in my room," Anna said to Carolyn. "You can read it if you like. Then give it to Janice. She can send it to my father."

As it turned out, no one was allowed to go with Anna. After the police car pulled away, Carolyn stood forlornly on the cobblestones, watching its lights disappear around the corner. "This is all my fault," she said.

"Now, Carolyn," I protested.

"No, it really is, Jason." She looked to be on the verge of tears. "Edie told Grace, who told me yesterday, that Anna had pushed her down the stairs at Mont-Saint-Michel, and what did I do? I thought Edie was lying. So did Grace. And I warned Anna. She probably panicked. She must have thought she was about to be arrested, and that's why she—why she bought a gun—and—and . . ."

Carolyn started to cry, and I put one arm around her while I fished for a handkerchief. I didn't have one. "If you'll let go of your purse, I'll find you a Kleenex, sweetheart."

"Why is it that only Southern men carry handkerchiefs?" she sobbed as she relinquished her purse.

Ah well, women say strange things when they're upset. I found her a Kleenex and let her odd remark go.

52
Best Western Revelations

Carolyn

Except for Denis and Laura, who followed Anna to wherever the police take prisoners, the rest of us staggered back to the hotel and headed, without even discussing it, toward the bar. I certainly needed a drink. I was horrified and confused and saddened. One wounded, one dead, not to mention all the other "accidents." Could Anna really have been behind all these things? Well, not the lunch box that broke Jeremy's leg. Not the wine cork that hit Childeric's forehead. I ordered a double Kir Royale.

Laura arrived twenty minutes later and ordered a double bourbon. "Denis is getting her a lawyer, and she didn't want to talk to me, so I came back." She looked depressed. "What an awful trip this has been. Has anyone thought to tell Janice what's happened? She obviously knew Anna better than the rest of us."

Hester said she'd make the call and left to do so.

"Isn't that just what I've been saying?" demanded Ingrid. "Perversions and—and illicit sex are a sign of moral decay. We shouldn't be surprised that—"

"Ingrid," said Carl sharply, "I don't want to hear any more of that kind of talk. Jesus told us not to be casting the first stone."

"He said, 'He who is without sin,'" she cried indignantly. "I've certainly never practiced perversions or illicit sex—or murdered anyone."

"We don't know the whole story," said Carl stubbornly.

Janice joined us, pulling up an extra chair, and listened to the account of the night's events. Then she said sadly, "If only she'd come back with me. I knew she was upset. I should have—"

"I'm sorry to say this, Professor Petar, but Anna didn't seem at all upset," Estrella interrupted. "She was perfectly calm until she realized she'd shot the wrong person or hadn't killed them both or whatever it was. Then she started to cry. I think that's terrible. It's bad enough to shoot someone, but to cry because you didn't kill them!"

"This tour was the first thing Anna had looked forward to in years, and having him here ruined it for her. She'd never have booked if she'd known Childeric had tickets, and he only came at the last minute because someone else dropped out." Janice shook her head. "It's really sad, when you think about it. She's always been such a gentle person, but this was just too much for her."

"Too much what?" asked Hester. "He is pretty boring, but most people don't shoot someone for being boring."

"Oh, he got what he deserved," said Janice.

"No one deserves—" Estrella protested, but was cut off.

"You don't know anything about them, Estrella, so there's no use your judging them," snapped Janice.

We all looked at her expectantly.

"Anna once had a good career building," Janice explained. "She'd probably have been promoted to full professor in a year or so. Before she was forty, which is extraordinary for a woman. The old boys' club pretty much tries to keep women in the lower echelons of—"

"I don't think we need a feminist lecture," said Macauley sardonically.

"I expect that you, of all people, do need one, Drummond. At any rate, Anna was doing well, and then she met

Childeric, who was interested in the changes in quality and length of life that could be attributed to changing diet during the Middle Ages. He got her interested, and she started doing research and even lab work on his project. Pretty soon she was devoting all her nonteaching time to Childeric's research, and she was in love. He said he was, too. He said he was going to leave his wife and marry Anna. They had an affair, which I doubt that Anna had ever done before. I don't know that. She's a reserved woman about sexual matters, but—"

"They committed adultery?" Estrella interrupted.

"That they did. It's fairly common in universities, in case you didn't know it, Estrella. Better watch your own husband, especially when you're further along in your pregnancy. That's a time, so I've heard, when men are particularly prone to straying, not that they don't at other times, too."

Estrella looked alarmed.

Janice continued imperturbably, "Childeric strung her along for almost two years, and then he dumped her. He said he'd discovered that he couldn't leave his wife, after all. Anna was devastated, but at that point she didn't know the full scope of his betrayal. That came later, when the article on their work was published. Her name wasn't even mentioned. She'd given the man her love, her loyalty, and two years of research on something that benefited only Childeric. He was given a research award and a chaired professorship, and she was passed over for promotion.

"I don't think she ever dated again, certainly never married, although she'd wanted to be married. She had enough trouble with depression after the affair with Childeric that her department would probably have fired her if she hadn't had tenure. So she kept her job, but she sort of faded into the woodwork, academically speaking. I wish she'd spoken up at the time, but she was humiliated, and she thought if people knew about the affair, she might get sacked for moral turpitude. Hell, maybe she was right. We'll never know.

"So he got away with it, and her life was wrecked. The best she could do was stay away from him, which she did. Anna stopped attending university convocations. She never went to social events. Then he turned up on this tour, and I think she just went a little crazy when she had to see him every day. It was too much for her. I only hope a French court will see it that way."

"I'm afraid that's unlikely," said Manfred Unsell. "In France, one is guilty until proven innocent. The Napoleonic Code. Nor do I think that a broken heart is considered mitigation for murder."

"Right," said Janice. "But then how would you know about broken hearts? As far as I can see, the only thing that flips your switch, Manfred, is the European Common Market." She stood up and slung a heavy handbag cum briefcase on her shoulder. "Well, I've got a couple of visits to make. One to Anna, if they'll let me see her. I want to tell her that she may have gotten her revenge, after all. And then I'm going to pay a call on Childeric."

Jason looked startled. "I hope you're not thinking of—"

"Finishing off the job? No, but I'm going to give him a bit of news that will ruin his day. In fact, I might as well tell the rest of you since at least two of you have a stake in this. The selection committee met today and named the new dean."

"And it's not Childeric," Hugh guessed.

"That's right, it's not."

"Then who is it?" Hester asked. "After all, it's my college too. And Jeremy's. He'll want to know."

"Laura, congratulations." Janice nodded to her.

"Me?" For once, Laura de Sorentino lost her amazing calm.

"Yes, congratulations," said Hugh, rising to shake

Laura's hand. "If you ever need input on the scientific mind, feel free to call on me." He grinned cheerfully.

"That's very gracious of you, Hugh. You don't mind?"

"Hell, as long as it's not that ass, Childeric, I'm as happy to see you get it as not. I've got an announcement of my own to make." He reached for Robbie's hand and pulled her up. "Robbie and I are getting married. We thought we'd try to do it tomorrow or the next day in Paris. The city of romance." He dropped a kiss on Robbie's lips.

"Ah, my friend, is very romantic," said Ivan, "but takes many months for French wedding. Papers for divorce. Papers for showing spouse is dead. Many papers, all with many stamps of officials. Many, many months."

Robbie laughed. "Well, that's all right. We can get married at home. I know your kids'll want to be there, Hugh."

I wasn't so sure that Hugh's children would want to attend the wedding, no matter where it was held, and Jason looked flabbergasted.

"A few more days of living in sin won't hurt us," said Robbie gaily. "Right, Estrella?"

Estrella shrugged. "Since you're not Catholic, your marriage won't be any more valid in God's eyes than your sinful conduct is excusable."

"How do you happen to know who was appointed, Janice?" Hugh asked.

"What? You think I'm making it up? I'm the selection committee's spy."

"Goodness, I thought Anna was." The words just slipped out of my mouth.

"Nope. I am. Won't Childeric hate to hear that. He'll think of all the nasty things he's said to me and wish he'd sucked up instead. Well, I'd better get moving. It's a shame about his wife, though. Bad enough to spend all those years with him, but then to die because of him. He's the one who should have died."

"He's the one she meant to kill," I said.

"That I can understand. I mean, why she'd want to. It's just hard to believe that she did all the other stuff." Janice seemed baffled. "She really is a nice woman."

"It's hard to believe none of us ever *saw* her do anything," I said. "Well, until tonight. Except for Edie's fall, we were all *there* when these things happened."

"She didn't push Edie," said Laura. "She told me that she'd been lecturing Edie for being rude to some tourist, and Edie ran off, laughing. She must have tripped."

"You wonder why you never saw Anna pushing anyone? Or why no one heard her give Childeric the wrong information about the tides—if she did that. I don't know; maybe he just misunderstood." Janice addressed this to me. "It's because no one notices older women. Unless you're beautiful like Laura, or pushy like me, or really famous in your field, no one sees you or listens to you. Give yourself ten or twenty years, Carolyn, and you'll see for yourself. When we're old and plain, we become invisible."

Epilogue

Carolyn

Jason and I left the bar shortly after Janice. Guilt ate at me as I thought of the clues I'd missed that might have told me Anna had an ominous interest in Jean-Claude Childeric. From the first night when she kept asking me questions about him and about our relationship to last night when I heard that Edie had accused Anna of pushing her, there had been clues, and I had missed them or ignored them. She'd wanted me to tell everyone when he came to my room; she'd hinted that his behavior that afternoon wasn't unusual; she'd believed Edie, whom she didn't like, when she heard that Childeric had kissed the girl; she'd disappeared from the dinner table right before the beef snacks for the mastiff appeared in people's pockets. So many clues, and I'd ignored them.

And her own story was heartbreaking, a shy, lonely woman preyed on by an unscrupulous man. "What a sad tale that was," I said to Jason as I began to prepare for bed.

"Anna's?" Jason stared out the window of the hotel room, his back to me. "It was sad, but if she'd handled the situation better when she first faced it—"

"She was seriously depressed, Jason. Childeric ruined her life."

"There are psychiatrists for depression, not to mention excellent drugs."

"Yes," I had to agree. "Laura thinks Prozac is a miracle drug."

"Laura de Sorentino takes Prozac?" Jason looked surprised. "I wonder if the selection committee knows that?"

"You're just upset because she was chosen over Hugh."

"I'm a lot more upset about this marriage he's jumping into. Robbie's had four husbands, and Hugh has children."

"Keep in mind that Robbie is a friend of mine," I reminded him. "Hugh knows how many husbands she's had, and he's a grown man. They're in love."

"That's what Anna thought, and now Childeric's wife is dead."

"Anna didn't mean to kill Mrs. Childeric. You heard what she said."

"What about all the others she attacked? Your friend Robbie, for instance."

"I don't know. That was after Robbie talked in front of her about the affair with Hugh. I'm sure Anna didn't want to see Childeric become dean. Maybe she thought she could frighten Robbie away before she ruined Hugh's chances. And the meat in Lorenzo's pocket, that did frighten him away, and he was certainly undermining Laura."

"What about Drummond? He said he was pushed."

"After Nedda read those passages from his book, I'm surprised the whole tour didn't attack him. He said something really mean to Anna at lunch before we went to the Bayeux Cathedral. But he was horrible to Childeric, too. Do you think Childeric pushed him? Drummond thought so."

"No idea," Jason replied.

"I'll bet he did. He was a bad person." Jason was frowning at me. "Well, I do realize that what Anna did was wrong, Jason. I just feel sorry for the miserable life the poor woman had, and now she's in jail. It doesn't look like things are going to improve for her."

"You're right, sweetheart. And I don't even like Childeric, but she put you in danger, too. Twice."

"Not on purpose," I replied defensively.

"Not on purpose doesn't count. You could have drowned."

"Well, it would have saved me from becoming invisible," I retorted, shivering at that depressing statement that Janice made about the prospects of older women.

"Carolyn, as long as I'm alive, you will never be invisible—or plain—or old. Love has very clear eyes about things like that."

While I was giving Jason a hug, which ended with me sitting on his lap, I thought how very lucky I was to have married such a sweet man. "You know, Jason, maybe we should stop traveling so much. We haven't been very lucky this year, at least when we're away from home."

Jason laughed. "That being the case, we're due for a run of better luck, sweetheart. It's like the man who takes a bomb on an airplane. His reasoning is: What are the chances of there being two bombs on the same plane?"

"How did he get the bomb on in the first place? If my wristwatch will set off the metal detectors, surely a bomb—"

"It's a joke, Carolyn."

"I don't think it's funny. Bombs are very—"

"—rare on domestic flights, thank God."

Jason gave me a kiss and pushed me off his lap, much to my surprise. Just because I hadn't liked his joke—

"Now I want you to take a deep breath, Carolyn, get out your computer, and write about eating Duck à l'Orange in Tours."

And I did just that.

Travel Journal
Day Eleven, Twelve? Whatever, Tours

They've actually been very kind to me considering that I just killed someone. I do feel badly about Mrs. Childeric. I hated her when I thought Jean-Claude was going to marry me. He kept saying that she didn't love him but still she refused to give him a divorce.

They gave me paper and a pencil, and they let Janice come to see me. He won't be dean. Well, that's good news. Maybe I won, after all. Everyone will know what he did to me, and I won't have to put up with their pity or disapproval. I' ll be here.

And he'll never be dean, and probably no one will ever love him. He'll be all by himself. Growing old. Losing the respect of his colleagues, maybe even fired for taking up with Edie. Maybe he'll become invisible. Just like me.

It's been so strange. Like a dream. Ever since I heard that Edie had accused me of pushing her downstairs. I wouldn't have minded doing it early on. I'm surprised I didn't. But the point is that I didn't do anything. Not that time. But when Carolyn told me what Edie was saying, I knew I had to act. Before people figured out that I was the one and stopped me from getting my revenge on Jean-Claude.

I wonder if I'm crazy. I don't think so. He just shouldn't have come on this trip.

My father. He'll be surprised when he hears about this. Mr. Tough Guy. Yelling at kids. Yelling at me. He never killed anyone. Big surprise, Dad. Your daughter's a murderer.

Do they still guillotine criminals in France? I don't expect that I'll feel invisible when they're cutting off my head. And maybe I can learn some French while I'm waiting. Maybe I can make some friends. At least, I don't seem to be invisible anymore.   *Anna Thomas-Smith*

Recipe Index